6-13

HOME RUN

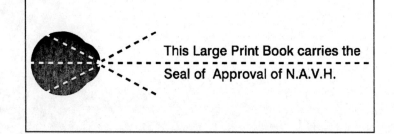

This Large Print Book carries the
Seal of Approval of N.A.V.H.

HOME RUN

TRAVIS THRASHER

THORNDIKE PRESS
A part of Gale, Cengage Learning

Detroit • New York • San Francisco • New Haven, Conn • Waterville, Maine • London

LIBRARY OF CONGRESS CATALOGING-IN-PUBLICATION DATA

Thrasher, Travis, 1971–
    Home run : freedom is possible / by Travis Thrasher. — Large print edition.
      pages ; cm. — (Thorndike Press large print Christian fiction)
    ISBN-13: 978-1-4104-5855-1 (hardcover)
    ISBN-10: 1-4104-5855-5 (hardcover)
    1. Baseball players—Fiction. 2. Large type books. I. Title.
    PS3570.H6925H66 2013
    813'.54—dc23   2013005559

Published in 2013 by arrangement with David C. Cook

Printed in Mexico
1 2 3 4 5 6 7 17 16 15 14 13

This book is dedicated to my uncle Jerry Ray Bagwell, who signed a contract out of high school with the world champion LA Dodgers in 1966. Before he could move up to the major leagues, he was drafted by the army to serve in the Vietnam War. Jerry went to be with the Lord in 1998. Something tells me he's still playing baseball.

Every strike brings me closer to the next home run.
— Babe Ruth

The devil says I'm out, but the Lord says I'm safe.
— Billy Sunday

These pieces of you, imperfectly sewn and patched all over, blur by like a blinding pitch . . .

Okmulgee, Oklahoma
1985

In the silent shadows of the abandoned barn, Cory Brand finished building the box that would keep their treasures safe from the rest of the world. He was eight and could already build things from scratch. Clay was only four and a half and didn't seem to be much of a builder. He just liked to watch and giggle. Cory wished he could take his little brother's funny laugh and lock it away in this pine box forever.

"Let me see, let me see." Clay was always there by his side, waiting, observing, nudging to see what Cory was doing. Cory made sure the rusting metal latch he'd found worked, then he opened up the box and presented it to his brother.

"What do you think?"

Clay held the box in his arms and looked like a kid on Christmas Day.

11

"See, Clay? It's all ours. Just ours."

Cory knelt on the ground and collected the stacks of baseball cards they had carefully organized. Streaks of sunlight cut through the misshapen walls surrounding them. The old barn with the leaky roof still had that straw-and-manure smell even though there hadn't been animals around this farm for years. Cory wondered if some smells sneaked inside the walls and never left.

"We'll put these in here, just like this," he said as he placed their prized possessions in the box. "Then we close it and hide it."

"Where?"

"It's our secret, okay?"

Cory knew Clay wouldn't tell anybody, but he liked making him promise just the same. The boys had spent more time sorting and trading and messing around with those cards than doing pretty much anything else. Each card represented a distinct hope. Hope that there was more to this world than a deserted barn decorated in cobwebs and a dilapidated white farmhouse as neglected as the five acres of land it sat on. Hope that beyond this battered-down address and small Oklahoma town, a world awaited. A world full of games and excitement and potential.

Cory took the box and walked over to a wall of junk that lined the one side of the barn. He carefully slipped the box under a broken wheelbarrow with a missing handle and a flat tire. An old black plastic tarp hung over it like a baby's forgotten blanket, hiding both the wheelbarrow and the box of treasures underneath.

"Let's keep it right here so we always know where to find it," he told Clay. "No one can mess with it right there."

Clay might be only four, but Cory knew he understood. It wasn't like they got a lot of strangers walking through their property and checking out their barn. Actually, Cory sometimes thought it would be nice if strangers did dare come on their property. Maybe they'd help them out a bit.

The box had only been hidden for a few minutes when something pounded against the decrepit wall of the barn. It felt like the entire structure shook. Clay just looked at him. They didn't say a word — they didn't have to. Daylight zigzagged through the open windows and the holes, but the boys still blended into the murkiness the old structure provided.

Another loud thud shook them. The question in Clay's eyes asked what they should do.

Cory hated that look. He hated seeing fear in his little brother's eyes.

"Pitcher's ready," a voice outside hollered.

Mom spoke about the fear of God, but for Cory and Clay there was only the fear of *him*.

Cory gave his brother a confident nod, then grabbed a couple of pieces of wood to prop up against the tarp on the wheelbarrow. Just to be on the safe side. He took Clay's hand and headed away from the pounding to the front of the barn, where two massive wooden doors stood wedged together by a heavy beam. Cory slid it out as he'd done many times before and then pushed Clay forward headfirst.

He followed, wiggling through the entrance, hoping they had made it in time. Hoping they could escape before the monster found them.

Clay standing there like a rock told him it was too late. Cory turned around to face the inevitable.

The man standing there looking down at them claimed to be their dad, though Cory didn't know any other fathers who treated their kids exactly like this. Mom said Cory took after his father, since he was good with his hands and could play ball, but Cory hated hearing that. There was nothing about

14

this man he wanted to take after.

He didn't need to see the look on Dad's face to know. The sound of the baseballs beating the barn wall had already told him. His dad had been drinking, and drinking a lot.

His voice boomed over them. "Batter up."

Michael Brand looked the same as he'd looked yesterday and the day before and probably the day Cory was born. His work boots were worn out, though Cory didn't think it was from working. He wore an old baseball jersey, dirty and frayed. His jacket was as battered as his boots, and he wore it whether it was twenty or eighty degrees outside.

This day was a hot one, and Dad's un-shaven face looked flushed and sweaty under his wide-brimmed hat. Cory hated the hat. He wanted to take the hat and the jersey and toss them into a fire.

Dad hurled a bat in their direction, and it landed near Clay's feet. The fear on the boys' faces must have amused him, because he looked at Clay with mock surprise.

"Are *you* first?"

Clay began to scoot backward, but there wasn't anywhere to go with the barn behind them. Cory stepped in front of his brother, not knowing what else to do. Dad just laughed as his eyes grew dim, the anger right behind them like a catcher planted behind a batter.

"Good idea," Dad mocked as Cory followed him around the side of the barn. "You need the practice."

The figure he followed wasn't extremely tall or big, but the very idea of him put a thumb over the brightness of the sun and snuffed it out. It didn't matter to Cory what got him so drunk, or why he needed to get this way. The only thing that mattered was that when he was in this kind of mood, he was mean. It was like he was taking the ugliness of the barn and the house and making the boys pay for it.

Sometimes Cory wondered what it would be like if he'd had a baby sister, or if Dad had two girls instead of them. The thought terrified him the same way seeing the beer can resting on the nearby tractor did. And the same way seeing his father take off his dirty coat did.

Cory swallowed, wiping the sweat off his forehead. He watched his father's dirty hand pick up the beer can and drain it, then toss it before picking up one of the baseballs scattered around the ground. Cory took his place in front of the barn, carefully getting into the stance Dad had shown him time and time and time again.

Glazed-over eyes glanced at him in that dull, not-really-there way. Cory had seen it all before.

The batter had the body of an eight-year-old but a much older heart. A much heavier heart.

The pitcher carefully wound up and then unleashed a frightening fastball that whipped past Cory and wailed on the side of the barn. Cory couldn't help wincing a bit as he forced himself to stay in position. There was no point in even trying to swing. All he could do — all he had to do — was stand there and take the pitches like a man.

And not get hit.

"Strike one."

His father's voice mocked him. For someone so unhealthy and underweight, Michael Brand could throw a surprisingly fast pitch. Today he seemed extra angry, so his pitch seemed extra fast.

Cory exhaled and rested the bat on the ground for a second. Just a second. He turned and saw Clay peeking out from a nearby tree.

Good for you, he thought. A very minor victory.

At least Clay wouldn't get hit. Not this time.

Dad had played some ball and obviously liked the whole elaborate routine of contorting to wind back and whip a fastball Cory's way. Cory stood his ground in the stance, eyes on Dad, making sure the ball wasn't going to land against his ribs or knee or cheek.

Each pitch he didn't bother swinging at pounded the side of the barn as Dad screamed out another strike. The third pitch was the fastest one yet. It soared by with fury.

"Strike three," Dad hollered. "You're out."

Full of adrenaline, Cory stood there facing his father, desperately trying to hang on. He wasn't going to cry. He wasn't going to give the man the satisfaction of knowing he was scared. He forced himself to say nothing, to just stand there and wait. Wait and wonder what would happen next.

Another pitch ripped by, and another. Some closer than others. Cory imagined the ball splitting his temple and landing him in the emergency room. Or maybe knocking out some teeth along with knocking him unconscious.

"Strike nine."

The voice taunted and terrorized. Each pitch twisted by him and bashed the side of the barn. Strike after meaningless strike.

Eventually Cory shook his head and put the bat on the ground.

"Get back in the box," Dad yelled.

Cory's whole body shook. A tear streamed down his cheek. His back was drenched with sweat. What else could he do? He couldn't outrun him. And even if he did, he'd be leaving Clay behind.

He resumed his stance, and the pitches continued. Each one tore through him even though they didn't hit him. Not yet. Dad looked like some demon standing there, clasping at baseballs and blindly hurling them his way. Eventually he ran out of ammunition. Gasping from being out of shape, Dad turned to get his beer from the tractor, then realized he'd already downed it.

"Go get the balls, Cory." The voice was without emotion.

Cory dropped the bat and wiped the tears off his face as he began to pick up the pieces of another shattered afternoon. He swallowed and blinked and tried to get a grip.

The good news was that Dad wasn't even watching to see his reaction. The fun was over, and he needed another beer. He always needed another beer. But there would never be enough to fill Michael Brand's thirst.

One of these days Cory knew he was going to hit a ball. He was going to blast one back at his father. And once he did, he vowed never to stop hitting.

Ever.

The ten-year-old doesn't want to budge. Doesn't want to look at his coach. He just stares at the ground, knowing he's going to get yelled at.

"Come on, Cory."

"I don't want to."

"What — are you too nervous to play?"

"No."

"Then what's wrong?"

"I don't want to."

"You don't want to what? You don't want to practice?"

"I don't want to play. Baseball. I hate it. It's stupid."

The coach laughs. "Cory — you can hit better than kids twice your age."

"So?"

"So — you have a God-given talent, kid."

"No, I don't."

"This team could use someone like you. Those boys — they'll look up to you when they

21

see you hitting. I promise. And trust me — it's a cool thing."

"Hitting?"

"No. Being liked. And being watched."

"I don't know."

"It'll get your father off your case. I promise."

"Really?"

"Yeah."

"Okay."

CHAPTER ONE:
FOUL TERRITORY

Fifty thousand fans filled the seats just outside the clubhouse, yet Cory Brand felt alone. Alone with an aching knee despite the handful of Vicodin he'd already downed.

There was no way he was going to let them start digging around his knee. The next thing they'd be doing would be telling him he'd have to get season-ending surgery. He wasn't going on DL, not this early in the season, not when he was in the middle of a slump in the final year of his contract with the Grizzlies.

I've been dealing with pain all my life. I can deal with this.

It was the middle of June, and he was moving slow. His knee wasn't getting any better, even though a week ago he'd told the trainers it was fine. If you hit the ball hard enough, he rationalized, you didn't have to kill yourself racing around the bases. All it took was one right smack. Something that had become a little more difficult as of late.

The mood before the game was about as exciting as the last five games the Denver Grizzlies had played. Cory took a sip from his thermal travel mug with the team logo on it as he sat in the chair in front of his lockers and glanced at the nearby television screen. His two lockers stood between those of the two other all-stars on the team. Once the idea of having a locker in a major-league clubhouse would have been unthinkable. Now it was just another one of those things he took for granted.

Sometimes you dream about something your whole life only to forget about it once the dream has arrived.

Because even dreams can be a lot of work. A whole lot of work.

"It's a blessed day here at the ballpark!"

The chirpy announcer on the screen sounded extra happy as he waxed poetic. Cory took another sip and rolled his eyes.

Yeah, another blessed day to take people's money.

"The spring heat is baking all this love into one slice of nostalgic, all-American pie."

On the screen a banner read *Young Life Welcomes You! Happy Father's Day!*

So that was the big deal. Explained why the announcer was giving it his A-game. Fog still filled Cory's head from last night — at least what he could remember about last night. Now he had to go out and smile and celebrate all the love and joy of fatherhood. *Fabulous.*

That's why it looked like a circus out there. The monitor showed the field littered with lots of fathers playing catch with their sons and daughters. The excitement was almost enough to make everybody out there forget about yesterday's loss. Or the losing streak the team was on. But not the subdued guys in the clubhouse.

"What's up, Brand?"

Rogers didn't seem to care much for Cory and his habits, but he kept his mouth shut and kept his faith to himself. Rogers had his cross and Cory had his coffee mug, but in the end both served the same purpose. Fuel and motivation to make it through another game in a very long season. They were men with jobs to do. Rogers had two lockers just like Cory did. Along with May-hee, they made up the all-star row of the Grizzlies clubhouse, the guys closest to the exit in case the media got a little too overbearing. Cory had heard that Willie Mays had had only one locker, but times

25

were different now, and stars got two and sometimes even more.

His mouth felt dry, and his eyelids didn't want to rise. Cory took another sip and thought of the kids out there playing. Personally, he'd rather be smiling at them than at those overbearing, overweight fans who only lived to ridicule you once your season was taking a nosedive into the dirt. Kids hadn't mastered the art of booing yet. Even though it just came with the territory, the criticism annoyed Cory, especially on days like today.

Cory's usual game-day routine involved cranking his iPod and listening to a little Foo Fighters, but his head hurt too much to do that today. He looked around and saw that Benny was rocking out with a pair of yellow headphones on that made him look like one of those guys on the airport tarmac who steered planes to their gates. Nearby, Gonzalez stood shirtless, showing off his carefully chiseled physique. You'd think a guy so disciplined and ripped could hit a ball a little better, but everybody knew it wasn't *just* about strength.

Cory once heard a guy sum up the science behind hitting a home-run ball. It had been interesting for the first thirty seconds, then began to bore him. He'd always been that way with baseball. The whole numbers game, for instance. Bored the life out of him. The history of the game. The incredible "aura" and all that nonsense. None of that did anything for him except make him thirsty.

He'd let others be enamored with this little round thing that you struck with a wedge of wood. The same way he'd let everybody else talk about his so-called batting slump and his so-declared career-worst .256 batting average this year.

Those things didn't bother him. What bothered him was the buzzing of flies in his head and the throbbing pain in his knee. He was already doing something for the former and decided to grab an ice pack for his knee.

Their relatively new clubhouse was eighty-five thousand square feet of space, with televisions all around and leather couches and love seats in the middle. On some days it still didn't feel big or luxurious enough. On days when the night games and flights back home seemed endless and it took a lot more to get the body and mind up for the game, Cory felt like he was in an expensive commercial made for someone else.

"Hey, Brand, how'd you make out with that chick last night?" It was Bruce, their tank of a catcher, asking.

"Same as always," Cory said, clicking on the flash of his grin.

Bruce just shook his head and moved on. *Yeah, right.*

Cory couldn't even remember her name, if he had to be honest. It was something ending with *ee,* like Stephanie or Emily. She'd wanted to come over to his condo, but he hadn't been *that* drunk. The last thing he needed during a season like this one was to come home and find some woman boiling a rabbit in his kitchen.

By the time Helene rushed into the clubhouse in her typical high-caffeinated manner, most of the players had already gone out to the field. The start time for the game was five. Cory was taking his sweet time. Because of the knee. And maybe because he knew what awaited him outside.

"What's this I hear about you chatting with Capano last night at the fund-raiser?"

"Relax, Helene. You're the only girl for me." He admired her legs as always and grinned. "Though he did offer me his first-born."

His fashionista agent looked as if she was dressed for a movie premiere and not a Denver Grizzlies home game. Cory laughed at her high heels that seemed to sparkle.

Her chocolate skin looked smooth and soft, but Cory knew the rough and tough fighter beneath the sexy exterior.

Helene barely paid his joke any attention as her thumb worked her iPhone.

"You'd have to be *really* drunk to think *that* was a good deal," Cory added.

Which, in fact, I really was.

"That animal would eat his firstborn if it meant signing a new player."

Cory tossed the ice bag on the floor and then rubbed his temple. "Last night was all pretty much a blur. I don't think I signed anything."

Helene ignored his comment. She was like a parent who was physically in the room but hadn't left her work and office behind. Not that Cory really knew anything about that.

"How's the knee?" she asked as her eyes moved from her phone to his leg.

She was probably noticing how he wasn't standing. Not yet.

"It's never felt better," he said. "Give me a minute."

There were lots of things he spoke about with Helene, but his knee wasn't one of them. If pressed, he'd tell her the same thing he told everybody else. It was fine. Wonderful.

A knee doesn't hit baseballs. A knee doesn't spend the game in left field waiting for pop-ups. A knee doesn't really matter unless it's completely gone.

Cory knew that Helene had other players on her roster. None as big as Cory Brand, of course. But that didn't mean she couldn't find the next young stallion ready to play ball and make everybody millions. She'd gladly hop off the saddle and jump on another if she knew that fame and fortune would follow.

His eyes followed her shapely figure out the door. With only Benny still left in the clubhouse, Cory stood up and shook his leg to get some feeling back in it. As usual, he could feel the click of cartilage — it was like hearing something not quite right in the engine of your car. Eventually you knew it was going to have to be looked at.

He sighed and reached for the thermal cup. A bottle of Ketel One was wedged in some clothes in his duffel bag — the first bottle he'd spotted at the condo. He wasn't picky. He found the vodka and emptied the rest into the Grizzlies cup.

It took him a quick swallow to drain it.

He didn't rush to hide the empty bottle, nor did he look around to wonder if any-body was watching. Nobody paid any attention to him in this room. It was out there, in the open air and bright lights under the heavens . . . that's when the world paid attention to his every move.

One hundred and sixty-two games. Those were the moments that mattered. These minutes right now, they were just throwaway minutes when he could do whatever it took to get ready for those games.

Some days, like today, it took a lot more than it used to.

He hears the screaming and makes sure that Clay is still asleep.

Some nights are worse than others.

He holds his breath, thinking that it might help the anger just outside the door go away. He can't make out the words, but he knows the conversation. Dad sounds like a bulldog. Mom sounds like a bird. But she holds her own.

Mom always holds her own.

He waits, listens, wonders if he should rush out there and help her. Wonders if there's going to be some big crash from Dad's hand. But Dad never touches her. He shouts and screams, but that's all.

It's enough.

Sometimes in the morning, Mom will smile and give him a hug and tell him everything's going to be okay.

Sometimes she even tells Cory he's going to grow up to be a great baseball player.

If he ever does, it'll be because of her, not because of the monster she married.

CHAPTER TWO:
LINEUP

On a day when he should have been celebrating and feeling a deep sense of pride, Clay Brand sat in the stands next to his wife, staring at the field and worrying that everything was about to go terribly wrong. They were just above the dugout, overseeing a team of ten- and eleven-year-olds, and so far everything had been perfect. The weather and the chance to get on the field and throw balls around and even the invitation for Carlos to be the batboy. It was a dream come true for Carlos.

Of course, Carlos was *their* dream come true.

For a moment Clay replayed the game of catch they had just enjoyed. For the ten-year-old kid born and raised in Guatemala, it had probably been just that. A game of catch while standing on the grass of Samson Field. But for Clay and his wife, Karen, who stood nearby taking pictures, it had been more. Much more.

Carlos was an answer to prayer, a prayer they had uttered hundreds if not thousands of times. A prayer that had gone unanswered for a very long time.

"What should I ask him first?" Carlos had said. "I got a lot of questions." The joyous smile and the bright eyes were lit up as big as stadium lights after sunset.

Clay had simply smiled, the proud father of a boy who was excited to meet his famous uncle for the first time. "Whatever you want, slugger. It's your big day."

Karen had shared her doubts, but every time, Clay had told her everything would be okay. In his mind he saw the picture of their family — not just the two of them with Carlos in the middle, but Cory standing next to them as well. Cory was always a part of this family, no matter what Karen might think or how little they saw him.

"I want to know his favorite player," Carlos said. "And how to hit a curveball. And what he likes to do on the weekends. You know — when he's not playing base-ball."

Clay could probably have answered that question himself, but the answer would have been R-rated. For now, it was simply impor-tant that Cory meet his nephew for the first time. And what better day for it than Father's Day?

"So Carlos. Ya think you're ready?"

"Only for like four hundred hours now," Carlos gushed. "I can't believe Cory Brand is my new uncle."

Clay had thrown his son the ball and then walked over to him. It was a good thing he was wearing sunglasses, because his eyes had teared up, and Carlos would have asked what was wrong.

The love — love he had questioned would ever come — burst out of Clay's heart and rushed into every inch of his body. He still couldn't believe God had granted it. Adopting a child wasn't a simple and easy process. Several of their friends had tried to no avail. But God had opened the doors, and through it had walked this ten-year-old bolt of energy.

Nothing is wrong, Carlos. I just still can't believe you're my son.

Clay had taken the ball back and joked, "Yep. Cory's a pretty big deal."

But inside all he could think was that Carlos was the big deal. And he hoped — he hoped and prayed — that Cory would get over himself for just a short while and realize the same thing.

■ ■ ■ ■

Now, as most of the players were already out on the field but Cory was nowhere to be seen, Clay began to worry. The commotion of getting all the Bulldogs and their fathers off the field and into their seats was an accomplishment in itself. Clay had kept stalling, hoping his brother would come out and say hello to everybody. He understood that Cory was about to play a really big home game, but he still had hoped . . .

No, I don't get it. Cory should've gotten his butt onto the field when we were all down there.

The look on Karen's face had said it all. It was the same look she gave him every time he mentioned his brother.

Now the typical look of cynicism was accompanied by concern.

"Do you think Cory will remember that's Carlos down there?" Karen asked.

Clay glanced out to the field, where Carlos was talking Jesse Rogers's ears off. The all-star pitcher didn't seem to mind.

"I have no idea."

"Or who Carlos is?"

Clay only shrugged.

I should've made 100 percent sure that Cory

got my messages.

But who didn't get three voice mails and four emails? Clay couldn't count how many times in the past he'd talked to Cory and his brother had said, "Yeah, yeah, got your messages." But this wasn't a simple *Happy Birthday* or *Merry Christmas* or *We're all thinking about you today.* Telling Cory about Carlos was a lot more than that.

He's gotta know we're all here. He's just busy.

Karen laughed and nudged his arm. "Oh my gosh. Look at him."

Carlos was now flanked by members of the Grizzlies team. They seemed to know who he was, because they were treating him special, letting him chatter and ask questions as he pointed to their shoes and gloves.

"What happens if Cory doesn't know?" Karen asked.

"It doesn't matter," Clay said, no longer thinking about his brother. "We still get to take Carlos home."

If Cory doesn't know, then he's going to miss out on the best thing that's ever happened to me.

"You know," Karen said in a voice that always reassured him, "he looks pretty good on that field."

Clay sighed. "Yeah. Well, judging by his

uncle's example, I'm sorta hoping he be-
comes a dentist."

Cory looks at the pitcher and smiles before stepping up to the plate. He doesn't do it to taunt or to tease. He just can't help himself. He wants to come up to this plate ten more times and swing away each time just like the one before. He knows now what it feels like — what the motion and the swing and the sound all feel like — and he doesn't want those feelings to go away.

The pitcher is tall, probably twelve years old like Cory, but he's got fear dumped all over him. The poor guy just wants to go home. He probably thought he was pretty hot stuff, whipping the ball like that and striking out all the other kids. But Cory knows now he's not like the other kids.

This is his fourth time at bat. The last three times resulted in three home runs. The last one got the entire crowd cheering like it was some championship or something. People even cheered his name. He hears Clay's voice above the others. His little brother never misses a game.

Cory still doesn't have any kind of routine for getting ready to hit. At home, the balls have always come fast and furious. At home, he's had to swing in order not to be hit. There's never been time for a routine.

The first pitch is way outside. The pitcher doesn't want another bomb over the back fence. The score is already eight to two, so it's not about losing anymore. It's about being humiliated.

Cory sees the eyes studying him. He knows they're scared. He knows that kid doesn't want to be here.

The kid throws the second pitch, and Cory knows it's his.

Something rushes through him, like the feeling you get when you curl up a fist as hard as you can, or the moment you leap off a tall bridge, or the instant you suddenly think of a brilliant idea. It's quick and thrilling, but it's also simple.

He feels like breaking something with the bat as he swings.

There's that glorious sound again, followed by the reaction of his teammates and the crowd behind him.

The ball soars into the sky.

For a brief second, Cory looks at the pitcher.

The kid doesn't bother to look at the ball; he knows.

It's an image Cory files away somewhere important. A mental picture that he knows he'll see a lot more in his life. The dejected, angry look of someone who knows something couldn't be prevented.

Cory jogs to first base, this time even more slowly and confidently than the last three times.

This is the place he needs to be.

Ripping that ball and blasting it far over the fence makes it all go away. For the moment.

But at the moment — *this* moment — as he runs toward second and sees the stares of the other team and hears the screams of the crowd . . .

It's enough.

CHAPTER THREE: TAG

Cory was usually the last player to leave the clubhouse before a game and the first person to leave afterward. Today was no different. As he walked onto the familiar grass of Samson Field, he heard the swell of the cheers greeting him. He heard and felt them, a feeling that was almost as good as taking a shot in a cloudy sauna. It never got old, to be honest. The only thing you had to get used to was the flip side, the boos and the curses. Especially if you were a star playing an away game. Especially if you happened to be a left fielder. And especially if you were in a bit of a slump and the opposition's fans knew it.

Yeah, those LA fans especially love me.

The afternoon sun felt brighter and the fans seemed more energetic and his head throbbed just a bit more. Cory scanned the seats above the Grizzlies dugout and could see a team of kids decked out in worn red

baseball jerseys and caps, laughing and smiling while their dads sat nearby. He was trying to forget about the whole Father's Day
marketing gimmick, though there were signs
everywhere celebrating it. Some of the Little
Leaguers waved his way, and he nodded in
response.

Cory chewed his gum a little harder as
thoughts crept over him like a pickpocket in
the shadows. He would fight the thief off if
he knew he'd forever leave Cory alone. But
sometimes there wasn't anything Cory
could do about him. This thief had been
taking from him his entire life. The noise of
the park and the vastness of the sky above
and the soft cushion of the grass and the
crack of the bat allowed Cory moments of
respite. But he'd never forget completely.

He glanced at the boy in the red T-shirt
who was talking to Ross, a batting coach.
Ross turned toward him with an amused
look, as if he was expecting Cory's reaction
for some reason. The kid, dark skinned and
bright eyed, spotted Cory and suddenly
stopped midsentence.

"Hey, man," Cory said to both of them
while offering the kid a high five.

The kid didn't say anything, and his high
five was weak. Cory noticed the logo on the
shirt.

"Bulldogs, huh? Got your whole team here with your dads?"

Cory looked out at the kid's teammates. They were all looking his way. Then he scanned the crowd like he usually did, his Oakley shades and cap allowing him to look around without anyone knowing where his gaze was focused.

"What's up, Ross?" Cory said. "Doing a little babysitting today?"

"Just like any other day. Except these kids probably hit better than some of the guys around here."

"Heh." Cory laughed. "So, you play baseball, buddy?"

For a second Cory wondered if the kid knew how to speak English, but then he heard a squeak of a *yeah* come out of the kid's mouth. Cory gave him a nod.

Cory knew the eyes of the crowd were on him, and as always, he didn't want to let them down. Not out here on this field.

"What position do you play?" he asked.

The kid once again gave a high-pitched *yeah,* which made Cory think perhaps he didn't understand English either. And Cory's Spanish wasn't so great, especially on the days when his head felt like a catcher's mitt after a doubleheader.

How do you say "Too much tequila last

45

night" en Español?

Cory tapped the kid on the back. "What do you say you and I get to work? Huh?"

He could have said more, but he walked away. He had made some sweet talk with the kid and had given the cameras a nice shot to show on ESPN. Now it was time to get down to business.

The crowd gave its loudest roar the moment Cory first approached the plate. The noise gave him a surge of energy and hope just like always. He wanted to answer their cheers with a nice long home run.

The pitcher eyed him, but Cory was used to that. Pitchers had never intimidated him. He knew they were trying to outwit him any way they could. Cory Brand wasn't just another player they were throwing to. He was one of the batters they needed to get by.

The first throw was outside. Cory stepped away and felt anxious for some reason. He quickly got back into his stance and waited for the ball.

He did everything right when he connected with it on the second throw. He had already started to burst toward first base, knowing he'd hit a winner. But for some reason, the ball seemed to pause in midair and then slow down. He could see the outfielder reaching, catching the ball, and the inning was over.

Cory cursed as he jogged back to the dugout, knowing his slump had continued, knowing these fans were all feeling the same way he did.

No-scoring games like this one drained the life out of him.

He didn't care about Father's Day and all those daddies with their sons and daughters. He didn't care about his team's losing streak and his batting slump that Helene was all over him about. Yeah, sure, he *did* care that it was a contract year, but that was about it. He didn't care about his ninety-year-old knee that needed a vacation in Maui to mend.

As the sun beat down on the field and the crowd grew restless at the lethargic offenses that had come to play on this day, all Cory could think of was finishing the game and getting rid of the pounding in his head. To scratch the itch, the slow-burning itch that got restless when the excitement wasn't there. Sometimes he found himself thinking this way in a game, already looking past the final pitch and looking forward to that first drink.

The first drink was usually the best.

Yeah, but your first drink came at about nine this morning.

The little Latino kid was still hanging around, handing everybody their bats and offering high fives to every player even though no player deserved one. It had been cute for a while, but by the time Cory stepped up to take the bat in the seventh inning, he'd grown a bit weary of this bundle of joy.

"Good luck, Cory."

He gave the kid a nod, his eyes already off of him, his focus on the subdued fans wilting under the sun. It was a hot day, and he'd give anything to be a fan in the seats, sipping on a beer. But he'd never really been a baseball fan himself. He never had time. He'd been given a bat and forced to hit, and then when it appeared that he was good at it, that's what he did.

He hit and kept hitting.

He'd been hitting so much that the actual game — the history and the love and the adoration and the mystique — was all a bit lost on him.

Those fickle fans out there didn't care about him, not really. They cared about CORY BRAND in all caps and all exclamation points. They cared about the autograph and the value of the card with his picture on it. And they *especially* cared about the hits. They loved you when you gave it to them, and they started to loathe you when you suddenly went dry. That was the reality of this world, this so-called dream he was living. Because at the end of the day, it wasn't a dream or a fantasy — not for guys like Cory. It was a job. A job that came with stress and expectations and the spotlight.

No, the dream came after the spotlight went away, when it was just him alone at the end of the day. Whether he was with the teammates or with a woman or by himself. That was when he could lose himself in his own fantasy. When he could buy into the hype and like that handsome mug smiling on his Facebook fan page.

The first pitch from Weller was a ball. Cory backed up, then stood back in place, shaking his knee out and getting set. He didn't scrunch down like some players when standing at the plate. Cory had gotten used to standing tall and just swinging when he was younger and didn't have an option. Yet he had grown into the habit of a leg kick as the ball came.

Hence the ninety-year-old knee.

The second pitch was a fastball the idiot behind him called a strike. He turned around and looked at the umpire, shaking his head. "Seriously?"

The least the guy could do was give in a little, considering the score and the little kiddies out there looking for some runs.

Cory stepped away and glanced out to the field. On the JumboTron, he once again saw a flashing sign that said HOME RUN CHALLENGE — $10,000. They especially liked showing it when everybody's hero stepped up to the plate.

So far there had been absolutely no money raised for whatever kids' charity it was going to.

His first two hits were a pop out and a groundout. Not exactly crowd pleasers. Nothing would get the fans going more than a clean crack right over the grandstands.

A couple more balls bored both the crowd and Cory. He positioned himself at the plate, the count three and one, feeling that buzz deep down inside of him.

He was a kid again, standing in the dirt, facing someone he hated. All he could do — the only thing he could ever do — was hit the ball the right way. Bash it far out on their property to make the old man shut up and go away. Make his haughty little smile calm down. Make his mockery and belittlement dry up so he could go have a few more beers.

Cory swung, every inch of him willing the ball to blast right through the nightmare playing in his head.

The whack of the ball and the roar of the crowd made the monster and the farm disappear. The ball soared toward center field as Cory hauled his way toward first base. He'd know soon enough if it was a home run.

He was waved toward second and he kept going, knowing the ball had hit the back fence.

The crowd screamed, and the figures around him blurred as he kept running.

I used to be a lot faster.

But he ran steady and hard, taking second and then continuing to sprint onward.

Then he saw the third-base coach telling him to stop.

Yet all around him were cheers and wails and screams telling him to keep running, to score, to "Go, go, go!"

Cory thought of the banners and the home-run challenge and the kids watching with their proud fathers, and he kept going, heading toward home plate.

This wasn't thinking anymore, just acting on pure adrenaline and the rush and the madness and the beating in his head. The defiant will that had always driven him, that had gotten him where he was.

He neared the plate and began to slide and knew he had made it even before the umpire signaled safe and the crowd went crazy.

Cory cursed in a triumphant, vicious manner. Then he laughed at the catcher, who'd taken the brunt of his slide, as he stood up and brushed himself off. He glanced out around the stadium and took it in. The sights and the sounds of over fifty thousand people cheering and high-fiving and finally being given something to see.

A group of fans in the stands waved signs that read *Young Life* and *$10,000.* He did his part, pointing their way and thanking them.

I'm just a humble servant, and I do this all for you.

That's of course how he wanted to appear. A meek and humble player who made seventy-four thousand dollars per game. A clean twelve million per season.

As Cory pandered to the crowd, something strange happened. The pitcher stepped off the rubber and threw the ball to third base. The basemen caught it and tagged the base, and the third-base umpire signaled an emphatic *He's out!*

An appeal? For a moment Cory wondered

if this was some kind of joke. Were they doing this for show, as part of the Father's Day celebration?

There's no way I missed third base.

The crowd began to show their displeasure as the image of him rounding third played on the JumboTron.

No freaking way.

The shouting and the madness around him went away for the moment as the fury inside of him began to swirl around. Everything suddenly turned red and upside down. Losing control, being unable to do anything, standing there stupid and helpless and out of place . . .

A feeling he'd had his whole life.

"Are you outta your mind?" he yelled at the umpire.

Suddenly logic and control ceased to exist.

Cory forgot where he was, forgot the cameras surrounding him and everything else. He just knew he was furious and couldn't take anything anymore.

He wasn't sure how long his hysteria lasted, hurling out curses and insults as the umpire threw him out. Soon he was surrounded on all sides by teammates holding him back, trying to calm him down.

One of them was his manager, but Cory

didn't care.

He didn't understand. Just like the ump and the rest of the world.

Nobody understood Cory's pain and rage.

It should've been a home run. God knows he should've been safe. For once he should have been *safe*. But once again something had been taken away from him.

He wanted to break everything around him.

He wanted to take the baseball and make the umpire choke on it.

Ross dragged him off the field and made sure he got into the dugout. Cory didn't want to look at anyone. He was done. He just wanted to get out of there and leave this stupid game behind him.

The first thing he saw was the Gatorade cooler, which he wished was the umpire's fat head. Cory kicked it and sent it tumbling over, with several guys jumping out of its way.

The booing around the field continued as his cursing in the dugout just got louder.

A little thing like neglecting to touch third base had managed to get him out.

It was unfair. It was stupid.

Cory grabbed a handful of baseball bats, taking them back out onto the field and throwing them in disgust. He heard Ross's voice behind him and knew the batting coach was trying to calm him down. But nothing was going to calm him down. Not now.

Don't you dare touch me or tell me what to do.

He jerked back, ready to shove Ross away from him, and suddenly he felt something crunch under his elbow. Then he heard a muffled wail and saw the kid in the Bulldogs shirt, holding his nose as it gushed blood.

Oh no.

The screaming and booing suddenly stopped as if someone had unplugged a stereo. For a second he stood there, wondering what the stupid kid was doing there in front of him. Wondering where he had come from. Cory started to go help him, but Ross and a trainer and a couple of other guys swarmed him before he could do anything. He started to object, but they grabbed him and made sure he was heading to the clubhouse.

Cory Brand was definitely done for the day.

He pried the hands off his uniform and tried to go back to see if the boy was okay, but the guys wouldn't let him.

Now the booing and yelling was intensified.

Suddenly Cory felt like he was part of the visiting team. Suddenly he felt like he was back in LA with all those fans who hated him because he'd beaten them so many times.

I didn't mean to hit him. It was an accident.

He was forced to go to the locker room by himself. Cory walked there in the darkness of the hallway, the sounds of the crowd fading behind him.

For a while he just stood there in the clubhouse, watching the incident replaying on one of the monitors on the wall. Seeing his own behavior made him cringe.

I gotta get out of here.

Yet he continued watching to see what happened with the kid.

The boy was flocked by the trainer and a couple of other guys, but soon he held his nose and gave a thumbs-up as he was led off the field.

The camera panned to his fellow Little League teammates cheering and yelling in the stands.

It wasn't Cory Brand they were cheering, however.

It was the kid Cory Brand had knocked over and bloodied on his home field.

"Come on, man. Nobody's gonna find out."

"I don't care if they do."

Rex is two years older than Cory but can't hit a ball like Cory can. Nobody can, to be honest. That's why the older kids look up to him, and why he's been invited to this house where the parents are gone for the weekend. Rex's older brother is a junior in high school and is taking care of Rex, whatever that means.

It obviously means Rex has the house to himself and is now searching for booze.

"Roger does it all the time," Rex tells him.

Cory could tell Rex that his father does it all the time too. He's not impressed with drinking.

"Come on. Roger got a case of beer. He won't care if we have some."

Cory doesn't tell the seventh grader in front of him that he's never had beer in his life.

"I don't want any."

"Why not?"

"Just because."

"You're not gonna get in trouble."

"Did I say I was gonna?"

"Lighten up, man. Come on."

Cory looks at the kid and doesn't intend to back down. One part of him is defiant . . . but another part is curious.

"I don't want any beer."

"Yeah, you told me that."

"Do your folks have anything harder?"

Rex looks at him and smiles. "They got a whole cabinet in the other room."

"Okay, then. What are we waiting for?"

It's the first time Cory takes a drink. The first time he feels the burn in his throat and his stomach. It's pretty awful. But he doesn't back down, not after Rex takes his second sip.

Cory never backs down. He decides to take another sip.

It won't be his last.

CHAPTER FOUR:
CLEANUP HITTER

Clay was dumbfounded. Not at the train wreck he and the rest of the country had watched up close as Cory flipped out and got thrown out of the game.

No.

What he couldn't believe was his son's response. The only thing that could possibly have topped the day for Carlos was if he had personally slammed a home run to win the game. He seemed to have forgotten what had actually happened and who had done this to him.

As the Bulldogs and their parents gathered around, Clay walked Carlos to the bus. His son held an ice pack like a trophy as several of his teammates rushed around him to ask how he was doing. His nose had gotten dinged, but it wasn't broken. He was going to live.

As for his uncle's career . . . that was a different story.

Karen hurried toward them, a concerned look on her face. Clay hugged her and gave her a kiss on her forehead.

This Father's Day hadn't exactly turned out the way they had imagined. Or at least the way *he* had imagined. Karen probably was biting her tongue to keep from telling him "I told you so." Because she had told him so, several times.

He was sure they'd be talking about it soon enough, but now wasn't the time. Especially since he had something else to tell her.

"I'm thinking about sticking around."

Now it was Karen who was dumbfounded. With the hum of the bus motor next to them, they were safe from being heard by the rest of the group.

"Are you serious? Why?"

"I can't leave him like this," Clay said.

Karen gave him a look of disbelief. "What can you possibly do for him?"

"I don't know. Just talk. Find out what's up."

He didn't want to share how he really felt. He wasn't just worried about Cory. His worry had turned to fear, the same kind of fear he'd felt growing up around Dad.

"That's ridiculous, Clay. How are you even going to get home?"

"I'll figure it out. I've got cash and credit cards."

His wife still didn't seem to believe what she was hearing. She waited for more of an explanation, but Clay didn't offer one.

"I would think — under the circumstances — you'd be heading back with us," Karen said.

He glanced over at Carlos. His teammates all surrounded him as he told about going inside the stadium to the trainers' room to be examined. One of his friends asked to hold the ice pack.

"Just for a second, Tyler," Carlos said in a serious tone that caused Clay to smile. "It's an official ice pack only for players and people who work for the team. And I need it."

"Dude, you were on that giant screen," the normally unfazed and cool Stanton said. "The whole place was cheering for you."

"I know! I was all . . ." Carlos acted like he was being led out of the parking lot and made his thumbs-up gesture again, which made the rest of his teammates laugh and cheer again.

Clay looked back at Karen and offered her a smile. "I think Carlos is fine."

Karen couldn't dispute it.

"Seriously, he's been checked out by the

team doctors. They completely indulged him in there. Used every state-of-the-art gadget they have."

"Good. Is there something to examine your brother's head?"

"I think they're still looking for that tool." He sighed, staring back at the massive brick stadium in the distance. "He's all the family I've got left."

Karen nodded her head slowly. "All right."

He glanced at his wife, who still looked so young and beautiful in her baseball cap and shirt. He leaned over and kissed her on the cheek.

"Do you think you'll even be able to get hold of him?"

"I don't know," Clay said. "But I have to try. I have to do something."

Cory deliberately skipped meeting with the media, and he also made sure he delayed leaving the stadium for a while. As he walked out of the empty clubhouse, after getting an earful from Ross, he recalled his conversation earlier with Helene. She'd barged in on him as he was watching the other team score five runs in the eighth inning.

"You're killing me," she'd said as she walked toward him, wearing her panic-mode face.

"Technically it's only batboys I'm killing," he replied, trying to make a joke. "And he's still alive, last I looked."

"This isn't funny, Cory."

"I know. They scored five runs now that I'm out of the game."

Helene stood next to him but didn't even look him in the eyes as she spoke. He knew she was already trying to figure out whom to talk to and when, and what she would say to get him out of this mess. All the reasons he paid her so well.

"This is serious, Cory. I mean it."

Cory yawned and nodded. He was tired and needed to get out of this place.

"You better get on your knees and pray that his family doesn't sue you and the Grizzlies."

"Get his family season tickets and some vouchers for free beer," Cory said. "They'll be more than excited."

"This isn't the year to be messing around like this," Helene continued.

"It'll change."

"What will change? The team or you?"

"Both," he said, flashing his grin and trying to convince her that everything was under control. "Once I start hitting again, everything will be fine."

"You have to stay in the game in order to hit."

They watched another shot to left field. The score was now six to nothing. "Yeah, they're dying out there."

Helene looked at her phone and shook her head. "I need to put out some fires. Can you just make sure you avoid the media?"

"What do you mean?" he joked. "Why do you think I'm waiting here? I got a seat warm and ready for Johnny Steiman."

"Stay away from them, especially Steiman."

"I'm not an idiot."

Helene brushed back her hair and gave him her trademark laugh. "You bloodied a kid's nose out there. No, you're not an idiot. You're just a jerk."

"Thanks for having my back."

"I'm here to *save* your pretty backside."

Her phone summoned her attention, and she left Cory in the silence once more. He liked the banter with Helene a lot more than the solitude and the waiting.

A little while after that, one of the trainers came up to him with a smile. "We took good care of him, don't worry."

He'd just coldcocked a kid, and yes, it was an accident, and yes, he was trying to tell himself that over and over again. But smiley-guy here was making it seem like everything was fine and he hadn't been just kicked out of a game they were now losing by seven runs.

"You should've seen the kid. He couldn't believe he was actually being examined by an official trainer. He was really proud of that."

"Yeah, great. Cool."

It was already dusk when Cory walked to his car. He'd had a few uncomfortable moments with the manager and gotten cold looks from some of the guys, but that was it. He'd managed to avoid the media. Heaven forbid he came within earshot or eyesight of another Little Leaguer or his mother or perhaps a 350-pound father waving a baseball bat at his head. He wanted to leave without any fanfare or without anything to do with a fan at all.

He was ready to go home and leave this waste of an afternoon behind. Hopefully the whole thing would blow over by tomorrow.

As he approached the last remaining vehicle in the players' lot, a black luxury Porsche SUV, he noticed someone standing by it, waiting. He wasn't worried, because security was top-notch and not just anybody could get in this lot without clearance.

But the last person he expected to find

waiting there was his baby brother, whom he hadn't seen in over a year.

"What's this, Clay-boy? You should've told me you were coming!"

To be honest, it was a relief to see him.

The relief lasted about the amount of time it took to drain a beer. The smile on Cory's face wasn't coming back from grim-faced Clay.

"I did." Clay looked like he'd been knocked in the face.

Cory tried to remember if they'd spoken about Clay coming even as he grinned and unlocked the car doors.

"That's right, that's right. You know — that's why I put on the big show out there."

"You gotta be kidding me." Clay glared at Cory. "What happened to you?"

Cory shook his head. He knew how to deal with Clay. "Aw, it's just show biz."

This was the last thing he needed, his little brother starting in on him. So he didn't know Clay was coming, and didn't play the part of the loving brother who met him on the field and introduced him to everybody and promised him a grand slam later in the game.

Yeah, maybe next time.

Cory casually tossed his bag into the back. Clay's expression didn't change. "That was some serious rage out there."

"Whatever." He opened his car door, unwilling to be lectured.

People didn't understand the pressure of the game. He could tell Clay this, but he was too tired and too thirsty.

"Cory, we should talk."

Oh no. I don't like that tone.

"Talk? 'Bout what?"

"About — you've got a problem."

Clay looked so dang earnest, like a judging parent or principal or priest. But the fact was, he was none of those things. Cory didn't have the time or the energy to be lectured by his kid brother.

"Okay, I think we're done here."

Cory climbed into the SUV and slammed the door, then watched as Clay opened the passenger door and sat down next to him. Cory ignored him, refusing to start the vehicle, refusing to say another word.

"I need a ride," Clay said.

"Then call a cab. I'm going home."

"I need a place to crash too."

Cory chuckled in disbelief. "Forget it."

"Hey, slugger, that *kid* you elbowed in the nose? He's my son. Karen and I adopted him two months ago."

Cory turned and saw the grim face looking at him. There was no punch line coming, no *Just kidding.* Clay was serious. In the black hole of his mind, Cory connected a few dots.

The team sitting behind the dugout, the kid stammering when he met him, the special attention placed on him . . .

"You know," Clay continued, "it'd be nice if you actually read an email or returned a call once in a while. Or remembered when you do."

Cory exhaled. He felt like a hot-air balloon shriveling up and dropping back down to the earth. Then he let out a curse.

No wonder he was so excited to see you, you complete and utter moron. No wonder he was the designated batboy.

"I'm sorry."

His words felt like a lone island in the middle of an endless ocean.

"Yeah."

It wasn't the first apology his brother had heard from him. But it was the first he'd heard personally in quite a while.

Cory rubbed the back of his head and then his eyes. For a moment, he just sat studying his brother.

The days of the two of them running around their farm seemed like a whole other life.

"You look kinda pudgy," Cory joked.

"I could kick your butt. And I could do it without a personal trainer and a masseuse. I *work* for a living."

Clay wasn't joking, yet he still made Cory laugh. Clay always made him laugh, when he wasn't making him feel the need to go find a priest and a confessional. Cory couldn't believe that the batboy was Clay and Karen's son, or that Clay had been in the stands watching the whole thing.

Uncle Cory. What a loser.

"So you're what. Mayor now?"

"District attorney," Clay corrected. "I get a parking place and a key to the restroom."

"Congratulations. Just tell me they're in different places."

"Your humor's not going to get you out of this one."

It had been a year since they'd seen each other, and a lot longer than that since he had been home. Cory wasn't even sure how many years, to be honest. When you were in this business it was hard to remember facts about others. Those details everybody else kept track of — stuff like birthdays and anniversaries and names of nieces — all drifted away like a fly ball soaring over the fence, out of reach.

"How's Emma?"

Hearing her name on his own lips was

strange. It was one thing to occasionally think of someone who used to be a big part of your life. It was another thing to utter the name out loud and realize you hadn't done so in a long time.

Clay got serious and sober so quickly that Cory almost laughed.

"She's good," Clay said. "It's been hard on her and Tyler since James died."

Names from yesterday, from yesteryear. Cory stared at the dashboard and for a moment lost himself in a strange cloud of memories.

"She says she likes being back home in Okmulgee," Clay said.

Good for her, and good for Okmulgee.

Cory wanted to crank up some Rage Against the Machine, but that might have been a little obvious, so he decided against any music. The cologne he'd doused over himself to cover up the smell of booze on his breath seemed to be competing with Clay's scent of sweat and nachos.

"I think she was geared up to see you at Dad's funeral," Clay said. "I think we all were, to be honest."

It's going to come any moment now, any second, just like that inevitable curveball you just know is gonna get thrown. . . .

"I still can't believe you didn't come."

Boom.

Cory had been waiting for those words since the moment he saw Clay standing by the SUV. They'd been waiting to be spoken for some time now.

"I couldn't."

That was all he would say. There was more, of course. A whole book more, but he didn't want to — no, he couldn't start that. Not after the kind of day he'd just had.

"I know."

Clay sounded as though he understood.

"You hungry?" Cory asked to try to figure out some way out of this conversation.

"Yeah."

He started up the engine and headed out of the parking lot. "It's gonna be a salad for you, chubby."

This time Cory did turn on the stereo, and for some reason the radio blasted an old song that seemed to be dedicated to Cory Brand.

This one's coming from all the batboys of the world, Cory: "I'm a loser, baby, so why don't you kill me?"

71

There's something different about the girl in his freshman class at Fremont High.

He knows this, even though he can't really admit it or articulate why.

She's more than just a pretty face.

She's shy when the pretty girls usually aren't.

She's feisty when the shy girls usually aren't.

She's generous when the feisty girls usually aren't.

She's pretty when the generous girls usually aren't.

There's nothing usual about Emma, and that's why he likes her. He's just not sure of one thing, and this is the thing that baffles him.

He doesn't know if she likes him or not. And that makes her even more unusual.

Chapter Five:
On Deck

"Okay, so you're totally serious, right? About the whole adoption thing?"

For a moment Clay didn't respond. He just watched his brother as he worked on the large steak on his plate like a person recently let out of prison.

"Why would I lie about something like that?"

"Because you hate your brother and want him to feel guilty for not giving you season passes."

"That would be a long drive from Oklahoma," Clay said. "Plus, I like my teams to win."

"Ouch."

They sat at a table in the back of the steakhouse. Clay had suggested they go someplace like Chili's or T.G.I. Friday's, but Cory laughed as if that was a joke. As if the very mention of those restaurant chains was so far below his lifestyle that they were a

punch line. Cory instead had driven to El-
way's. The servers were professionals who
apparently didn't pay attention to baseball
games. Clay had actually felt a bit silly in
his jersey and cap, walking into the fine dining establishment.

"I thought you said you were hungry,"
Cory said.

"I was thinking more of fast food or something."

"Should've gotten the rib eye. I told you
I'm paying."

"Such generosity."

Clay thought of the last time they had
spoken, over the phone after their father's
funeral. He'd just wanted to know why Cory
hadn't been there, but all he got was a
drunken rampage about a messed-up childhood and the pressures of the game. Cory
obviously didn't remember the conversation, because he'd ended it with some harsh
things to say about Clay.

"You guys all should've spent the night,"
Cory said as he took a sip of his beer.

"Did you want a team of Little Leaguers
spending the night with you?"

"I'm talking about Karen and you. And
the boy."

"Carlos."

"Yeah, Carlos."

Clay picked at the pasta in front of him. Nothing about this felt natural. The fine linens at the table, the hushed atmosphere, the expensive clothes Cory wore. At least back in the stadium, things made a little more sense. Even with the hysterical Cory Brand going off. *That* was a picture he recognized. This was something that belonged to someone else's life.

"It took a lot for Karen just to agree to the ball game," Clay said.

Cory shook his head, obviously not wanting to talk about it. He was a good-looking guy — always had been. The resemblance was there, of course, but with Cory everything was always just a little more. He was a little taller and a little broader. His eyes were a little more striking, his smile a little more shiny. Clay could play sports, but not like Cory. Living with someone like that day after day, this brilliant bursting sun that was impossible for the world to miss, simply made the shadows in Clay's own life all the more noticeable.

"I really thought you knew we were coming."

"It happens," Cory said in a casual, everything's-going-to-be-fine manner. "I'll make up for it. I'll make sure Carlos doesn't regret coming."

75

Clay chuckled. "Are you kidding me? He's already on top of the world. It's his mother I'm worried about."

"Yeah, well . . ."

Cory obviously wasn't so worried about Karen. Perhaps he'd given up on her the same way Karen had given up on him.

"You know, this past year — with Dad passing away and our adopting Carlos — a lot has happened."

Cory nodded but didn't look at him, not really.

Don't push him like you usually do. Don't force the issue.

"There's just — it's been a pretty wild year."

"You and me both," Cory said with a knowing laugh.

Clay knew what Cory was talking about. He didn't want to admit this to his brother, but every day Clay kept track of Cory Brand. The name and the number. One of the first things he did every morning was Google the name to see if there was any news on him. He was interested in the games, of course, and he watched all of them that time allowed. But Clay couldn't care less about stats or streaks or any of that stuff. He cared about the news items that linked Cory to some latest bit of trouble. A fight in a bar or being seen in public with some floozy actress. Clay wanted the star athlete to go away and his brother to come back home. To get straightened out and to be in his life — *their* lives — once again.

The server came, and Cory didn't hesitate to order another glass of beer. Clay wanted to say something about the drinking but knew he couldn't. Not here, not tonight. All it would do was make Cory shut down.

I said enough in that last phone conversation.

He was here with his brother and spending the night at his condo. That was a start.

Clay would pray that this was indeed just the start of something bigger and better for the two of them. The start of Cory finding his way back home. One way or another.

Sometimes the condo felt like another hotel room in another state. Or another home belonging to another person.

Cory made small talk with Clay and set him up in the living room to sleep. The guest bedroom was a complete disaster, a storage place that he used for everything, including his baseball gear. He never had guests. Usually Cory was the one staying overnight somewhere else. This was a bachelor pad. Designed for a bachelor who

77

didn't spend a lot of time at home.

It was late and he was tired, and more than that, he was starting to feel something he hated. Something that he tried to outrun but that sometimes caught up to him. It was a feeling like trying to steal a base and then realizing he'd started to slide way too early and there was no way to avoid being tapped out.

Cory turned on his bedroom light, wishing he could forget everything that had happened in the last twenty-four hours. Yet thoughts crept in like moonlight into the dark room. He found his noise-canceling headphones underneath a pile of clothes on the floor and slipped them on, hoping the rock music from his iPod could cancel out the memories as well. He found something loud and upbeat, meant to ruin this melancholy moment. He was Cory Brand, and he didn't have time to mope around thinking about yesterday.

Tomorrow was already here, and he had a new chance to step up to the plate and hit the ball out as far as he could. Few people understood it like he did and lived it out like he did.

As he closed his eyes he pictured Emma's sweet smile.

Don't.

He hated thinking of her. Thinking of Emma reminded him of all the things left unfinished. Like a game with only six innings. Like striking out with only one strike on the count. That story hadn't been finished, yet it was over. It was over and done and everybody had moved on, especially him.

So why are you thinking of her?

It was just because Clay's silly little face had come out of nowhere and surprised him. No, more than that — Clay and his surprise had gotten the best of him. So now he was feeling guilty and letting his guard down. Normally if he felt like this he'd grab a bottle and head out to a gentlemen's club. To forget. To have some fun and to enjoy himself.

He liked enjoying himself, and having Clay back wasn't very enjoyable.

After searching for a few minutes, Cory found half a fifth of rum in his closet and decided he deserved it after the day he'd had. Rum wasn't his favorite, but it would do.

The music and the alcohol helped. But he knew sleep was going to be an enemy tonight. He'd need the rest of this bottle in order to find slumberland and forget.

"Don't go believin' in something that's never gonna happen."

The words don't surprise Cory. He just doesn't realize they'll never go away.

His father drives the beat-up truck with Cory on the other side and Clay in the middle. As usual, Clay is ignored, which is part of Cory's plan. The less attention Dad pays to Clay, the better. Dad smells like cheap cigarettes and cheaper beer. If a cop pulled them over, he would definitely get arrested, but they're in the middle of the country, and nobody's going to pull anybody over.

"A dream's just that — a dream. Something you do when you're sleeping. Keep it at that."

Cory doesn't say anything. They're coming back from a game where Cory was the hero. Dad only showed up after the game was over. He obviously heard about Cory's success — hence the pep talk.

"Life's gonna come and crush you," Dad tells

him. "You mark my words."

Cory stares out into the dark countryside and marks the words loud and clear.

He grips the armrest just like he might grip a bat.

Deep down inside, he answers back to his father.

I hear you, and I'm going to prove that I'm different.

"You hear me, 'cause I don't want you crying like a baby when your knee goes out or when you realize you're not that good compared to the really great ones."

"Yes, sir," Cory says.

Yeah, I hear you.

But I'm going to prove you wrong.

Dead wrong.

Chapter Six:
Called Game

His bare feet brushed against the hardwood floor of the condo. The small hallway opened up to the large open space that comprised both his main living area and the kitchen with an island that served as the only barrier between the two. Cory could see the back of Clay's head popping out of the blanket, his hair sticking up like a potted plant just starting to grow. It wasn't even eight o'clock, but Cory had already been up for a while, his mind racing around a room he felt trapped inside.

For the first time since moving to this condo, Cory noticed how bare everything looked. The walls, the counters, the tables. There were decorative pieces here and there that an interior decorator had placed when he first moved in. But there were no pictures, either hanging or framed and standing on the tables. There were no books or magazines anywhere. The last book Cory had tried to read was a horror novel by a guy named Dennis Shore, but he'd only gotten halfway through. This condo didn't looked lived in; it was just a pretty shell.

As the cupboard door squeaked in a way he'd never noticed before, Cory grabbed a glass and carefully put it on the counter. He glanced back at his brother, still snoozing away.

Probably best sleep of his life, now that the ball and chain isn't anywhere around.

He opened the almost-empty freezer and found the bottle of vodka. As he opened it and began to pour, the bottle seemed to have a mind of its own and clanked down hard against the glass. Cory tore off a silent curse as he stood there, like some grade-school kid caught in his father's liquor cabinet. Clay didn't move.

Cory had forgotten how Clay could sleep through anything. How both of them could, in fact. You grew used to sleeping through noises and bangs in the night when you had a lush for a father.

He took a sip of vodka and exhaled. Some guys needed to sip their morning cup of coffee or light up a nasty cigarette to get their morning fix. This was what he needed. It hadn't always been like this, and he was sure it wouldn't always be. It was what he needed now, in this season of his life. Nobody, including Clay, would necessarily understand. That was why he didn't want his brother noticing. It wasn't his business, and really, it was no big deal.

The sound of birds outside soothed him. It looked like it was going to be another hot day, and they had another afternoon game scheduled. He began thinking about his knee and about taking something for it when a flurry of sounds interrupted the peaceful moment. First came the pounding knocks, then a key fit into the lock, and the front door banged open.

Even before hearing the tip-tap of expensive heels, Cory knew who was bursting through his doorway at this time of the morning. Helene strolled past the head suddenly sticking up on the couch and went straight to Cory.

All business, all the time. That was Helene Landy.

Cory set his glass down on the island but didn't have time to do anything with the bottle behind him. As usual, Helene looked as if she'd been up for several hours, her hair perfectly in place, her business suit tailored just right around her figure.

"You're on an eight-week suspension," she said as she picked up the glass and continued striding past him.

"Good morning to you, too," Cory said.

For a moment Helene glanced at the couch; then she continued on toward the dining room table, obviously not interested in the half-clothed figure now sitting up. It could have been a half-naked woman or half-alive corpse, yet Helene would still be getting down to business. She pulled the laptop from her briefcase and opened it on the table, then waved Cory over like he was a puppy getting ready to start potty training.

The glass stood next to her computer like a dog treat. If Cory had a tail, it would probably be wagging.

"Come on," Helene said. "I have something interesting for you to watch."

Cory didn't think it was going to be interesting. He didn't even think he wanted to see it.

Helene clicked something on the computer screen and then moved out of the way so he could see the monitor. It was a YouTube video that showed him yelling and kicking the Gatorade cooler and elbowing the poor ten-year-old kid in the nose.

That looks worse than it did yesterday.

"Cory Brand injures batboy," Helene said as if reading a jury's verdict. "Almost one

85

million hits. Already."

Over by the couch, Clay quickly slid into his jeans with an uncomfortable look. Cory would make a formal introduction in a moment. For now he watched the video, wanting to shut it off but unable to keep his eyes off it.

"It was an accident," he said. Then, as Clay began to strip his makeshift bed on the couch, Cory said in a quieter voice, "Can we do this later?"

He walked back toward the kitchen.

"Hold on just a sec." Helene typed something else and brought up another video. "Cory Brand boozing it up in Vegas. 364,902 hits."

Cory let out a loud laugh. Someone had shown him that video, which he had laughed about at the time. He still didn't exactly know when the Vegas video was filmed, or who filmed it, but he knew it was in the off-season when he was blowing off some steam. So what? People did it all the time.

I was really bombed there.

"Jon Stewart thinks I should move in with Roethlisberger and start a reality TV show," Cory joked.

He said it to Helene, but the statement was really directed more at his brother. Clay was folding a blanket like the good little boy he'd always been, but Cory knew he was listening to every word.

Helene pulled up another video and just studied the screen. "Cory Brand drunk at a strip club. 217,408 hits. You're a disaster."

"I'm a career .327 hitter."

Nobody was laughing at his attempt at humor. Clay began to walk over toward them, since Helene wasn't finished.

"Cory's DUI arrest caught on tape. Over one million hits."

"Who doesn't want to be on *Cops*?"

Helene was still looking for more, but Cory had seen enough.

"Hey, when you look at it all at once like that, of course it looks bad. But I'm sure you'll find a lot of videos where I'm sober and doing something good."

The computer snapped shut, and Helene picked it up. She wasn't trying to shame him. Helene didn't operate like that, not with Cory. She was probably just trying to show him what she was dealing with. She looked like she was already negotiating, trying to figure out the next move they should make.

"You still have the condo in Miami?" Helene asked.

What's that have to do with anything? Is that where I need to spend my suspension?

87

"Yeah, but did I tell you I popped the water bed?" Cory glanced at Clay the way one frat boy might look at another. "Floor's a little warped now."

Clay gave him that adult look, the look that Cory hated, the kind that most adults seemed to inherit from their self-righteous and fun-bashing parents. The look that said *Shame on you.*

Helene slipped the computer into her bag and checked her phone for a moment, answering a text or an email. Cory introduced Clay, but she wasn't extremely interested. She found something in her bag and gave it to Cory. It was a boarding pass.

"Here's what you're going to do. You'll fly to Tulsa with your brother and make nice with the kid in Okmulgee while you're there."

This wasn't a round of brainstorming here. Helene spoke to him like a mother to her son.

"Okmulgee? No."

She gave her polite but bullheaded smile. "Okmulgee, yes. We'll arrange a *very* public apology to the kid —"

"The kid has a name," Clay said with a bit of an edge in his voice. "It's Carlos."

Helene paused for a moment, the annoyed look filling her face, then stepped away while she continued to talk to Cory and ignore Clay.

"Well, whoever he is, he's getting a bag of goodies from the Grizzlies and a photo op with a celebrity. Then you can go chill on the beach for eight weeks."

She still doesn't know that's my nephew she's talking about.

He was about to argue with her, telling her there was no way he was going back home, not now. He'd promised himself he was never going back there.

"One other thing," Helene said. "The Grizzlies want proof you're attending a twelve-step program."

"Twelve-step?"

This was unbelievable.

He accidentally hit a kid in the nose. It wasn't like he ran over the kid with his car while intoxicated.

The kid has a name.

"The team wants you out of sight until you've completed eight weeks. So you do the press conference, then go to Miami and find some kind of program. A low-profile sort of thing."

Then what? There has to be a then, right?

He waited. Helene wasn't going to tell him anything else. There wasn't any *but* this time.

Cory sighed as she began walking toward the door. He wanted to ask her about an appeal process, and whether he could talk to the Grizzlies owner, and maybe a hundred other questions. But he knew she was done for the day.

"Oh, and Cory?"

Well, maybe not.

"You're writing a ten-thousand-dollar check to Young Life for the homer you screwed up."

"What?" Cory slumped onto the nearest couch and moaned in a way that sounded like he was dying.

"I promise you," Helene said, "you won't feel a thing."

The door slammed shut, and she was gone as quickly as she had come.

For a moment Cory just sat there, staring at the ceiling and wishing he didn't feel anything. Clay didn't speak.

There really wasn't anything more to say.

"That smile is dangerous," a tenth-grade Emma teases.

"I know. It's like a James Bond kind of smile."

"No way."

"What do you mean?"

"You're the farthest thing in the world from James Bond."

"But you just said —"

"That your smile is dangerous."

"I don't get —"

"James Bond is cocky."

"So I finally met a girl who doesn't think I'm cocky."

"Deep down, there's someone else. Not a superhero."

"A baseball player?"

"No. An actor. A comedian. Used to stepping up to the stage and making everyone applaud and laugh. But I've seen you when the lights shut off and there's no one else around."

"Uh oh. Emma Johnson knows me."

"I think I do. And that's what scares me. Because I'm falling for that guy. The one no one else knows."

Chapter Seven: Fly Ball

"This is a bad idea."

Clay knew Karen would say that because she didn't want Cory near their family. She didn't want him anywhere remotely close to the state of Oklahoma, much less Okmulgee.

"It's not like I bought him the ticket," Clay said. "I thought you'd be happy."

"I'll be happy when Cory stops thinking of himself and cools his temper."

"Isn't that the point of recovery? Karen —"

"Now isn't a good time."

"A good time for what?" His cell phone was almost out of juice; he had to wrap this up quickly. "It's not like he's moving in with us."

"I know people like Cory."

"He's my brother."

"And you're my husband, who has better things to do than having to go around cleaning up for him."

"That's unfair."

Their flight was a couple of hours from leaving the Denver airport. Cory had wandered off somewhere, saying he might not see Clay until they landed. "First class" was all Cory had said in an amused, we're-taking-an-adventure sort of way.

"So where is he going to stay? And what's he going to do?"

"His agent is taking care of it. You should see this lady. She's something else."

"Cory's something else."

"This might be the change we've been praying for."

"Recovery doesn't happen overnight," Karen said.

Clay couldn't say anything to her. He understood. He also knew that this wasn't Cory's decision, but his determined agent's. An agent trying anything she could to make the publicity nightmare go away.

Karen didn't need to know all of that. Clay just wanted her to know where he was and what was happening with his brother.

"How's Carlos doing?"

"He's still talking about the big game," Karen said, her defensiveness dialed down.

"He's going to love having Uncle Cory in town."

"As long as his uncle doesn't run over him with a truck."

"Wow."

"Well, it's true."

"This is a side of you I haven't seen," Clay admitted. "Mama Bear protecting her new cub."

"Do you blame me?"

"No. I mean — I like this side of you. It's kinda sexy."

"Oh, stop. See — you've been around your brother twenty-four hours, and you're already starting to talk like him."

Clay laughed. "I just want us to be a family."

"You have a family."

"I want Cory to be a part of it. To maybe start from square one, like Carlos is doing."

"Cory has a long way to go to be as loving and *mature* as that beautiful ten-year-old boy."

"Can I tell him you said that?"

"Please," Karen said. "And tell him I'm saving a nice spot for him to sleep. In the barn."

Clay couldn't help smiling. "I'll see you guys soon."

Cory sat in a booth in the corner of a restaurant, having a conversation with the love of his life. The beauty of this private chat was that she didn't talk back. She comforted and soothed him, allowing him to vent without saying a single word. She understood his deepest and darkest feelings. She didn't judge him, either. She simply let him be Cory and let him enjoy as much of her as he wanted.

He finished his "conversation" with the vodka and tonic and crunched an ice cube as he glanced up at the screen above the bar. The volume was down, but ESPN was replaying the glorious highlight of him going ballistic at the game and striking the batboy. A couple of commentators followed to share their own thoughts, and judging by their expressions, they were doing the whole good-commentator/bad-commentator routine. Several pictures came up showing Cory; first his official team picture, then a few other at bats for the year. Cory laughed and looked back at his empty glass, thankful to see the skinny little thing walking up to refill it.

"Another?"

The young woman didn't smile like the ladies usually did. That was because she was oblivious to who was sitting there. And that was fine with him. The last thing he needed was to cause a commotion and have people start asking for autographs or pictures.

It wouldn't be good to be seen drinking in a bar at the airport.

But he was inside and facing the back so that he couldn't be seen. To the waitress, Cory was just another businessman traveling for his job and worried about the wife and kiddies at home.

"Give me a double," Cory said, knowing the flight would be taking off soon.

He'd spent enough time "catching up" with Clay and making sweet chitchat. He could already see his brother's mind working. Clay had seemed glad that Cory had to go back home, even if it was for a brief visit. Now Cory could get to know Carlos a little more and try to make amends with some of those he'd lost touch with. In particular, with Emma.

That was why Cory was sitting in this place, in the muted light and the soft hum of conversation. He needed some peace of mind. Some time to not have to think about all that twelve-step nonsense.

Missing one step to tag third base shouldn't mean I have to enter a freaking twelve-step program.

Helene didn't care what it meant or what he thought. She didn't care whether he actually believed in the recovery program.

She just knew he needed to get his rear out there in the spotlight to show he was doing something about his "problem." He had to go through it so he could get back on the field and start producing. Already he'd made her job more difficult in terms of negotiating a new contract. But the idea of talking about a new contract now made him think of NFL coach Jim Mora answering a reporter's question about the play-offs — "Play-offs? Don't talk about play-offs!"

Cory couldn't help laughing a bit. The waitress brought him back a drink, and he gave her a few twenties to cover the tab, telling her to keep the change. He took a sip and stopped thinking of Helene and the team and Clay and all the other stuff. It was just one downward spiral that wouldn't stop. Feeling bad didn't change a thing. He'd spent his entire youth feeling bad about his father, but that had gotten him nowhere. There was never anything anybody could do, and then one day not long ago he heard his father had finally died.

Boom.

Just like that. There was no dramatic deathbed scene where his dad gripped his hand and asked for forgiveness.

No, if Cory had been there, Dad probably would have started complaining about the way he'd been hitting.

Feeling bad couldn't bring Dad back, couldn't make him replay his youth.

It is what it is.

This was a favorite saying of his because it spoke so much truth. You live, you die. You excite some people, you let others down. You bat a ball over the wall, you knock a batboy over.

Life was full of surprises.

Cory glanced at his first-class ticket and then thought of what awaited him back home.

He wondered if he'd see her, and what she'd say to him after all these years.

It starts to be amusing.

Ten straight hits in three games in the middle of his junior year.

Cory Brand knocking them down.

Home run.

Single.

Double.

Single.

Home run.

He finds a group named Queen, and he starts playing "Another One Bites the Dust" after each game.

People aren't just watching him with interest anymore.

People are talking about him.

And they should be, because he'd be talking about someone like him.

Cory doesn't know what it feels like to be arrogant because he's still some poor kid living on a farm with a freak of a father who berates him every single day. And every day he bats back and shows him. Maybe not his father, because his father isn't anywhere around, but he's showing someone something.

CHAPTER EIGHT:
HIT AND RUN

The first thing he thought about when he stepped off the plane and waited for his brother by the gate was how he could get another drink. He felt too good to waste this buzz just for Clay.

Cory never wanted this feeling to stop. It was like playing. The game, the moments, the rush, the thrill. It was a tangible, living and breathing thing, something he could scoop up in his arms and then let go to the amazement of the crowd. They burned inside his head and his heart, these strangers who watched and waited and cheered every movement. Time stood still and breaths would be held all while they waited. Hoping for the same rush and thrill. Hoping for the ride.

Sometimes — no, all the time — it was hard to come down. It was hard to turn off the switch. Normal human beings couldn't understand being put into a situation like that. The pressure and the madness and the adrenaline and the joy. To feel yourself blast a ball out of the park and then to see a whole host of fans under the bright lights, cheering you on . . . Nothing compared to it. Nothing.

Eventually the lights were turned off, and the fans went home.

Eventually, Cory was left alone.

And this was just a little help to get to the next game. To the next rush and thrill.

It used to be enough. The immense spectacle of it all. The spotlight on him. The favors that came with it. The women. But eventually none of those nothings could fill the inevitable void.

Drinking did that.

To an extent.

His mouth was dry when he simply nodded at Clay coming toward him. Cory needed to do something about that dry mouth, and quickly.

"Whose closet did you raid?" he asked his brother after noticing what he was wearing for the first time.

Clay wore a matching Nike athletic shirt and a pair of sweatpants, both of which were too large on him. He simply nodded at the joke. "A vastly overpaid and overrated baseball player."

"He obviously works out to fill those duds."

"Yeah, but he's also got chicken legs."

"You know — if you worked out you might look good in my clothes."

"I'll never be as pretty as you."

Cory rolled his eyes at the brotherly jab. There were only a thousand of them they shared. It was nice to have that one person on this earth who would never think of him as *Cory Brand* but simply as the annoying older brother who never let him win at anything. The big brother who liked to tease and bully, but who'd spent his whole youth protecting this kid's butt.

Soon they were in the parking lot, looking for the car Cory had rented. Cory pressed the unlock button on the remote, and a black Corvette nearby greeted them with a chirp.

"You didn't need to waste money renting a fancy car."

"I've never met an upgrade I didn't like," Cory said. "Don't worry about it."

When they got into the car, Clay mentioned he was hungry. And Cory was thirsty. He figured they could kill two birds with one well-thrown stone.

"What do you say we make one last stop in civilization?"

Cory started up the engine and then revved it as he smiled and raised his eyebrows at his brother.

After loading up on roast beef sandwiches and jumbo-sized drinks at Arby's, Cory and Clay walked back to the car to eat their food on the way to Okmulgee. It was an hour to town and another fifteen minutes to the old farmhouse, which Clay and Karen now owned. Before getting into the Corvette, Cory looked through the bag he carried and let out a curse.

"Mr. Arby forgot my curly fries."

Clay glanced at him across the top of the car with a look that said, *What do you want me to do about it?*

"Don't make me go back in there," Cory said.

"Oh, come on."

"He nearly cried when I signed his hat. A grown man."

His brother looked at him in the same old way he used to as a kid when Cory was pulling his leg. "He did not —"

"I swear to you. There were tears."

"Right."

Clay's eyes seemed to be in a perpetual state of rolling whenever he was around Cory. He headed back into the restaurant.

"Don't forget the Arby's sauce," Cory called out.

His brother could only shake his head. This was their typical banter and shtick. It never changed even as they got older.

When the door closed and Clay was inside, Cory popped the trunk on the Corvette and then walked around to the back of the car. He quickly walked to the nearby trash can and tossed the box of curly fries into it. Then he riffled through his duffel bag till he found the thing he'd been thinking about since deplaning.

His eyes scanned the parking lot as he casually poured out most of the Diet Coke in his cup and refilled it with vodka. He closed the lid, then slipped the bottle back into its place. He had a feeling he'd need it later this evening.

The sun began to drift off to sleep in the west as they headed south on the rural two-lane road toward the farm outside Okmulgee. Cory remembered heading the opposite way very well; it had been his escape route out of this place. It seemed like something that had happened to another person, one who'd died just like his mother and father had in the time that had passed since then. That kid was long gone, buried underneath a thousand blurry memories that tried to bury another hundred thousand bad ones.

Cory took a sip from his nearly empty Arby's cup as he turned up the Led Zeppelin song on the radio and cranked up the engine. Sandwich wrappers shifted on the console next to them. Clay seemed to brace himself. Not another car in sight. The Corvette drifted over the double yellow lines as if it owned them.

"Careful," Clay shouted above Robert Plant's wailing voice.

The open road and jamming music summed up exactly how Cory felt. "I love this stretch. Wanna see what this bad boy can do?"

"Not really," Clay said, holding the handle on the door next to him.

Cory could tell his brother was looking at him, but at this point in the evening he didn't care.

"Did you drink on the plane?"

Cory laughed as he glanced over at his brother. Then he punched the engine to see how fast they could go.

They flew past a sign saying that Okmulgee was only ten miles away. They were close to the tiny town and the terrible past and those nagging, constant reminders.

Don't think of them now — just drive.

Cory did just that, trying to outrace the

demons following him. The snapshots and the pictures and the running tape and the running figures and the dancing balls and the screaming faces.

Clay shouted something, but Cory didn't hear the words. He was just thinking about when the levee might break and the past would come gushing out over him like a Gatorade bucket full of hurt and disappointment.

"You coulda been so much more, boy."

Thanks, Pop.

"I miss you, son."

But I had to get outta here, Ma.

"You never loved me and never loved us and you left us to fend for ourselves."

This voice hurt the most, and now Cory drove out of anger.

Mean old memories are just as mean as that levee, aren't they?

In the blur of the past and the present, Cory saw it but couldn't react quickly enough. A fastball that he didn't have time to hit. Like swinging the bat, Cory instantly jammed on the brakes

no no no it's coming up too quick

as the slow-moving tractor jutted across the highway

going down going down

and he swung and tried to make it but the

car shook and veered off and struck a side and smashed and all the while Cory could only think of one thing in the madness of his mind.

Clay

He walks down the street in the middle of the black night with no car around for miles, and he vows to keep walking until he passes out or he's struck by a semi. The blood he spits up is all over his hands and his shirt and pants, but it's so dark in the middle of this nowhere that he barely knows how bad he looks. He can taste blood, but he thinks it's from his cut lip.

Soon he'll realize that a couple of ribs are broken and it's not just his lip bleeding.

Tomorrow he'll see crimson-splattered Nike shoes and jeans and a shirt. His right fist will show bloody scrapes from trying to fend off his father. Punching the side of the house and the railing on the deck didn't help either. He will see the black eye and the J-shaped gash along his cheek.

But mostly Cory will see those eyes that finally know. That finally understand.

He can count on one hand the amount of

110

times his father's hit him. But earlier tonight, everything that happened — with Mom screaming and crying and eventually taking off with Clay in the car and Cory standing off with his father — it was pure and utter insanity.

The games had gotten to him. Cory was starting to feel big, and maybe his dad thought he didn't have many more chances to make his son feel small. The old game of standing beside the barn and taking in the blistering pitches no longer worked. Cory would hit every single ball. He'd try to stop the grin from washing all over his face. Every single hit was a message.

You're not better than me, you foolish old man.

But on this night, the old man was better than him. Because Cory decided to make a stand, and he got beat up. Badly.

His father shoved him back once. Then moved in and punched him over and over and over again. With punches that felt like they'd been stored up inside for a long time.

When Cory finally fell to the floor and bent over and spit out blood, something clicked.

Good old Dad stood there looking at him in horror, his drunken eyes suddenly sobering up and realizing. Then he spoke Cory's name, but it was all done.

Cory needed help standing up, but then he stood before the monster and asked if he was done. His father started to cry like a baby, and Cory just cursed at him. Then he walked out the door.

He doesn't care about baseball or Emma or this farm or Okmulgee. All he wants is to get far, far away. He is going to walk to California and start a new life.

But sometime around midnight, Cory stops on the side of a lonely two-lane rural highway. He sits down and puts his arms around his legs and begins to cry. Everything leaks out. Everything.

CHAPTER NINE: ERROR

Cory wasn't sure if it was the collision with the tractor or the ambulance ride to the hospital that sobered him up. If he was forced to blow in a Breathalyzer, it would surely reveal that he was technically inebriated. But as he sat in the chair in the lonely waiting area in the hospital, he felt the cold, hard slap of reality striking him across the face again.

He already felt hungover, even though the buzz hadn't completely worn off. And Cory knew all too well that not all hangovers are created equal.

He could still remember his first and last encounter with Jack Daniel's in high school. It hadn't been pretty. The last thing he remembered was sitting in the backseat between two pretty girls while holding a bottle between his legs. The next memory was ten hours later, when he woke up in his boxers in the basement of one of those girls' houses. The parents knew, of course. *All* the parents knew, including his own. He'd gotten in a lot of trouble for that one, but the worst thing had been how bad his head and stomach felt.

Cory hadn't blamed it on himself, however. He blamed it on the awful taste of the whiskey.

There was a time while playing baseball in college that he'd decided to drink only wine one evening. His stomach was beginning to hurt from all the beer he'd been drinking, so like an idiot he decided to try to drink cheap wine instead. As if he was drinking beer. That had made the Jack Daniel's hangover seem like child's play.

Now he sat in a hospital waiting room, the throbbing in his head minor compared to the guilt he felt. Like every drunk driving cliché, Cory had walked away from the collision with the tractor with only some bumps and bruises. A nice square bandage on his forehead was taped over a cut he'd received from the broken glass flying everywhere. He also walked away without getting another DUI, all because of Clay.

Clay was going to be fine. He *looked* awful — broken arm and some broken ribs and other bumps and bruises — but the guy on the ambulance was confident that Clay's injuries weren't serious.

'Course you thought he might be dead the moment you looked at him once the careening car came to a rest and he just sat there hunched over and bleeding.

Cory had gotten a response from Clay, thankfully. Then when the county cop arrived, Cory was out of the car while Clay still sat inside. The guy's name was Murphy — that's what Clay said when he saw him. Clay told him to call an ambulance but made up some excuse about Cory and him being distracted in the car. Murphy recognized Cory, of course, and seemed a bit starstruck.

Once the ambulance came and Cory climbed in with his brother, he was off the hook. The other cops who didn't know Clay as well and weren't as starstruck as Murphy were going to ask questions, but they couldn't do a thing. Clay said once Cory got in the ambulance and left the scene of the accident, the police could no longer arrest him.

The last hour after arriving at the hospital had been like the accident itself: a twisting and turning crash that never seemed to stop. Cops were swarming around him.

"I don't care who your brother is," one yelled. "And I don't give a rip who you are.

You should be going to jail."

This wasn't the first time someone had yelled in his face. Cory ignored them all. He had mastered that art.

His phone vibrated, so he checked the incoming text. Helene.

I'M OUT FRONT. WHERE ARE YOU?

Cory thought about making a wisecrack, then decided against it. Even he knew when to stop joking around. He stood up and began walking to the front of the building. As he moved through the hallway, he could hear steps approaching quickly. The clean, stark look of the hospital seemed to match Karen's face as she rushed past him in the hallway.

Cory couldn't think of anything to say to her as she glared his way and kept walking.

He went on outside to meet Helene, hoping he wouldn't run across anybody else he recognized. Or who recognized him.

Helene smoked a cigarette the way she did everything else, sucking the life out of it with no time to waste and then tossing the butt onto the curb and forgetting about it until she lit up again. Cory hated the ugly habit but knew she hated some of his habits even more.

"I can't watch over you 24/7," she began

without even a *how are you doing* or *glad to see you're okay.* "With the new collective bargaining agreement in effect, you're gonna be dealing with more discipline from the league on top of whatever the Grizzlies decide."

"You can't smoke here."

"Watch me."

They were in the entrance of the hospital, and Cory glanced at the sliding glass doors leading to the dark night outside. A part of him wanted to dart through them and head back into the shadows. Not just a part of him, but every inch of him.

"What do I need to do?" he asked his agent.

"Pray your brother can swing a suspended sentence. And try, *try,* to stay out of trouble while I cover your butt."

He knew that when Helene told him to pray, things were bad. Very, very bad.

"Clay already bailed me out," Cory admitted.

"How?"

"He knew the county cop. A young guy. Clay said things were fine — that he needed medical attention. He told me to just shut up and act quiet. I went with him in the ambulance."

Helene knew how lucky Cory was at

times. This wasn't the first story of this kind he'd told her. She was probably going to say as much when they heard the sound of a group of people coming toward them. A bunch of kids in faded red T-shirts with *Bulldogs* printed across the front were walking up the sidewalk like little possessed dwarves haunting his nightmares. A couple of mothers were following them as they all marched into the hospital.

"Oh, man. The kids are here."

"Who are they?"

"My brother's baseball team."

Helene let out an incredulous moan as the group converged in an animated circle nearby. "Your brother is the kids' *baseball coach*? Next time why don't you just shoot Bambi?"

Then yesterday walked in with the kids and glanced over in Cory's direction.

For a moment, he couldn't move or do anything as he stared at her.

Emma Hargrove stood there looking a bit shocked herself, staring at him as the kids ran around her. She crossed her arms and suddenly appeared uncomfortable, like she was freezing in her short-sleeved shirt even though it was still warm outside.

She looks the same as that young girl I left ten years ago.

118

Helene smiled as she took a drag from the cigarette.

"Uh oh," she said to Cory in a hushed voice. "There's a story here."

Not just one story, Helene. A whole book of them.

Cory was about to act when a couple of obvious newshounds sniffed their way into the hospital and spotted him standing there.

"There he is," one of the reporters said.

"Cory Brand," another announced to the hospital and the rest of the world.

Like all paparazzi and reporters, the couple suddenly mutated like a pack of zombies. Yet Cory almost welcomed them, since it ended whatever moment was about to happen between Emma and him.

Helene dropped her cigarette and prepared for battle. "Game face, Cory."

He could say a lot about her, but Helene Landy knew how to sweet-talk strangers and how to work a hungry crowd. The reporters seemed to scurry toward them from all directions as Helene fronted Cory with a smile and a sharp look. Nobody in the entrance to the hospital would doubt that this woman would plant her heel in your foot if you didn't watch yourself.

"Good evening, folks. I'm Helene Landy —"

Which meant nothing; they were here to see the ball player with the bandage on his forehead.

"Cory Brand. Did you sustain any injuries?"

"Cory, what happened?"

The reporters were elbowing to get a quote and a sound bite, but Helene remained on guard, trying to shield him as he stepped up beside her. He knew the routine. Running away or not saying a word only made things worse.

"As I was saying," Helene said in a commanding voice, "Cory Brand is happy to report that, other than bumps and bruises, he is just fine —"

One of the more aggressive reporters, a blonde-haired woman obviously not impressed with Cory or his agent, barked out, "Cory. How's your brother?"

"He's, uh, okay."

"Clay Brand is resting comfortably, and while sustaining other injuries —"

"What injuries exactly?" Ms. Barbie-Doing-Barbara-Walters demanded.

"Cory, have you been suspended by the Grizzlies?" a wrinkled-faced journalist asked.

"Was alcohol involved in the accident, Cory?" asked another plain-faced, suspicious stranger holding a recorder.

Cory wanted to take the mini-recorder and jam it down the guy's throat.

Helene put a hand on his arm and held it firmly as she continued to talk. "A tractor was involved in the accident," she said, elevating the mood and defusing the intensity. "And Mr. Brand, out of love for his brother, has offered to stay in Okmulgee and take his brother's place as coach of the local kids' baseball team."

Say what?

Cory looked at her with a disbelieving glance, just like the rest of them. There was laughter and some levity now as the pack of reporters picked up on this latest news.

"Cory Brand's coaching kids' baseball?" the blonde asked.

Nobody seemed to be buying it.

"That's one lucky team," the older reporter said.

"Do the parents know their kids are getting Cory Brand as their coach?" Mr. Don't-Drive-Drunk roving reporter asked.

Cory had no idea what to say. First Helene got him roped into taking some twelve-step program, and now he was coaching Little League?

Next I'm going to be working in a soup kitchen and sewing clothes for the homeless.

121

"Does this mean you're moving to Okmulgee?" another journalist asked.

The others were scrambling, trying to get more details and sending others off to try to interview more people for this big story in sports.

The questions began to assault them, and Cory couldn't answer a single one because he had enough questions of his own.

"Mr. Brand's had a long day, guys," Helene said, waving the white flag with her hand. "We'll release another statement tomorrow when he attends his first practice with the Bulldogs. Thank you very much."

I've gone from batting cleanup with the Grizzlies to chasing ten-year-olds on the Bulldogs. Wonderful.

Helene tugged at him to follow her back into the hospital. He gave his routine smile even as more questions came.

"Is the Bulldog venue big enough to handle the anticipated crowds?"

That was a good question, but he didn't have the answer. The lights of the cameras went off as reporters and photographers knew this was their last opportunity to capture a moment.

Out of the entryway to the hospital and standing alone in the hallway where they could still be seen, Cory looked happy and calm on the surface, but inside he wanted to tear into his agent.

"You're way out of line this time," he said.

"No, you are. And I'm fixing it." Helene raised her eyebrows and grinned as she glanced at the crowd. "Man, I'm good."

"I'm not doing it."

"Oh, that ship has sailed. It's online by now. Next conversation."

Cory glanced down the hallway leading to the room where Clay lay.

"Go see your poor brother one more time before I take you to your new home sweet home."

Before he could tell her no or ask her another question, Helene was moving, on her way to fix things. That was her job.

He headed inside to see his brother. Not that he particularly wanted to, but he knew that was the only place he could go right now.

"It's okay, Cory."

"No. I'm not — I don't know."

"It's fine. We're all alone."

"I know. It's just —"

"Just what?"

"I'm just not sure."

"Don't tell me you're afraid."

"I didn't say that."

"Then what are you saying?"

"It's just — I don't know."

"Cory Brand."

"What?"

"Why are you the one being shy?"

"I'm not being shy. You know — you know how I — Emma, you know."

"I know. So come here."

"I just —"

"Suddenly you want to be a gentleman after we've known each other four years?"

"Don't make fun of me."

"Then what is it?"

"I just —"

"You already said that."

"I don't want you to feel like this has to happen."

"I want this to happen. Are you saying you don't?"

"Em —"

"Well . . . ?"

"You make me — I can't stop — all I have ever — you just don't get it —"

"Cory? Just hush and come over here."

CHAPTER TEN:
BRUSHBACK

Some things get buried not because they're too painful to remember but because they're too precious to forget.

Emma Hargrove had discovered this the hard way.

She sat quietly in the shadows in her truck, breathing in and out and trying to get control of her emotions. That face from the past was the last thing she'd expected to see as she walked into the hospital with the Bulldogs. With Tyler. And while the reporters had thankfully broken up a possible reunion, Emma still had excused herself to go to the truck and freak out.

She wasn't sad or happy or angry or shocked. Those emotions had withered up in the dry heat of exasperation long ago. Cory had left this town and everybody in it for bigger and better things. And Emma had moved on and gotten over him.

So why am I hiding out here?

She couldn't leave because she still needed to take Tyler back home. They had all come to see Coach Clay, but Emma knew she wouldn't be going into that room. Each question churning in her mind gave way to a dozen more.

What was Cory doing in the car? Is he going to be in trouble? Is he staying around here? What does that mean for them? What does it mean for Ty?

She wanted to take Tyler out of the hospital and make sure he stayed fifty miles away from Cory. She wanted her son to stop loving Little League and get into science projects. She wanted him to stop growing and stop being so stinking cute and charming.

She wanted him to stop being a walking and talking picture of his father.

These fears deep inside of her had drifted away after she met and fell in love with James. But then she lost him. *They* lost him. Baseball took Cory, and a war took James. Now it was just Emma and Tyler, with the help of the good people of this town who had welcomed them back.

We're doing fine on our own because God's taking care of us.

But if she really believed that, then what was she doing hiding out in the parking lot, afraid of seeing Mr. Fireworks himself back in there, afraid of hearing him ask about his son, afraid of all the awful things that could happen? Cory had never bothered keeping in touch, never asked about Tyler . . . but what if he suddenly woke up and wanted his son in his life?

I lost James. I can't lose Tyler, too. I won't.

Cory had made his choice long ago, when neither of them realized the consequences of choices like that. He had gone on his journey and she on hers. And whatever might have been and could have been between the two of them, that was long gone.

Yet Tyler was here, and he was more beautiful than she could have ever imagined. Out of heartache and mistakes came a blessed baby who was growing up to be a fine young man.

Lord, don't take him away too. Please, God, don't let anything happen to him. To us.

The room was silent as Cory opened the door and peeked inside. He hoped that Clay would be the only one there, now that the little monsters on the Bulldogs team appeared to have left the premises. But he could see Karen standing there by Clay's bed.

"Sorry to interrupt. I just —"

Karen walked over toward him, her face registering a lot more than simple disappointment or anger. Her stern jaw and expressionless eyes clenched the fury just beneath the surface.

"He's awake," she said tersely. "Concussion. Broken arm. Broken ribs."

All because of you, big brother. All because of you.

"Clay wants two minutes, and then I want you to leave."

It wasn't a request or even a demand. The statement came across as a threat.

Cory could hear her steps as she left the room and walked off down the hall. He went up to the bed rail and felt a bit like the tractor they'd struck. Seeing Clay there, in this bed, all bandaged up and aching, made him want to throw up. To say he was sorry wouldn't even begin to express what he felt.

"Hey." Cory's voice came out soft and weak.

And even though Clay was the one resting in bed in a hospital gown, looking like a fighter who'd lost in the ring, his eyes seemed to stare at Cory in pity.

"So do you usually try to get soused

before sunset? Bit early in the day for a DUI."

"I don't know what to say. I'm so —"

"So don't. Don't even try."

Cory gripped the rail on the bed and wished he could just squeeze this messy picture away.

"I did what I could to help you legally," Clay said in a matter-of-fact way. "You're lucky Murph was the one who came out. God forbid it was Pajersky. You'd be in a lot worse trouble then."

"Yeah. Never thought my kid brother would be bailing me out."

"I didn't bail you out. I vouched for you. You still have to . . . don't be skipping town okay . . . ?"

It probably took Clay all the energy he had to say those words to Cory but not to tell his brother how he really felt. Cory watched his brother drift off to sleep, succumbing to the sedatives he'd been given.

He looked around this room and knew it would forever be one of those ugly snapshots he carried around with him. A photo album of shame, courtesy of the great Cory Brand.

Cory sits in the shadows of the barn with the night purring around him, feeling like a Roman candle with endless amounts of fiery shells to blow off.

He'd always known this moment would come. And always dreaded it.

All he can think about is Emma.

Should he take his dad's truck and go tell her? He's been wondering that since the call came around eight. Some guy named Stan from the Denver Grizzlies "expressing his interest" in Cory. Arranging a meeting to talk about the upcoming draft.

Cory doesn't know what he's going to do when he graduates high school.

Another kid — a better kid — might be sitting in this barn praying. But Cory is sitting here going through his baseball cards, arranging them, organizing them in a different way. He's got these cards memorized by now. He knows the names and the faces and the stats of every one.

It's crazy to think that he might one day be among these guys.

But that's not the craziest thing.

All he can think of is Emma.

He doesn't want to leave her. He won't leave her. But how's that going to work out? What will he say?

He's not sure about anything except these cards in his hands. The players and their numbers and their cards.

It's a simple reality he can focus on. For the moment.

CHAPTER ELEVEN: BACKSTOP

The silence in the motel room felt louder than a full stadium screaming his name. For a while Cory drained the remaining juice from his iPod, listening to Kings of Leon, but now he was bored and thirsty. Helene had found this dump and brought him here only to leave him once again. This wasn't a place meant to spend a lot of time in. There was no place to work out, no main lobby for meeting people, no room service. This was a one-story, off-the-highway motel with bare-bones rooms for people who simply needed a bed and a bathroom. God only knew what usually went on in this small space. Cory certainly didn't want to try to imagine.

He was sitting there on the bed, tossing an empty glass, mindlessly waiting for Helene, when she burst into the room using her own key. This wasn't the first time a pretty woman had torn into his hotel room, but the circumstances now were quite different. Her arms were full, and she dumped their contents on a nearby table. Cory just watched her, knowing she had something to say and a plan in motion.

For a moment Helene looked around the room. "Ugh. Just looking at those polyester bedspreads makes me itch."

"You should check out the bathroom," Cory joked.

She ignored his wisecrack as she pulled a fifth of vodka out of a brown bag, along with some plastic cups. Cory noticed the expensive brand and liked what he saw.

"Okay, listen up . . ." she said as she dropped a brochure on his lap. She grabbed the ice bucket on the table next to him. "I found you a twelve-step program."

Cory looked at the pamphlet in his hand as Helene disappeared outside.

What the . . .

It didn't say AA or Rehab Central or Destination Margaritaville. It said *Celebrate Recovery.*

Helene returned at her regular galloping pace, carrying two full cups of ice.

"You couldn't find me a normal twelve-step?" Cory asked.

She gave him a smirk as she poured their drinks, then handed him his cup as if they were commemorating a new contract or a three-homer game.

"It is a normal twelve-step. Just . . . with Jesus." She emphasized the last word for effect.

"I'm not doing church."

"You're doing whatever it takes to get back on the roster. Besides, it's the only game in town."

Cory opened up the brochure. "Celebrate? Recovery?"

This was turning into something far worse than a nightmare. He was in his own personal *Twilight Zone* episode.

Helene gave him her trademark smile, almost as phony as his. "If your career recovers, I *will* celebrate."

She took a sip, then set the cup down, clearly finished with it. Now *that* was alcohol abuse, in Cory's opinion. She picked up her purse and car keys.

"You're leaving?"

Her eyes scanned the room as if a glowing plague was starting to cover the walls. "Staying in Tulsa. I'll drive back here tomorrow."

"What for?"

"An apology to the kid? A press event?" She sounded more than fed up. "The whole reason we rode into this one-horse town."

"How am I getting around?" His drink

was already empty.

She stood by the open doorway as the sound of vehicles rushing by on the highway mixed with the hum of crickets. "You're a big boy. You figure it out. See you at the field tomorrow."

He sighed and glanced at the bottle on the table. Helene still stood there.

"If you're smart, you'll come ready to coach. Just remember, you're *happy* to be doing this for your brother and the children."

He was about to ask where he could find the nuns, but Helene was gone. She closed the door without tucking him in and saying good night.

For a moment, Cory sat looking at the empty wall with the off-white paint. Just a couple of nights ago he'd been at this wild fund-raiser and had hooked up with this amazing girl whose name he still couldn't recall. Now he was suspended and staying in a roach motel with a television that had ten channels. No ride, a license still under probation from the last DUI he got a year and a half ago. Another DUI and he could have kissed his driving privileges away for half a decade or more.

He got off the bed and refilled his cup. At least he had a bottle to keep him company.

And at least there was something other than ESPN that he could watch.

He was tired of hearing about Cory Brand.

Cory holds Emma's hand as he sits on the bench beside her. "They're going to draft me."

She doesn't say much because she knows. Emma is smart and doesn't live in denial.

"I'm happy for you."

"I'm turning them down. I'm going to OU."

Emma looks at him. "Stop it."

"No, I'm serious."

"No, you're not."

"Yes, I am."

"What do you mean?"

"I mean I'm playing college baseball. I mean you can't get rid of me that easily."

"Cory —"

"I thought you'd be happy."

"I am. It's just — are you sure?"

"I'm sure. I've already told everybody. Well, everybody but you. And my father."

"He's going to come over here and burn our house down."

"Over my dead body."

Emma's concern showed in her sweet face. "Cory, are you really sure?"

"Yeah. It's good — it's going to work out great. Trust me. It's going to be great."

"But what if you don't . . ."

Emma can't finish what she's thinking, but Cory already knows her reservation.

"This is what Coach Weideman has always said: nothing good happens when you hang back."

"But isn't that exactly what you're doing?"

"No. No way. This is — this is going to be great. Everything's going to work out, Em. For both of us. I promise."

CHAPTER TWELVE:
OUTFIELD

Voices woke Cory. For a moment he thought it was another morning in his condo in Denver, that he was lost in his soft king-sized bed, trying to figure out how he made it home last night or who he might have ended up with. Then, as he turned over, the unforgiving mattress beneath him solid as a rock, Cory realized where he was.

He climbed out of bed and noticed the empty bottle on the floor. Too bad it didn't have a full brother to say good morning to. He pulled back the heavy drape and saw a man in his late forties holding a brush in one hand and a can of paint in the other — the maintenance guy or the motel manager. Or, considering this sorry little inn, both. Talking to him was a college-age guy pushing a shopping cart full of stuff like toilet paper and towels and linens.

A makeshift janitorial cart. This is a classy joint.

Near the manager's office stood a beat-up pickup truck.

This gave him an idea.

He got ready, trying to get in and out of the dingy shower as fast as he could. The Little League practice was later this afternoon, and there were a few things he needed to do. Well, one in particular. Something he had to get out of the way before he could manage to do anything else around this tiny town.

Cory walked outside toward the older of the two men. "Your truck?" he asked, nodding toward it.

The man shook his head and aimed his paintbrush at the kid. As he did, the young guy instantly got that look of recognition on his face. His eyes were wide, and he appeared to want to say something.

"Wanna rent it?" Cory asked the kid.

"Rent my truck?"

"Rent your truck," he said, confirming the ridiculous.

"Yeah, sure."

The manager shot them both a suspicious glance. Either he didn't recognize Cory, or he did and wasn't a fan. Cory just smiled and said that was great. He walked over to the truck, urging the kid to come with him, away from his boss. As they neared the side

141

of the old Ford, Cory pulled a wad of cash from his pocket.

"Hey, listen. My mini-fridge is empty. Know what I mean?"

This kid had recognized him, and he was no dummy. He knew exactly what Cory meant.

"I could fill it for you."

Bingo.

Cory smiled. "The little fridge. You fill it, and charge me five times what it cost you."

The guy nodded in agreement, his face looking like he just won the lottery. Cory handed him a hundred dollars.

"That's for filling it with adult beverages."

Again the kid nodded. Cory gave him another couple hundred.

"And that's so you remember to keep filling it with adult beverages. Every time you remember, you'll get paid again. Sound good?"

"Uh, yeah."

"How about another five hundred a month for renting the truck?"

Cory knew he'd made the kid's day. Make that year. The big smile confirmed it.

"What's your name?"

"Chad."

"Where are the keys, Chad?"

Oh, yeah, he seemed to say as he dug into

his pockets and produced a set of keys. He handed them to Cory.

"Thanks, Chad. I'm Cory Brand."

"Yeah. I know."

"Promise I won't crash your truck." Cory thought for a second, then added with a wink, "But if I do, you'll get an even better one."

He found them at the bottom of the hill, a place that appeared abandoned and unremarkable. The grass hadn't been cut in a long time, and there were weeds growing everywhere. The summer breeze seemed to sigh as he scanned the area.

Cory didn't think it would be like this. So — simple. So detached. They died, and he moved on. Just like that.

He studied the pair of bronze plaques.

You should've been here.

Alicia Brand

He had no memorized speech to share. No apologies or afterthoughts. There was nothing he could say to undo the past. He'd tried to outrun this place and these plaques beneath him, yet Cory had known that one day he would need to face them like a man.

He glanced about at nearby graves and spotted a lone red silk flower resting on a nearby stone. He took it without hesitation and set the flower down by her name.

How that woman could have stood by her husband for all her life, Cory would never know. Maybe life back then was just different. His family had always gone to church, though his father stopped going as the boys got older. Mom would drag them there every Sunday no matter what had happened the week or even the night before. It was her sanctuary and solace, probably a lot like how the baseball field felt to Cory. She was a strong woman, but she'd never threatened to leave his father, even when Dad's drinking got completely out of hand.

With his toe he scuffed the dust and weeds off the plaque next to his mother's. For a moment, Cory looked at the name the way he might have looked its owner in the eye.

Michael Brand

In a clear, loud voice, Cory cursed his father and hoped that wherever he was right now, the old man could hear him.

There was no apology that could give Cory back his youth. There was no way to make amends for the years of fear and anger. Even after leaving this place, Cory felt like he had the weight of his father on him, watching him, swearing at him, scolding him. There was nothing he could have done to be acceptable in his father's eyes, even when the old man got older and more feeble and tried to get right with all of them.

There's a reason I've been gone a decade, and it's this corpse rotting six feet underground.

For a moment Cory looked at the sky, wiping a drop of sweat off his forehead. Thick stubble covered his face, and he was as thirsty as a man trapped in a desert.

He thought back to his childhood. What did a kid like him know anyway? He'd thought this was all there was to life. This place off the map, this tiny existence where the lights and the crowd were nowhere to be found. Cory had been stupid enough to believe he could get away unscarred. He was dumb enough to think he could leave all this behind.

A heaviness filled him. Not regret, not anger, but a deep empty feeling, the way a stone might feel being dropped into a discarded well.

There was nothing to make him cry for his parents, not even for his mother. He couldn't bring them back and couldn't make them fill a snapshot that never existed. He'd done everything he could to survive his youth intact and to keep Clay from being damaged.

And Clay made it to adulthood just fine.

He knew his mother would have been disappointed in him. Not because of the mishap with his elbow that got him suspended from the game. Not even because of the accident that sent Clay to the hospital. She had lived a life with Dad and understood how those things went.

No, she would've been disappointed that he'd left them behind and never bothered to come back until he was forced to.

Cory left the graveside. Regrets were for losers, and that wasn't how he lived his life.

It is what it is.

And he kept saying this over and over, even though he didn't believe a word of it.

He sits in the locker room, trying to find the will to leave.

He's the last one there. He's taken his time, and now he just wants to escape this room and this campus and this life.

He wonders if he made a mistake.

What if the slump continues?

He ignores the thought.

What if my game doesn't improve?

He shuts the voice off.

What if I threw away the one chance I had because of some silly girl?

Cory stands and gets his gear and knows he needs to just get out and stop thinking. Emma isn't some silly girl, and this slump and his game are just some rocky stretch of road he's traveling over.

It's all gonna be fine.

He knows what he needs to do.

Go see Em.

But that's not what he needs. He needs to

find the rest of the guys and blow off some steam just like they'll be doing.

He needs to stop thinking so much and just start being Cory Brand again.

CHAPTER THIRTEEN: SIGNS

Some women might have been up in their walk-in closets with the boxes opened and the old memories pouring out. But Emma refused to do that. She couldn't even remember where a lot of the mementos from her time with Cory were. Every day, she walked with and talked to and hugged and loved the only memento that was important to her. Tyler was more perfect than a pitcher throwing a no-hitter. He was more beautiful than a grand-slam homer to end a World Series. He was indeed the best part of her life now that James had died.

What if Cory decides he wants to be back in Tyler's life?

Cory was his legal father. No court could prevent him from wanting time with his son. The man she saw at the hospital yesterday, the man she occasionally saw on a highlight clip on the evening news, was a complete stranger. There had been a kid she'd fallen in love with in high school and accompanied to college, a guy scared to death that his dream of playing baseball was over when she told him she was pregnant. That guy ran away.

She could see Tyler playing out in the backyard with some friends. He always had someone he was hanging around and having fun with.

Of course he does. He's got Cory's charm.

It wasn't the only thing Tyler shared with his father. And that scared her.

She threw away the uneaten sandwich she'd made for herself. The Bulldogs practice later this afternoon would be a nice way to take her mind off things. She just hoped that Cory wouldn't show up for some reason.

Sometimes, in her imagination, the Cory Brand she used to know would hold her with his massive frame and whisper that everything was going to be all right. Whatever she was worried about, he'd say that things were going to be fine. For a long time she had believed him. Even when he left them behind, she tried to remember those words and let them soothe her.

But like everything else in Cory's life, the words had just been for show. He had never meant them, and surely he didn't believe them himself.

The young girl who fell in love with that young boy was gone. They were both gone.

Not entirely, and you know that.

Emma took a sip of iced tea and closed her eyes as the squeals of the boys outside grew louder.

"Lord, help me get through this, to get through having him around. Please don't let anything happen to us. To Tyler. Protect us the way You always have."

Emma knew she no longer needed some stud athlete to put his arms around her and tell her everything would be okay. She had someone much stronger and bigger, someone who loved them and took care of them.

She thought about James. While God did indeed love them and protect them, He didn't always answer their prayers. That was one of the great mysteries of life. But that didn't prevent her from continuing to have faith in Him. It just made it a little harder.

The kid had delivered. In spades.

Now Cory sat on the bed, the buds of his iPod in his ears, the music cranked, the glass almost empty by his bedside, a worn photo of Emma and Tyler in his hand.

He laughed.

This was so pathetic. All of this. Every bit of it.

Look at him. Sitting in this dump a street-walker would think twice about visiting, looking at the one and only picture of Emma and Tyler she had ever sent him, drinking the day away while counting the minutes to practice. Not regular practice, but Little League practice.

Pathetic.

At least the guy named Chad had loaded up this fridge. It looked like something that could be in a frat house, all the booze. Cory hadn't even thought twice about opening the pint of vodka that sat on top of the fridge along with the other bottles. The kid had been selective, which was great.

For a moment he laughed, thinking of the utter ridiculousness of his collision with his adopted nephew at the ballpark. The only thing that could have been worse was if it had been a girl he'd hit. In a wheelchair.

That's cruel.

And yeah, he knew it was cruel, but it still amused him. Being thrown out of the game and now ending up here.

All he ever told people was that he was just trying to have a good time.

Knocking a kid over in anger?

And he was passionate. That was all. What

was the big deal? He got a little excited, and things happened. A little angry, and an adopted nephew suddenly popped out of the magician's hat.

Oops.

A little bit reckless, and a tractor suddenly appeared out of nowhere.

Double oops.

Thinking of the tractor driver made him laugh again.

"I've had that tractor forty years," the farmer had said. Insurance would pay for it and give him a brand-new tractor, so again, he was getting off good. Like Carlos and his teammates. Like this whole town that was about to be put back on the map.

He filled the glass and hit shuffle on his iPod, and a familiar song came on — Gerry Rafferty's "Baker Street." It had been one of his father's favorites.

For the first time in his life, Cory sat and listened to the song all the way through, draining his glass and then filling it again to drain it one more time. The sax and the guitar soared, and Rafferty's laidback, cool voice sang about life and loss and dreaming big.

Then a wave of goose bumps drifted over him, and Cory got it. He suddenly heard the song not the way a kid might listen to it

153

on the way to school as his father blasted it from the truck's tape player, but the way a grown man might listen to it, thinking of the man who was once the same age he was now.

This Baker Street wasn't a place, but a fantasy. It was a dream of hope imagined by a restless, troubled soul. A man who was trying but could never find the home he was looking for, even though it was right there in front of his face the entire time.

Suddenly Cory didn't like how he was feeling. His amusement was gone.

The booze wasn't working the way it should have. The picture next to him mocked him. The sun outside beat down and cut through the blinds. Cory changed the track. But he couldn't find his own personal theme song to soothe his troubled soul.

He was far beyond that, and he knew it.

The moment she walks into the room, Emma bursts out crying.

"Hey — come on — I'm not dying or anything."

He still feels drunk and surely sounds the same. She walks over to the side of the bed and puts her head against Cory's chest.

"If you think I look bad, you should see the other guy," he continues to joke.

"The cops aren't going to file any charges."

"I know," he says.

The bar fight was stupid. Cory knows the only guys who would've been arrested were the two who helped make his pretty face look ugly. He could've gotten a drunk-and-disorderly, but they're letting the baseball star of OU go.

"They just wanted to take a look at me," he says. "It's just a concussion. First one I've ever had."

Emma looks at his right hand, which is

bloodied and cut up, especially around the knuckles.

"Good thing I'm not a pitcher."

"Cory."

"It's all good," he says. His way of apologizing.

CHAPTER FOURTEEN:
INFIELD

Cory looked like a bona fide Little League coach, dressed in his red Bulldogs polo shirt and matching baseball cap, all thanks to Helene. She had stopped by his motel shortly before the practice to give him the gear. She'd also told him to clean himself up and look like the Cory Brand in the magazines and not the Cory Brand in the tabloids.

Now he was back on a field, though this one was a little different from the one he was used to playing on. Helene was directing everything; she shuffled and moved photographers around as Cory greeted his nephew with Karen by his side.

"Hey, big man," he said, smiling and greeting the kid like he was his own. "Looks like you've got your nose on straight."

Carlos was still wide-eyed and excited to see him, though the same couldn't be said about his mother. She forced a polite smile on her pretty face. It was just for show, like everything else going on.

There were a couple of duffel bags full of Denver Grizzlies swag that Helene had brought for Cory to give to Carlos and the rest of the team. Right now, she was making sure that the shots of Cory greeting Carlos were just right. Cory knew that they were being watched, not just by the photographers, but by the other parents. He made a big deal of stepping up to Carlos and offering his hand to shake.

"I am *so* sorry about that."

"Aw, that's okay," Carlos said in a voice that was a little more audible than last time.

Cory smiled and shook the kid's hand, and the clicks of a hundred photos being taken went off. Helene, who looked dressed more for a night on the town than for a Little League baseball field, nodded approval.

"I got some Grizzlies gear for you and some other stuff you might like," Cory said as he opened one of the duffel bags.

"Awesome," Carlos shouted as he took the T-shirt Cory handed him. "Thanks!"

Karen still didn't look impressed. Cory had casually asked her how Clay was doing and received a very short and cutting "Fine" in reply. He hadn't asked her any more questions.

"Okay, Carlos, let's see that famous thumbs-up for the camera," Helene called.

Carlos eagerly complied, embracing his role as a celebrity for a few extra moments. Cory followed suit, smiling shamelessly for the cameras.

Emma deliberately arrived late. As she walked onto the field and saw the commotion by the pitcher's mound, she let her son carry his bag and follow her. The bag was almost as big as he was. She hadn't told Tyler the news she'd learned this morning from Karen. The news about Cory being at practice today. Hopefully she could keep it from him just a little while longer.

You mean hopefully you can keep Cory away from Tyler just a little while longer.

She slowed down by the dugout as she saw half a dozen photographers taking shots of Cory giving Carlos hats and jerseys and other bribes. He looked different from the guy who'd left ten years ago. Not just older but bigger, fuller. *Stronger* was the word that came to mind, but nothing about the man standing out there represented strength to Emma. Not anymore.

A man scrambling to keep his squadron alive, that represented strength. Scrambling

159

to buy drinks for everybody in the bar was stupidity.

Tyler kept trudging along with the duffel bag over his arm. Emma signaled to Karen and mouthed the words *Come here!*

She couldn't go out on the field. Not just yet.

Karen walked up beside her with a serious look on her face. "You ready?"

"Does he know yet —"

"I don't think so."

Emma sighed.

"Like I told you, things are going to be fine," Karen said. "You'll get through this. Don't worry about a thing."

Karen was the sister Emma had never had. She was the picture of strength, a woman who had gone through so much and yet remained optimistic and giving.

Emma glanced back out to the crowd and noticed a glamorous African-American woman talking to the cameras, making some official statement. A publicist for the Grizzlies, or someone official from the league? As soon as the lady was finished, Carlos started talking Cory's ear off once again.

"I can't believe you're our coach. We need major help. You'll see. We're not even close to as good as the Roughnecks. They can hit the ball so far. Like as far as that building

160

over there. Which is where you get the best ice cream ever."

Karen couldn't help smiling as she glanced over at Emma.

"He just adores Cory," Emma said.

"I know," Karen replied. "Scary, huh?"

Several other parents were beginning to walk up around Cory now. Emma knew it was almost time.

You can do this. You have nothing to worry about, not a thing.

Just as she was drumming up the confidence, still feeling like the shy high school girl that the handsome and popular Cory Brand decided to ask out, Emma glanced over to see Suzanne Fairchild standing by the side of the field, refluffing her hair.

You've gotta be kidding me.

Emma looked back onto the field and noticed the striking businesswoman next to Cory commanding everybody's attention. Perhaps she'd get some competition now in the form of a blonde bombshell about five years past her prime. Not that Suzanne knew that, since every man around her still managed to look her over. Perhaps it was because of her tight clothes or the fact that she had enhanced that already shapely figure of hers. Everybody knew it, and Suzanne didn't seem to mind that they knew it. It was impossible *not* to notice.

"Oh, please. Suzanne's here?"

"In heels," Karen added.

"Haven't seen her all season."

This was pitiful. Emma standing there afraid to go onto the field, afraid to go face the kids *she* helped coach, afraid to face a man who was the coward and ran away.

Enough, Emma.

She had a job to do. So she walked over toward the team — *her team* — and called out to them. "Let's warm up. Come on. Take a lap!"

They were typical ten-year-olds, taking their time, distracted, moaning about having to run. Even her son wasn't immune.

"Aw, Mom."

"No way." That was Wick, a tiny mouse of a boy with chocolate-brown skin and big glasses.

They began to run while Emma awaited the inevitable intersection of her past with her present.

As the team began running, Karen urged her son to join them.

Her son, Cory thought.

It was amazing to think that Karen and Clay were parents now. This bright-eyed kid was their son. Carlos headed toward the rest of his teammates, then turned back to Cory.

"Do we get to call you Coach?" he asked.

Cory knew the cameras and reporters were still nearby, still waiting for any and every opportunity, good and especially bad.

"Of course," he said. "Just don't call me late for dinner."

As the obligatory laughs came, Helene urged Carlos to leave as she stepped forward to bid farewell to the reporters. "We're done here, everyone. Thank you."

But of course, you don't tell reporters you're done.

You're *never* done with the media. It's if and only if they're done with you.

"Cory, your suspension hit the wires today," a young guy in his twenties began. "How long do you think you'll be doing community service?"

Before Cory could even try to answer, Helene cut him off.

"Thank you, everybody." The way she said it sounded like a president, or the father of a family of five.

Helene was finished. Cory knew to just remain silent and go his way. No small talk and no eye contact and nothing between him and the media. He stood with Helene and acted like he was debriefing on how the session with the media went, but really they weren't debriefing about anything.

Emma still didn't know who the lady in the fancy suit and even fancier heels was. "Who is that woman?"

Karen shook her head. "His agent."

"Since when do agents look like that?"

"Well, she is representing Cory."

Emma tightened her lips together, glancing across the field. "Ugh, I gotta do this. I have a stomachache."

"Breathe," Karen told her.

"I haven't breathed this much since having Tyler," Emma said, straightening up and walking toward the outfield.

Helene was already working her phone and ignoring him. It always fascinated him that in front of the rest of the world, she would take a bullet for him. But one-on-one it seemed like she never stopped and looked him in the eye or stayed around long enough to be considered a partner or a friend or anything.

"My work here is done," she said without looking at him while she texted.

"Where are you going?"

"Home." She glanced up and ignored his needy look. "We're good. I'll call you in a few days."

"A few days? What am I supposed to do now?"

The Energizer Bunny began walking again, always walking, always on the move, always ignoring the obvious. She glanced back over her shoulder and smiled. "Start coaching."

Helene said he sometimes acted like a baby, but it was because she treated him like one. He watched her walk off the field and then turned to go see the kids and try to figure out what in the world he was supposed to do.

Then he saw her.

Walking toward him.

For a moment he turned back around, but Helene was gone. She couldn't help him anymore or protect him from unnecessary questions.

His buzz was already wearing off, and he had summoned all his energy and goodwill for the reporters. For a moment he felt like a trapped animal with nowhere to crawl to.

"Cory Brand."

She still looked the same as she did when he fell in love with her. Sweet, innocent, with eyes that never ceased to make him smile. Yet she wasn't smiling back at him. She wasn't trying to be sweet or innocent.

"Hey there, Emma Johnson." He tried to

be his usual confident, casual self.

"It's Hargrove," she said in a softer tone. "I mean — it's been Hargrove for the last ten years."

This was an invitation to say more, but Cory never responded to invites like that.

"Right. I'm sorry. Wow — great to see you."

He said it as though he had run into her on the street corner in some big city. But this was her home. *Their home.*

Emma responded with a timid "Yeah," but her eyes weren't on his anymore. She was nervous, just like she'd been that first time he came up to her in the hallway. The pretty cheerleader who didn't think she was as pretty as the other girls.

You haven't changed a bit. You've only grown more — But he stopped that train of thought quickly. He dipped his head down so he'd catch her glance again.

"Hey, that is so cool of you to come out here today," he said.

"I'm actually the Bulldogs' other coach."

Hence her T-shirt and cap, you moron.

Cory looked at her and laughed. He had to laugh because this was too much to take in.

"You? Seriously? Come on."

His lighthearted Cory Brandish mode of

166

talking was quickly reigned in as Emma grew serious.

"Yeah. Listen. I know you're caught up in some kind of PR mess, but let's be real —"

Cory wiped his brow as he glanced around, making sure nobody could hear their conversation.

"The parents are never gonna go for you coaching their kids," Emma continued. "These are salt-of-the-earth people, and you're . . . pretty much a wild-child felon to them."

For a moment he looked at her in disbelief. The smile filling his face was genuine, and genuinely amused.

You think I don't know the kind of people living around here?

She thought she had him all figured out. Which was fine.

Suddenly he liked the idea of coaching this team.

He liked it a lot.

"Well, wild-child felon or not, the Bulldogs are out one coach."

Emma took a deep breath. "Yeah, but we don't need you."

A couple of fathers approached them, so Emma finished quickly. "Here comes the truth. They probably have a volunteer all picked out, and then you can be on your way."

Cory was about to say more, but one of the fathers/fans/freaks forced a handshake and a smile on him before he could respond.

"Dan Stanton," said the man with the round face and rounder bald head. "I own the hardware store and gas station. Welcome home, Cory."

Of course you own the hardware store and gas station. If Cory was to picture someone who owned a hardware store and a gas station in Okmulgee, it would be this guy.

"Thank you very much," Cory said, avoiding the wisecracks going off in his head.

"Greg Kendricks," the other guy said, shaking his hand. "Honor to meet you. Thrill to have you here. You're a dream come true to these kids."

"Not to mention us dads. If you need anything at all, feel free to call the store."

Cory smiled and glanced at Emma.

I win. I always win.

Emma didn't say anything, but stepped away from the chattering fans as she looked to see what the kids were doing. She escaped the man-love and went over to where Karen was standing on the side of the field.

"Unbelievable," Emma uttered.

Karen could only give her a knowing smile. "He's not going anywhere."

"You'd think those guys would have a little better sense."

The two women began walking toward the group of kids, who were finishing their lap. The team really was an odd assortment of misfits and lovable losers. A team that seemed destined for someone like Cory Brand to coach.

There was Tyler, by far the best player, following in his genetic father's footsteps. Carlos had energy and enthusiasm for the game, but he also had a lot to learn.

She scanned the others. There was Stanton's boy, Mark, whom everybody just called by his last name. Stanton was a cynical kid who acted a little too cool for anything. He was talking to Wick, whose real name was Theodore Washington. The kid was a walking encyclopedia whose ready stock of minutiae had earned him his nickname. Near them was a redheaded, freckled-faced kid named Wellsey, who was lost in his own world.

One of the best players on the team, Kendricks, was a lanky eleven-year-old with a wicked submarine slider. This kid's biggest problem was the one being demonstrated this very moment — complaining about having to run. Kendricks hated practicing but liked playing the game.

And yeah, Kendricks was a girl. The only girl on the team and definitely the only player with french braids.

Clay and Emma had made a good team of coaches, though their styles differed greatly. Clay was all about technical head knowledge — educating the kids on how to hit and slide and catch and throw. Some-times he forgot that baseball had to be played from the heart.

Cory knows this better than anybody.

It surprised her when she heard his voice calling out behind her.

"You ready to get started, Coach?"

Emma turned and forced her tough game face on again, giving him a nod and leading him toward the infield. She knew she'd have to be honest with Cory. Brutally honest. Hurting his feelings wasn't something she needed to worry about.

I doubt I could hurt his feelings if I really tried.

"Look, these kids will like you, and you will leave them. So keep your distance." She looked ahead of them. "Third base is yours. That's your only responsibility."

Suddenly a brown-haired, blue-eyed

bundle of energy burst between the two of them.

"Mom? It's so hot. Can we do something else?"

This was the moment she had been fearing, an inevitable moment that had taken only ten years to happen.

Coach Straubel looks at him with grim eyes and an expression even more serious than usual. The door is shut, and Cory sits there knowing why he's been summoned but wondering what's going to happen.

"Look, I'm not going to make this long. I've made this speech before. Some listen to me and some don't; that's life. But the difference is that I've never had this sort of talk with someone like you, Cory. Never. So don't smile or play the victim or any of that. Just listen."

Cory nods.

"You got a gift. I know you know it too. Everybody knows it. But you have to realize — you only have a certain amount of time. I know — I know."

"It was a stupid bar fight involving some idiotic —"

"I'm not talking about the brawl. I'm talking about you. A guy who's wasting his talent away."

Cory listens. This is not his father berating him, telling him to stop dreaming. This is Coach Straubel telling him to wise up.

"Listen, Cory. God gives some people certain abilities, and He sure gave you one. To hit home runs. So remember that, okay? Wake up thinking about it, and go to bed thinking about it. Because that talent can take you places if you let it. If you don't waste it away being a typical college student."

The coach doesn't say any more.

For Cory, he's already said enough.

Chapter Fifteen: ChangeUp

You can try to outrun and outmaneuver your past, but eventually it's going to catch up to you and tag you out.

Cory was learning this the hard way.

He stood there looking at a kid who was still just a baby in his mind. The ten-year-old was tall and strong and looked like a nice kid. A real nice kid.

Nothing like his father.

"Tyler," Emma began, lost for words in the face of Tyler's sudden appearance. "You can't just walk over here. You're interrupting."

"It's just so hot."

As the boy glanced his way, Cory found himself at a loss for words too. It wasn't that Tyler was a surprise. He'd been a surprise ten years ago, a big one. But since that time, the surprise had lessened with each fading sunset.

Now the sun had just risen right in front

of his face, and it was standing there burning his eyes.

The boy stuck his hand out. "Hi. I'm Tyler."

Yes, you are.

Cory shook the hand, noting the firm grip. Tyler didn't just look cute but appeared well trained.

Look at his mommy.

He glanced at Emma, who was watching the scene with an expression he didn't want to read.

"Hey, man," Cory said, ignoring her. "Cory Brand."

"Tyler," Emma yelled. "Get back out with the rest of the team."

Tyler smiled and ran off to the outfield. As he ran, Cory felt a strange sense of déjà vu. He knew he hadn't played this field before, but somehow it still reminded him of being that age and playing Little League.

He looks just like you. That's why, you idiot. He smiles and runs and breathes just like his father.

The reality was a lot to take in.

For a moment it seemed that it was too much for Emma to take in as well. So many days and months and years, and now the two of them stood in matching red Bulldogs shirts and caps, looking like an ordinary

American couple ready to coach an ordinary American Little League team.

But nothing about this was ordinary.

Cory's head felt a strange buzz that had nothing to do with liquor. He turned to face her. "Hey, Em —"

Her eyes grew thin, and her voice was barely audible but forceful nonetheless. "I'm begging you, Cory. Please. *Please* keep your distance."

She stared him down, and Cory knew that the Emma he remembered was still there. Not the Emma who fell in love with him, but the Emma he fell in love with. The intense and strong and careful and safe Emma Johnson who now was staking her ground.

She waited for him to say something, anything, but Cory couldn't speak.

He still wasn't sure what to say.

"Third base," she said, speaking to him in the same tone she had used with Tyler.

Cory went toward the base, thankful to have somewhere to go and something to do.

Thank goodness Emma didn't expect anything more from him, because he wasn't capable of much coaching this afternoon. Not after that.

The rest of the afternoon and evening

played out in slow motion like some sad country song. Eventually the practice was over, and Emma finished up with the kids without saying another word to him. Cory found himself locked into conversations with more parents, including a big-haired blonde who might have proposed to him if he hadn't excused himself. He saw the kids shuffling out and piling into cars to go home with their parents.

Before getting into his rented pickup, Cory glanced out to the field where Tyler was walking with Emma.

It was a beautiful picture, the mother and son walking like that after baseball practice.

Both of them were so beautiful.

And you left them and didn't think twice.

Driving home under one of those endless ceilings of streaked blue brilliance, the sun finally drifting off, Cory tried to get rid of the whirlwind going on in his head by playing the radio. Unfortunately, the two stations that came through didn't provide any relief.

When he got back to his motel, the emptiness of his room depressed him. He felt like a prisoner.

You made your choice ten years ago, and it wasn't to walk off into the sunset with those two people.

His choice had led him to this unfortunate place.

The bed squeaked as he sat on it, the bedbugs surely waking up and wondering who was visiting them tonight.

His mouth was dry. He stood back up and tossed his cap onto the table across the room, then opened the mini-fridge. It was fully stocked and ready to rock.

He opened the bottle of vodka and took a wallop of a shot, the kind more suitable for a beer, then filled a glass and found some ice cubes. It didn't take long to drain the glass again.

Cory breathed in. Took another drink. Began to calm down.

Then it dawned on him that in another hour or so he'd have to show up at one of those Praise Jesus for Sobriety meetings or whatever they were called.

He needed *a lot* more to drink before he could endure one of those things.

She tells him the news as they sit in darkness by the side of the barn, underneath a sky full of brilliant speckles. Cory holds her hand but looks up and away, lost for a moment.

"I'm sorry."

He shakes his head, looking back at Emma and then squeezing her hands. "It's going to be fine."

He doesn't know what else to say or how to react.

Of all the things she could have told him, this wasn't something he could have imagined.

"Have you told anybody else?" he asks.

"No."

He looks out and sees the hulking outline of the barn behind him. He suddenly sees himself never leaving this place, stuck living in a hollowed-out shell of crushed dreams and empty promises like someone else he knows too well.

"Cory — I don't want — I know what you're

thinking, and this — it doesn't have to change things —"

"I know," he says, still holding her hands, now looking at her again. "We'll figure it out, okay? It's gonna be fine."

As he hugs her, Emma starts to cry.

They're twenty-two years old, and up until this night the future looked a lot like the heavens above. Now it looks and feels a little more like the old structure next to them.

Cory holds Emma. He can't picture himself as a father, or picture the two of them as parents. Ten years from now, sure, maybe. But not now, not when everything is happening, not when life is working out exactly the way he wanted it to.

For the first time in a long time, he feels fear sinking back into his soul.

Chapter Sixteen:
Sinker

"Everything looked fine on the outside. But the inside was a definite mess."

The average-looking guy stood in front of them in the average-sized church. He'd said his name was Phil. He wore dress pants and a dress shirt, as if he'd just come from work at some job requiring a tie, which he'd taken off before speaking. He read in a solemn tone from a sheet he'd brought with him to the podium. Along with Cory, there were thirty other people sitting in the pews.

"What started as a private curiosity became something I couldn't stop. Eventually I was looking at porn at work, with my office door shut."

Did he just say porn?

Cory glanced around to see if there was a reaction from anybody else, but nobody seemed to be surprised. All the faces of the people around him listened attentively to Phil.

"And even with the door open, when I thought I could get away with it. The sad thing was I actually thought I was getting away with it. Until the day two security officers confiscated my computer and escorted me out of the building in front of my coworkers and subordinates. They had every website and every minute I spent looking at 'em logged right there in black and white. I've never felt such shame and embarrassment."

You're not the only one feeling embarrassed.

Since he was sitting near the back, it was easy for Cory to slip out and leave the sanctuary behind. He figured he was in the right place but the wrong meeting.

"My porn addiction and unwillingness to face it led to the loss of my family, my job, and my self-worth," the speaker continued.

The door provided relief from poor old Phil and his sad story. In the lobby, Cory looked around to try to find where he was supposed to be. That meeting inside was indeed a Celebrate Recovery gathering. Except they'd neglected to tell him it was for porn addicts.

Maybe the crackheads were down the hall and glue sniffers were in Sunday school rooms.

Don't put them there — there's glue!

The joking in his head didn't ease his nerves. As he was about to wander down a hallway leading away from the main entry, a figure approached him.

"John Townsend. Folks call me J. T." The man had a warm and welcoming face.

"Hey," Cory said with relief as he shook the man's hand. "Yes. My agent told me to look for you. You'll be signing my paperwork, right? Listen, I think I landed in the wrong room. I'm looking for, uh . . . your basic twelve-step program. I think I connected with the sexaholics instead. Not that I'm judging."

"You were in the right room. Just takes a while to know it. Come over here."

Cory followed him across the foyer to a bulletin board, the ache in his knee acting up since it was getting later in the evening.

"There are three different group meetings in Celebrate Recovery. The large group is the one meeting right now in the sanctuary. That's held every Friday night for our group here in Okmulgee. Anybody can come — and there's no obligation to share."

"I like the sound of that."

"Following that, we gather into smaller groups called Open Share. There's one for eating disorders, one for victims of childhood abuse, and so on."

Cory glanced at the board with the various room assignments. Besides the ones J. T. had named, he saw Sexual Addictions, Chemical Dependency, and Codependency.

"So what if you have 'em all?" Cory asked, trying to be funny.

J. T. smiled. "You take it one day at a time. I'm the ministry leader, so if you have any questions, concerns, or jokes worth telling, I'm here for you."

"And what about the other meeting? You said three?"

"Step studies. Those are held here on Tuesday nights with a small group of men."

"And those are mandatory?"

J. T. nodded.

"So all together, how long do I get to celebrate being in recovery?"

"Hopefully the rest of your life. But for official purposes, you're supposed to attend eight weeks. The program is designed around studying eight recovery principles."

Well, I guess there's a case to be made for not having to go twelve weeks for a twelve-step program.

"Guess I should head back in there then. Though I still can't believe people are talking about things like *that*. In a church."

"Surprise," J. T. said.

"Well, it's good TV."

J. T. held the door for him and followed Cory back into the sanctuary. Phil was still up there, still talking.

"Depression followed, and prescription drugs made me feel better. But I was never able to reveal the true reason for my depression and addiction. But God changed everything. He changed me. Long story short — my wife and I renewed our marriage vows last August. Our three children and their spouses stood up with us as we recommitted our marriage to God and each other."

His wife came back? Is she meeting with the Bad Decision Makers?

"Because of my time in Celebrate Recovery, I know how to run to God — and His people — when I need help. And He does help me, every time. Thank you for letting me share."

Phil smiled and went to sit back down. Cory still felt like he was at the wrong place. The wrong building and the wrong room and the wrong celebration.

I'm so going to kill Helene for this.

A short while later, in a smaller room in the church, a group of nine men sat in a circle just like at any AA meeting. Cory had been to a few of those due to some of his run-ins with the law, so he wasn't sure what made this Celebrate Recovery any different. Until J. T. started to talk.

"We always read these small-group guidelines," J. T. said, more to Cory than to anybody else. "They help keep this group safe."

Cory glanced around and then nodded at the group leader.

"Number one: keep your sharing focused on your own thoughts and feelings. And limit your sharing to only a few minutes."

I bet I can limit mine to a few seconds.

"Number two: there is no cross-talk. That's when two people engage in conversation that excludes others. Everybody is free to express their feelings without interruptions."

J. T. had a sheet in front of him, but it was clear he was reciting these from memory.

"Number three: we are here to support one another, not fix one another."

A couple of the men around Cory gave knowing nods.

"Number four: what's shared in the group stays in the group. Unless someone threatens to injure themselves or others."

Cory liked number four. He didn't want to hear anything he might say showing up on ESPN later that night.

"Finally, offensive language has no place in a Christ-centered recovery group."

For a brief second Cory thought of blurting out a profanity as a joke, but the guys around him looked pretty serious.

With those "rules" now read, everybody started to go around and introduce themselves, starting with the leader.

"I'm J. T. I'm a grateful believer in Jesus, and I currently struggle with alcoholism."

As everybody greeted J. T. and told them they were glad he was there, Cory wondered if any of them were ungrateful believers. Surely a few of them weren't *that* grateful, right?

A fiftysomething biker dude next to J. T. went next. "My name is Rick, and I'm a Christian who struggles with cocaine addiction."

This would certainly be a strange Sunday school class to be a part of.

J. T. gave Cory a relaxed and friendly nod to go next.

"Oh, uh . . . hey, I'm Cory. I'm currently struggling with — my agent."

The group laughed as they welcomed him there. J. T. gave another nod, which was nice. Cory didn't want to have to go overboard and suddenly become someone he was not. He was here anyway, sitting in this room, doing as he was told.

Soon each person in the group began to share something going on in his life. The hard-edged rocker type named Rick cursed, then apologized to J. T. for his language.

Cory wanted to ask if he was kidding, but Rick didn't appear to be the comic type. This group took their rules seriously.

A man named Herb was talking about his neighbors being loud and obnoxious, and without thinking Cory chimed in. "Man, I hear you."

J. T. politely reminded him there was no cross-talk.

So this is AA with a bunch of rules and a hallelujah at the end.

Yet as the men around him spoke, none of them seemed churchy or phony. There was Abe, who had once been in prison and was now serving at local prisons, helping other inmates. There was Steve, a businessman who had been abused as a child and still had major trust issues with everybody. But most of the sharing was optimistic and hopeful.

The meeting lasted an hour. There was still a lot that Cory didn't understand, like "chips," for instance. Or the step studies. Or other lingo that went over his head.

Afterward J. T. came up to Cory and

shook his hand. "That wasn't so bad, was it?"

"That was pretty heavy, what Abe was talking about."

"One of the things about small groups is the need for confidentiality. As I said, what's shared in the group stays in the group. We don't talk about it anyplace else. We want this place and these groups to be safe."

"And no cross-talk," Cory quipped, trying to play the game.

"There's a reason for that. It avoids people giving their personal opinions. We're not here to fix each other. We're here to support each other."

"So how is this different from AA?" Cory asked. "Besides letting overeaters and meth users in?"

"Celebrate Recovery is based on Scripture. It gives you God's perspective while you're working through the steps."

"Okay."

J. T. smiled. "This place changed everything about my life, Cory. But it wasn't the people or the program that did it. It was the Lord who brought me here. I have a feeling He brought you here too."

"Can I blame my recent batting average on Him too?" Cory cracked. All this God talk was making him tired.

"You can certainly try," J. T. replied. "But believe me — that blame game doesn't work. I've tried every sort of way possible."

"So are you my sponsor?" Cory asked. "Or do I have to ask someone else?"

"We call it accountability partner."

"That means if I don't show up, I'm accountable?"

"Something like that," J. T. said with a smile. "But remember — I am responsible for signing off on your official paperwork. And I'm not fudging the facts."

J. T. told him he looked forward to seeing Cory next time they met.

As Cory walked outside the church and felt the cool night air hit him, he wondered who in this town had started Celebrate Recovery, and if any other churches in Oklahoma were doing the same strange thing.

The open sky and endless stars beckoned to him, but Cory ignored them as he tried to ignore the comments swirling around in his head from the last hour.

He remembered one of the guys referring to "God the Father."

It was a nice thought to think that God was like a father who sometimes heard you, but Cory knew better. He didn't need some father figure in his life. He'd made it thirty-three years without one. He could make it a little farther.

Cory's never been inside Hank's Tavern, but he knows it well. It's the place his dad has gone to drink most of their lives. Just a small square building that looks abandoned except for a few neon beer signs in the windows.

Cory wants to get some answers. He knows his father is inside. He wants to meet him on his home field. He wants to talk to his father man-to-man.

Emma is three months pregnant. He's gone with her to a couple of doctor's visits. Both times the doctor has hinted at other options, but they've never spoken about it because Cory knows Emma.

The question has never been whether to have the baby.

The question is what will happen with the two of them. With Cory and his baseball career.

A thousand different scenarios have played out in his head, and that's why Cory is here.

He doesn't want to ask his mother. He already knows what she'll say. He doesn't want to involve Clay or his friends or anybody else.

There's a man drinking his life away in this tavern, and Cory knows that man will tell him the straight-up truth. For better or worse.

CHAPTER SEVENTEEN:
STRIKE ONE

When Cory woke up Monday morning, he wasn't sure where he was. He knew he was in Oklahoma. But his last memory of the night before had been getting a call from Clay inviting him over to their house. Cory told Clay maybe, and he genuinely thought about going.

But the thought had turned somewhere else, just like his truck had. He skipped the Sunday evening family outing and instead found some watering hole to visit. The bar had been full, and the patrons had gotten a kick out of his stopping by. Especially the cute college-age girls who seemed barely old enough to drink.

The last thing he could remember was taking shots like a frat boy with those girls.

He looked around his motel room, checking to see if there were any signs of one of the girls coming back with him. But he knew he was alone. It was almost ten in the morning, and he was alone with a dry cotton mouth and a splitting headache, not to mention a throbbing knee that wouldn't stop.

The two days after his first Celebrate Recovery meeting had been a blitz of drinking. Cory had woken up Saturday morning and found himself bored and more bored, with a fridge full of booze. Obviously there was only one thing he could do. The same went for Sunday morning.

When he found his phone and plugged it in to charge, he saw he had missed several calls. A couple from Clay and another from Helene.

He didn't listen to them because he already knew what they said. It was the same old stuff. Clay trying to fix things and placate him, and Helene trying to fix things and placate him.

Thank God the Bulldogs' practice wasn't till later this afternoon. If he had to go looking and feeling like this, there might be some more drama on the field.

He remembered dancing in the bar and kissing some stranger's lips. Cory winced. Then he thought of Emma and Tyler, knowing that was the last thing the two of them needed. Some bar-hopping daddy stumbling home in the middle of the night.

■ ■ ■ ■

"Any word on Cory?"

"You think *I* know where that man is?"

It was Clay's first day back in the office. His arm was doing okay in the cast and sling; it was his ribs that were slowing him down. He was taking pain medication, but he hated that stuff. He knew well enough that certain things ran in the family, like addictions. The less Vicodin he could take, the better.

It was around lunchtime, and this was the first time today he'd been able to call to see where Cory might be. Emma was obviously as clueless as he was.

"I invited him to our place last night and he said he was going to come, but he never made it," Clay said.

"That sounds familiar." Emma's voice sounded cynical and annoyed.

"I just wondered —"

"I'm sure he'll be out on the baseball field later today. Walking around like a coach."

"Emma —"

"What?"

"I didn't bring him back to Okmulgee."

"I know," Emma said, her resistance gone and her voice more relaxed.

"Please don't blame me for my brother's mistakes."

"I don't. It's just — ever since I heard the team was going to the Grizzlies game, I had this sense of foreboding. Somehow I knew that Cory Brand was going to come back into our lives. *All* of our lives."

"It's funny how so many people say his whole name," Clay said. "Like a product, you know. Folgers coffee. Nike shoes."

"Idiotic baseball players."

Clay laughed. "Look, if he doesn't show up at practice, let me know."

"I'm sure Karen would do that for me."

"Yeah, I'm sure she would too."

Clay told her good-bye and sat at his desk for a few minutes, thinking. Part of him wondered if he should head down to Cory's motel.

He's a grown-up man who needs to take care of himself.

The phone rang. There was too much work to do here for Clay to take off and start searching for Cory. He'd lost enough time because of his brother.

He would keep praying that Cory was okay. And that this was the wake-up call Clay had been asking God for ever since Cory left Okmulgee to pursue his dreams.

There was nothing wrong with dreams unless a person forgot himself and where he came from in pursuit of them.

The question is: the love or the dream.

Cory knows they're a world apart.

The dream of playing professional baseball isn't just an idea that's never going to happen. It's there. It's reality in his hands. It feels as real as holding a bat and belting a home run. It's as real as hearing and seeing the world applauding around you. Of cracking that bat and knowing. Just knowing.

But what about love?

Love can conquer all, right?

There is no rule book to show him what's right or wrong. There's no parent to show him the way. All he knows are his gut and his instincts. All he knows is the now.

There is something blinding and crazy about the world out there. And he wants it. He wants to escape. To go far from Okmulgee.

Is it the right decision?

Maybe he should be asking that, but he doesn't.

He just wonders how to tell Emma he's leaving.

How to make sure she's going to be okay when he knows she won't be.

No one else can understand. Because they aren't him. They don't have this gift that he has. To be able to stand there and face the fears head-on. To launch the unlaunchable. To hit all those balls the pitchers don't want hit.

That is a talent.

That is something.

And Cory is leaving knowing he has the talent and that's something and he's going to go far and that's okay and if love can survive then so be it.

CHAPTER EIGHTEEN:
STOLEN BASE

Driving this beat-up Ford truck reminded Cory of his father and the steady supply of useless vehicles he went through. Sometimes Dad would total a truck and need to find a new clunker for the road. They all learned you got what you paid for.

Being in the pros had been one of the easiest ways to forget about Dad and everybody else around here in Okmulgee. It wasn't just playing baseball, which was a relentless sport that took your time and took your energy and sometimes took your soul. It was the money that came with playing, especially if you were good. Once the money really started to roll in, Cory could spoil himself with fancy cars and gadgets and toys and whatever else he imagined.

It was hard to imagine much while driving in the country in this jerky truck and listening to country music.

When Cory arrived at the baseball field,

parents and kids were already filing onto the field. He could see Karen walking with Carlos as he parked the truck and climbed out.

"Hey, Cory. Did you have some huge boxes delivered to the house?"

No how are you or how'd you sleep or how's life treating you.

He ignored her abrasive tone. "Oh, yeah. They arrived. Great. Hey, Carlos."

The two of them walked onto the field while Karen followed behind. Cory much preferred the peppy little guy to his mommy. He wanted to tell Carlos that sometimes his mommy seemed to be crabby for no reason. He wanted to add that all women at some point were going to be crabby for no reason; it was just a fact of life. But something told Cory that Karen might not appreciate this . . . wisdom.

"So how's your daddy?" Cory asked.

"He went back to work today."

"Good for him. Did you join him?"

"No," Carlos said. "I'm only ten."

"What? Only ten? Come on, I thought you were at least twenty-seven."

Cory knew the juvenile humor was lame, but Carlos indulged him. Soon they were joined by Tyler, who came sprinting up behind them.

"Hi, Coach."

"Heeeey, Tyler." Cory knew he was over-doing it a bit, so he scaled back. "Ready to work hard today, guys?"

They both told him yes. Cory liked watching Tyler right next to him, literally walking in stride with his father.

"What are we going to work on first? Sliding?" Another kid joined this group. For a moment, Cory struggled to remember the kid's name, and then it came to him. Stanton. The know-it-all of the team, the one who was never going to be much of a player because he acted like he was great when he wasn't exceptional at all. Acting the part of a great player only made you an actor.

"We need to work on our hitting," Tyler said. "We suck. I mean stink —"

Cory only smiled at him.

"We could work on winning," Stanton said. "That'd be nice."

Cory was glad that this smug, sarcastic kid wasn't his son. He liked the fact that Tyler was the nicest kid out here. And among the best players on the field.

Just like his daddy. A nice guy and a great player.

He wanted to tell Stanton that winners didn't talk, but he kept his mouth shut.

203

Stanton would learn that the hard way, like all kids.

At this age everybody played the game. Then year by year, play by play, the game weeded out the weak and the worthless. Soon only the strong played the game, and even they couldn't play it very long.

Cory wondered how many years he had left to play professionally.

Not many, if I keep coaching Little League and never get back to home base.

The two mothers followed Cory and the boys at a slower pace, watching them converse as if it was the most natural thing in the world.

"How weird is this for you?" Karen asked.

"Weird." Emma just watched Cory and Tyler and how they both walked the same way. There was the big version and the little version. The more she thought of this, the more her head hurt. "Actually more like — scary."

"Are you feeling anything for him?"

"Well, now that you brought it up, I have to tell you — he came over last night and spent the night. It was the most amazing night of my life. Until, of course, he burned down our house."

Karen laughed.

"You can't be serious," Emma continued. "Yes, I'm feeling like he's in my space and needs to go back to his big faraway life."

"That big faraway life might not take him, you know. There are rumors about whether he'll be able to go back to the Grizzlies."

"I don't pay any attention to those things. Never have."

"I can't help it," Karen said. "Clay does it for me. I call him obsessed."

"He called me wondering where Cory was."

"He told me."

"I'm not Cory's caretaker. I have one boy to take of, and that's enough for me."

"Amen," Karen said, putting her arm around Emma as they walked out onto the baseball diamond.

Emma assumed this wasn't going to be any ordinary practice, not with Cory being around. But this time it wasn't Cory's fault that the practice got off track from the very start.

It was Wick's fault.

He'd brought an old yearbook to show his fellow teammates. A yearbook that just happened to have Cory Brand smiling like he always did as a hunky senior in high school. Then there was the skinny and big-haired

205

Emma Johnson, who happened to be in a lot of pictures with Cory Brand.

Especially the infamous "Cutest Couple" picture.

When Emma and Karen arrived at the dugout, they saw the mischievous grins and the secretive conversation going on with the team. Right away, Emma knew this wasn't going to be good.

"Mom. Why didn't you tell me?"

For a moment her heart stopped beating, knowing there was no way Tyler could know, yet wondering how he did. Then she saw the yearbook in his hand.

"Where'd you get that?"

"Wick brought it."

She snatched it out of Tyler's hand and glared at little Wick.

He shrugged. "My dad got it out for me last night."

"Really. Remind me to thank him." She held the yearbook up like a trophy. "I'll keep this until after practice."

The team giggled and groaned and continued talking about the photos they'd seen.

Cory stepped into the dugout looking curious. "Keep what?"

"Nothing," Emma said.

She hid the yearbook behind her back and suddenly felt like that senior girl again, looking at Cory in a playful way. She knew he would go overboard once he found the memento of their teen years.

"Let's see."

"No."

For a moment Cory played it cool, then he quickly reached around her and snatched it. Emma couldn't believe how fast he was for such a big guy. When he saw what she was hiding, Cory laughed in amazement.

"Oh, this is classic," he said as he opened up the yearbook.

"We need to get to practice."

He immediately found one of the first few pictures of her, a smiling shot by her locker. "Look how cute you are."

She knew this was just Cory being Cory. A guy being a guy. A jock being a jock.

He pointed at another picture and couldn't help bursting into laughter. As he did, Karen stood behind Cory and did her bug eyes while Emma smiled.

We're seriously still acting like we did back then.

"Those clothes are classic."

She glanced at the page and saw the two of them, high school kids during the era of grunge — Emma in her floral dress and boots while Cory looked like a Kurt Cobain wannabe with his flannel shirt and long hair.

It still felt like yesterday to her.

Just a decade and a ten-year-old son later . . .

Carlos couldn't resist sticking his nose in the fun as well. "Hey, Coach, does this mean you and Coach Emma K-I-S-S-I-N-G-ed?"

The rest of the team howled and gave a chorus of "ewwws." Emma knew she needed to get control of this situation fast.

Cory grinned and glanced over at Carlos. "How about I K-I-C-K all you Bulldogs' B-U-T-T-S-es out onto that field. Now."

The kids all started to run onto the field, laughing and joking while Cory followed them, slapping the rears of the slower ones. Emma glanced over at Karen again, disbelief and humor and horror all mixed into one expression on her face.

She could only mouth the words *Oh my gosh.*

As she followed, she couldn't help smiling. The yearbook thing could have gone down a lot differently. Been a lot worse. But they'd been laughing and joking about it.

She couldn't help feeling a bit of relief.

The girl with the french braids was undeniably cute, but she could also play some ball. During the practice game, Cory decided to give her a few pointers before she went up to hit.

"You're a lefty, kid, like me, so that gives you two extra steps to first on the drag bunt. I promise you —"

"There are two outs," Kendricks said with disbelief.

"Trust me, think like a gazelle," Cory assured her. "Lay it down and don't look back."

She went up to the plate and went with the bunt on the first throw. Everybody was surprised, just as Cory had said they would be, and Kendricks easily made it to first base. Cory clapped and cheered her on as he beamed over to the pitcher, who didn't even have time to field the bunt. Emma picked up the ball and gave Cory that look he remembered. She hated losing, and she was a fierce competitor.

"Nice bunt, Kendricks," Emma shouted.

Kendricks wasn't her competition. But Cory knew he was another story.

Near the end of practice, the team sat around third base while Cory took the stage and gave them a new set of batting signals. Some of the kids, like Tyler and Carlos, listened attentively while others, like Stanton, seemed bored, or, like Wellsey, seemed in a slight daze. Even though the signals were a bit too complex for the kids, Emma couldn't help being impressed. Cory kept surprising her moment after moment, whether it was something he did for one of the kids, or some ridiculous display of talent, or simply by making her and everybody else laugh.

Why are you so surprised?

This was just Cory being Cory.

So what about that guy who went ballistic during the home game? Or the guy who nearly got his brother killed in a car accident? Or the wild party animal in the tabloids?

It was so easy to be swept into the whirlwind that was Cory Brand. But Emma knew that tornadoes were beautiful but also furious, leaving only wreckage and destruction in their wake.

Cory was still talking. "Back of my hat means we're going to bunt, double steal, suicide squeeze."

Most of the kids sat cross-legged and watched with confused looks on their faces. Emma knew they had no idea what Coach Cory was talking about.

"Anything goes," he said. "We are going to smoke 'em, shock 'em, scare 'em. We're gonna fart in some runs if we have to."

Obviously Cory had noticed they were

beginning to fade out, so he used the good old fart trick. But it worked, getting their attention and making them wake up and laugh. Wellsey, the redheaded kid who was usually off in outer space, particularly liked this joke and couldn't stop laughing.

Cory glanced at Emma, and she caught herself smiling at him. Giving him one of those grins she gave him years ago when they still wore grunge clothes and listened to Pearl Jam.

What are you doing, Emma?

She looked away quickly and tried to remember where she was and who he was.

She was staring the center of the cyclone in the eyes. Emma knew she needed to get as far away from it as possible.

Wreckage and destruction, a voice reminded her. Over and over again.

"It's going to get better," they tell him.

"Just major-league blues," they say.

But he feels like he's managed to come all this way to get nowhere.

On the plane late one night, his body aching and his mind and heart tired, Cory wonders if he made a mistake. A huge mistake.

He cranks up the music. But something is wrong, because instead of enjoying inspiring power rock, he's suddenly listening to a bunch of ballads about long-lost love, and he's thinking of Emma and Tyler.

Everybody loves Journey, right? Their greatest-hits album rocks. They're always playing "Don't Stop Believin'" at the parks, and he's gotten into it.

But now these songs are making his hitting blues even worse. Songs like "Who's Crying Now" and "Separate Ways" are making him wish his Nine Inch Nails album was nearby.

But he keeps listening and can't help thinking of them.

What if he only makes it a year or two? a voice asks.

What if they don't invite him up to the show?
What if he's forced to go back home?
What if . . .

The plane wings its way through the night sky, and he feels lonely and empty. He wants to do just like the song says and send her his love.

Broken hearts can always mend. Can't they, Cory Brand? Can't they?

Time has faded, and it's too late to send her his love or to send her anything because she has moved on.

He needs to get sleep for the game tomorrow. But he can't. He finds the bottle of vodka and takes a few sips to try to lighten up.

The night devours the weak, but Cory vows not to be among them.

CHAPTER NINETEEN: CHECKED SWING

The four walls around him felt like a prison. A prison that allowed you to go through the drive-through at McDonald's on the way back to your cell. Cory's stomach felt full on fast food, but he still felt empty. He'd been in the room only a few minutes before looking to see if the fridge was fully stocked. Chad hadn't let him down.

He closed the door without taking anything.

I don't need anything tonight. I'm fine just hanging out in this room by myself without the need to drink.

He took off his shoes and turned on the television and checked his email. He felt bored now after the full, fun day. At least the full, fun afternoon. Being around the kids reminded him of something good that had been gone for a while — that wonderful "love of the game." Those kids loved the game, even if they had a hard time picking it up.

Emma's smile filled his mind. Being around her had been a good thing too.

This humming deep inside his soul never turned off.

For a moment he thought of tomorrow and looked forward to the game. Emma had said there were four practices a week along with a game or two on the schedule. Cory found himself eager to go back out on the field with the team.

He looked at the fridge, ignoring the television. He knew he was going to open it, that he was going to drink tonight.

I don't have to, but I want to. There's a difference.

There was no point in making some grand stand, because it didn't mean a thing. He could drink tonight, or he could not drink. But not drinking meant he'd be more bored and restless for no reason.

I can stop whenever I want.

It was hot, and he slipped off his shirt, tossing it over a chair. Once again he glanced at the fridge, as if he thought it might start talking back at him.

Nobody was there. His brother wasn't around, and Emma wasn't about to come by tonight. It was just him.

He checked a few messages he'd gotten from some of his female friends. He wouldn't mind one of them stopping by, but Okmulgee was a bit far for all of them.

Cory cursed and turned up the volume of the television, resisting the urge to get something to drink.

I don't have to, and it's that easy. If I don't want to, I won't.

But nobody watched and nobody cared. Not in this motel room. Not now.

Tyler smelled like shampoo and was dripping water onto his bed. It was a little past his bedtime, but Emma still did their regular routine of reading to him. They were going through The Prydain Chronicles and were on book three, *The Castle of Llyr*. James had turned Tyler on to fantasy classics like this. Of course, the first series they'd read to him was The Chronicles of Narnia. James had wanted to read some of these easier series before diving into Harry Potter and then graduating to The Lord of the Rings.

Emma fully intended to read all of those books to Tyler even though James was no longer there. Normally Tyler was enthralled with the nightly chapter, but tonight he didn't seem to be paying attention.

And I bet I know what he's thinking about too.

When Emma closed the book, Tyler looked at her with curiosity.

"So you, like, dated Cory Brand in high school?"

There was the inevitable moment of Tyler meeting Cory that Emma had feared. Then there was the next inevitable moment, of Tyler learning who his real father was.

Not "real," but technical. James was and will always be his father.

"Yeah, sweetie," Emma said as she tucked his blanket around him.

"Was he a good baseball player in high school?"

"You kidding me? Of course he was. People would come from other schools to watch him play."

"Really?"

"You bet." She smiled. "He was fun to watch."

"So then why — why didn't you keep going out?"

Emma brushed the wet strands of hair away from his face. She couldn't help being amused at his logic.

Cory Brand is a great baseball player, so naturally you'd want to keep dating him, right, Mom?

"He moved away to play baseball."

She'd once thought those six words would forever sum up her life.

"Oh, cool."

But then two other words entered her life and would forever define it.

Tyler Hargrove.

"You think I could do that one day?" he asked her.

"Do what?"

"Play baseball like Cory Brand."

"Then you'd have to move away from your mother," she said, feigning a deeply serious tone. "Sorry, but I can't allow that."

"Mom."

"Nope. I think you need to be a veterinarian or something."

"No," Tyler said. "I want be like Cory."

You already are. So much so it scares me.

"Well, you keep practicing like today, and who knows," she said.

Tyler had been through enough in the last year. The last thing Emma was ever going to do was tell him he couldn't dream.

He needed to dream for the both of them. She'd stopped dreaming.

The problem with dreams was that deep down you always hoped they'd come true. And hope was a dangerous thing for Emma these days.

It had found her in a dark spot the moment James entered her life. It hurt too much to expect that hope could come walking into her life a second time.

The numbing feeling was like someone wrapping a warm towel around his knee. Except in this case, it was his head. And instead of the throbbing stopping, it was the thinking. He drank so he could stop all that thinking running around in circles in his head.

Cory wanted to call Emma. He wasn't going to, but he wanted to. He remembered how they used to be, and he wanted that back. She was fun. And she was wild herself. She certainly enjoyed herself around him. There had never been anything that Cory had done with Emma that she didn't want to do. That was the complexity of Emma, and one of the things he loved about her. Or had loved about her. This contrast in personalities, being this cute and innocent and lovable girl one moment, then the feisty and assertive and take-control woman the next.

This same girl who had fought for him and been so loyal and loving to him had also helped him dream for something more. Until, of course, it became more than what either of them wanted, and the dream turned into something bigger. Something heavier.

Cory worked on another bottle since he'd already drained the vodka. He needed to tell the kid to buy more vodka. But it didn't matter. He was tired and drifting in and out of sleep. He'd seen himself twice on ESPN and swore at himself both times. If he didn't change the channel, the third time he might break the television screen with a flying bottle.

Emma.

He wanted to call her and say come on over. Just to relive old times. There was still something between them. He'd noticed it all afternoon.

Yeah, idiot, it's a ten-year-old kid, and his name is Tyler.

What a buzz kill. The boy. The buzz-kill boy. Oh, he was loving Tyler, but when it came to Emma, there was always going to be Tyler. Cory couldn't escape that reality.

He felt warm and slow. The pictures and words on the television plodded by. He caught bits and pieces. He didn't know what time it was, didn't care. He couldn't sleep, because he wanted Emma next to him. And if it couldn't be Emma, then maybe some-one else, but he hated feeling alone.

He'd only felt this way his entire life, and after thirty-three years he still wasn't used to it.

Boo hoo cry me a river suck it up you pathetic loser.

Maybe that was his father talking. At this point Cory wasn't sure.

His last sip of the night spilled a mouthful on the bed, but he didn't mind because he didn't notice.

Soon he was out cold, sitting up in bed with the television blaring and empty bottles around him, and somewhere in the back of his blurry mind Emma and Tyler were watching with the rest of the disappointed world.

The pounding in his head from the night before gets a little worse when he cranks up his iPod to the familiar song. Freddie Mercury and crew sing "We will rock you," and Cory drowns out the rest of the world. Not just the locker room and the stadium, but the memories and shadows that follow him. He moves his head, and the dull throb feels better. The voices and the whispers fade away as he feels his body getting ready. It's always the same. This crowd in his headphones cheering him on right before the guitar wails, muffling every other voice wanting to speak.

Nobody out there knows where he comes from or what he's had to do to get here. Nor do they care. What they want is the long ball and the chant of the home run. What they want is a W and a good time and to leave the ballpark with a good feeling in the gut from a few beers and a few runs batted in. Cory knows there's one reason he's here, and that's it, and that's all he cares about. To go out there and do this thing that he's heard is a blessing and a gift, which is all fine, but it's just about hitting a ball. He doesn't really love this sport, just because he's getting paid an insane amount to hit a little ball. That's all. Hit a ball and become a champion.

Chapter Twenty:
Strike Zone

Cory couldn't remember the last time he'd wanted to win a game so badly. He stood over by the dugout and glanced out at the largest crowd this Little League field had ever seen. The stands, nothing more than several rows of wooden beams over concrete blocks, were jammed full. People lined both sides of the field. He wanted to show a great game to all these townspeople who had come to see the first official Bulldogs game with Cory Brand as coach. He wanted to give them a win.

He also wanted to beat the other team. The Roughnecks were the "unbeatable" champions who always crushed the Bull-dogs. Cory wanted to show them that you didn't have to wear fancy new top-of-the-line black-and-gray jerseys and look like some New York team to win on the field.

He also wanted to show them that you didn't have to be a jerk to coach a team. He recognized the Roughnecks' coach from the hospital: Pajersky, the cop who had wanted to throw him in the slammer for driving drunk. His idea of coaching seemed to be yelling at his players.

It was the top of the fourth, and the game was tied three to three. The Bulldogs were hitting, and the tall pitcher, who looked as though he knew what he was doing, just walked another batter.

"C'mon, Caleb," Coach Pajersky screamed. "What are you thinking?"

The way he said it made it seem like this was beneath them. Not just being tied to the lowly Bulldogs, but the mere fact that they had to play them.

It's a Little League game, buddy.

Several of the parents seemed embarrassed at the spectacle. The most embarrassed, however, seemed to be the pitcher himself.

"Throw strikes," Pajersky continued. "You can let this team try to hit, just don't walk 'em."

Something deep inside of Cory started to vibrate.

This isn't the scene of any crime, and this isn't some random car you pulled over. It's a Little League game.

Cory walked over to the edge of the

Roughnecks' dugout, looking cool and collected behind his shades and cap. He watched the game for a moment, then turned to Pajersky and tried to be as friendly and affable as possible.

"Hey, what do you say we lighten up a bit, Coach?"

The guy was average in every way. Average build, average face, average haircut, surely living an average life. He waved Cory off, like someone who didn't want to be bothered at this crucial juncture. A freaking Little League game that his team might tie. Or, heaven forbid, lose.

"That's my boy out there, Brand. You coach your team, I'll coach mine." The guy didn't even glance at Cory when he spoke.

Cory looked at the mortified kid on the mound, standing there with his head hanging down. Then he let out a disbelieving chuckle at Pajersky's comment and clapped to try to cheer the cop's poor son on.

"Let's just play ball," Cory said, walking back to the Bulldogs' dugout.

Tyler was stepping up to the plate. He stood several inches away from the plate, just like he always did — just like Cory had tried to get him to stop doing.

"Okay, Tyler-my-man, move in tight. Let's shore up our stance."

Tyler moved in a painful inch.

Cory smiled. He understood why Tyler was scared. "It's all right," he said in an assuring voice. "Little more, now."

"You're okay," a voice from first base said. "Stand where you want, Ty."

He's never going to learn, Emma, if he doesn't try.

"A couple more inches and you're there."

Tyler moved another inch.

"You stand wherever it feels right, Tyler."

Tyler looked at his mother and then back at Cory. The pitcher, Caleb, was watching with impatience from the mound.

"Batter ready?" the umpire asked.

Tyler nodded, then immediately scooted back into his original position. Cory gritted his teeth. Caleb pitched, and Tyler's swing wasn't even close. He was out by the third pitch.

Pajersky was laughing and shaking his head. Cory wanted to ram that smug look down the guy's throat. He didn't care if he was a cop or a father or the humanitarian of the year. People who gave Cory that kind of attitude usually ended up regretting it.

Kendricks was having a great game for herself on the mound. Now she was facing Pajersky's kid with the count two balls and two strikes.

Even before she threw it, Cory knew. He could tell Caleb was hesitating. The ball whizzed by, and the umpire called a strike. The Bulldogs all cheered as Caleb threw his bat into the dirt.

"You can't watch it, Caleb," hollered Pajersky. "Two strikes, you gotta be swinging."

As Caleb reached the bench, he gave the Gatorade cooler a karate kick that sent it flying away and spilling out on the ground.

Cory felt a weird sense of déjà vu.

Coach Pajersky yelled at his son and then yanked him by his jersey, thrusting him back down on the bench as the rest of his teammates went back out on the field. For a moment, Pajersky held him with an uncomfortable force. "You're benched, young man," he snapped.

Cory couldn't believe what he was seeing. He crossed over to their dugout. "I'm warning you, Coach."

Pajersky turned to him. "*You're* warning *me*? Where do you think he learned that behavior? Watching idiots like you!"

"Dad."

"Shut up," Pajersky shouted back at his son.

Everybody around was quiet. Cory had seen and heard enough. He wasn't a kid anymore, and this wasn't his father, but that didn't matter. All he could think about was a poor helpless kid who had never hurt anybody being belittled and beaten down day after day after day.

This stops now.

Pajersky stepped away from Caleb and out of the dugout to confront Cory. Others had started to walk their way. Emma from first base. Clay, with his arm in a sling and a bit of a limp.

Cory didn't care. It didn't matter that the whole town, including the two teams, was watching them now.

"Apple doesn't fall far from the tree, Cory," Pajersky said. "You're a showboat and a drunk, just like your old man."

Cory's fist slammed against Pajersky's jaw, and the cop dropped like a ten-year-old boy. But as he lay sprawled on the grass, alarmed cries coming from the people around them, players rushing to the coaches' sides, Pajersky smiled.

He smiled in a way that said *Gotcha.*

He tries not to think of home. It's easy not to.

The grind and the game allow him to focus. Then other things allow him to forget.

The nights are endless, and the days are a blur. Sometimes time races, and sometimes it seems to stand still.

He thinks of the old farmhouse and the crippled barn and the aging parents and the lonely brother, and he wonders how this could be his fate, to find his dreams on an empty platter.

When Cory stops, he can still see it like a lone cloud in the sky as the sun begins to drift away. But he closes his eyes quickly and sees the black hole in the place of the sun.

Nobody knows these empty feelings inside. Nobody.

This is what he tells himself as he makes others laugh. As he faces others who might easily relate to what he's feeling, but wouldn't share even if they did.

They're all grown-ups playing a kids' game. They're just kids having fun and doing whatever they want to do.

It's easy to forget that tiny Oklahoma town with the hard-to-forget name.

He forgets. Sometimes.

But sometimes he remembers, then tries even harder to forget.

Chapter Twenty-One: Cellar

The humid night air felt thick. Clay steered his truck with his one good arm. He had the window down to feel the breeze against his skin, but it felt like the hot breath of a disappointing sigh. Karen hadn't wanted him to go to the police station, of course. Neither had Emma. Karen was tired of Clay trying to bail his brother out. Emma, on the other hand, was simply scared of Cory and what his stay in Okmulgee might mean to her and to Tyler.

Every time Clay thought there was something good coming out of this, something went terribly wrong. He'd been persistent about taking the team to the Grizzlies' home game on Father's Day. He had hoped that Cory could meet Carlos and make a connection. That Karen could see the good in his brother. That Cory might want to see more of them. It could have been the start of something special.

Yet all Clay kept doing was bailing Cory out. This time, the bail was literal.

God, help me figure out something to say or do.

The list of possible words and actions was growing thinner by the day. Clay had tried everything. Backing off from Cory's life, intruding in it, bringing up the past, letting the past go. He'd tried to be his brother's drinking buddy, had also tried to be his counselor. Nothing had worked.

He parked in front of the police station and turned off the vehicle, and for a moment he sat in the silence.

He wondered why people God gave so much to always turned out to be the biggest idiots in the world. Cory was tied in that spot with their father.

No, Cory owned the *numero uno* position. He'd had a chance to be different. He saw what a failure looked like, day after day.

Clay loved his brother, but this was pathetic. He was embarrassed to have to go inside this station and see guys he knew and then accept responsibility for Cory.

He wiped his forehead and took a deep breath as he climbed out of the truck. His ribs ached even though he was still taking pain meds. As he shut the door, he still wasn't sure what he was going to say. It seemed every single thing had already been uttered.

Clay had hoped, after signing the papers and seeing them release Cory, that he might get an apology. Maybe "I screwed up again" or "I'm a moron" or "Man, I need help." But instead, Clay knew his brother was just angry with the whole world.

Staring at a dejected and angry-looking Cory only made Clay more infuriated.

"Nice going, Cory," was all he could think to say.

"I wasn't drinking." Cory looked at him in defiance.

You are such an absolute fool.

Clay stood right in Cory's face. "You weren't arrested for drinking," he shouted.

"Hey, I stood up for that kid the way no one *ever* stood up for me with Dad."

Now Cory was trying to act cool and calm and collected. But this was how he did everything. Exploding first, then later either laughing it off or playing the victim.

"Well, you're looking more like Dad every day."

Cory lit up again like a fuse for a dozen fireworks. "Maybe that's because I took all your hits."

"All my hits? What do you think happened

when you weren't around, Cory? You have no excuses."

Poor Cory Brand. What a victim. What a tragedy. Blame it on Dad. Blame it on Clay. Blame it on everybody else but never, ever try to blame it on Cory.

Clay didn't look away. He used to be unable to confront Cory, the big brother he idolized and would follow to the ends of the earth. But that big brother wasn't so big anymore. He was just another man with a list of broken, failed promises.

"You turned a nice day into something ugly," Clay said. "Again."

Cory just looked at him in disgust and disbelief. He chuckled and then paused for a moment, staring at Clay. "Sorry I don't have it all figured out like you, little brother."

Cory turned and walked away from the parking lot and down the road.

Clay didn't know if his brother even knew where he was going, but that was fine. He'd find his own way home just like he always did. He'd get by without anybody else's help.

Weeks blur by.

He hears the crack of the bat in his nightmares and sees the spin of sliders in his daydreams. Some days he opens his eyes to find himself on foreign land in a visiting field. He keeps his smile close at hand like a pistol at a sheriff's side, using it whenever forced to, whenever confronted and confused.

Sometimes the night sky waves good night and he looks out the plane windows in awe.

Sometimes he sees the face of a beautiful woman smiling at him, waiting for him.

We're not in Kansas anymore, Toto, he thinks. *Oklahoma either.*

A day leaps over into a week, into a month. Then it's all about the repetition, about making it through, about making it count, about making it to October.

He's wide awake in October. He sees the sights and the sounds in October.

But the rest of the season blurs by. Letters

never arrive. Phone calls never reach him. Invitations never get answered. Promises never get fulfilled.

It's all about the Grizzlies. It's all about Cory. It's all about this little round thing called a baseball.

The blur. The bite. The roller-coaster ride. The blindness.

Only to wake up empty in the off-season, wondering what happened.

CHAPTER TWENTY-TWO:
INTENTIONAL WALK

Cory was still walking in this inkblot of a town when Helene's name showed up on his phone.

"Helene," he said in a way that politely said, *I don't need any more guilt trips from anybody else, thank you very much.*

"Assault? This is your idea of lying low? You are killing me."

"It wasn't assault," he replied.

"*Killing* me. An uploaded photo went from Facebook to a Grizzlies blog to ESPN."

Cory stopped near the curb and looked at the sleeping center of Okmulgee. Now the world at large had another image of Cory Brand: slugging a fellow coach and, oh yeah, a police officer besides.

Everything was crumbling down around him, and all he could do was watch. Everybody wanted his entire world to get smeared and wiped away, and they just wanted to stand by and laugh. Nobody understood.

Nobody got it. Nobody ever would.

He wanted to reach out and hit something, blast it far away deep into the night where the shadows watched from hidden bleachers.

Helene continued to moan and critique and chastise, and he just wanted her rambling mouth to shut up.

"Just fix it," he eventually interrupted. "That's what you get paid for. It might take a little effort, but I think you soak enough out of me to put in the time."

He clicked off the phone and kept walking, kicking a metal trash can and sending it hurling into the road.

The night seemed as though it would never end. Cory wasn't sure how much time had passed or where exactly he was going. When a car slowed down and then stopped by him on the edge of the road, Cory figured it might be someone with a gun who was going to take the little cash he had and then sink a couple of rounds in his skull. That would show the world, as they grieved his passing and wished they had treated him a little better.

"Need a ride?" a familiar voice asked.

It was J. T.

Wonderful. Another face to feel guilty in front of.

"Well, my truck's at the field."

"Hop in."

He didn't ask why Cory was out here in the middle of the night walking. Cory knew J. T. had heard about the game. Everybody that had *anything* to do with his life knew about it. But he appreciated not being asked. He climbed in and sat in silence for a few moments as the car moved down the road.

"I used to be a road warrior," J. T. said out of the blue as the car coasted along. "King of the road. Spent a lot of my time driving. That was when gas was a lot cheaper. And when people didn't connect by computers."

Cory didn't want to hear it. Another sad story from another sad soul. It didn't matter.

"I was in sales. I might seem a bit laid-back for a salesman, but I wasn't back then. I was relentless. I'd force people to go my way just so they could get me off their backs. Relentless."

For a moment, Cory glanced at J. T. It was hard to believe the mild-mannered guy could be anything resembling relentless.

"I gave everything I had to the job, and I

drank because of the pressure. Meanwhile my marriage was falling apart, along with every other part of my life. It was on the road late one night when I finally called out to God. I needed help. I needed — well, I was tired. Tired of trying to control things and not being able to manage any part of my life."

The sleeping town of Okmulgee passed them by. Cory looked out his window while J. T. continued talking.

"You know, when I was about three or four weeks clean, I thought I had this thing licked. But then life would happen, and before you know it I was at it again."

J. T.'s deep voice sounded like an authority on pain. Cory could only say "okay," but he didn't really want to talk about recovery.

"It wasn't until I finally understood *why* I drank that I could see my way out of it."

Cory didn't say anything. He knew why he drank. Because he liked how it tasted and how it made him feel. Pure and simple. Sure, there was his irritating knee, and also his irritating agent — those were two more reasons to drink.

You could fill a phone book with reasons why you drink.

They pulled up to the lone truck in the parking lot next to the baseball field. Cory

241

wanted to jump out of the car and sprint away from this man with his deep thoughts and deeper history, but he couldn't.

J. T. parked the car but left it running as he looked at Cory. "It wasn't about my drinking. It was about my pain."

Cory nodded and tried to give him an earnest, heartfelt, *I-feel-your-pain* look. "Okay, well, thanks for the ride."

As J. T. drove away, Cory looked at his truck sitting in the middle of nowhere. Nobody around here could possibly understand what he was going through. It didn't matter what kind of curveball life had thrown at them. They couldn't possibly begin to understand the stresses and temptations and struggles of being Cory Brand.

Unless they walk in my shoes, they won't ever get it.

Just one more day, and you'll change.

Just one more day, and they'll see.

Just one more season, and the season will pass.

Just one more year, and the needs will go away.

Just one more failure before you make things right.

Just one more apology before you make amends.

Just one more outburst before you finally relax.

Just one more drink before you actually can.

Then another. But just one more. Just a few more and just a few more after that, and then tomorrow you can go ahead and change.

Just one more day, and peace will finally come.

CHAPTER TWENTY-THREE:
BACKDOOR SLIDER

The back roads were like wrinkles forever etched in Cory's skin from all the times he had walked and ridden over them. They seemed to lead to nowhere, just more Oklahoma countryside with flowing fields and endless sky. But this five-acre plot of land was the place where he'd grown up, where his father had made his childhood miserable. Cory hadn't been back in a long time.

As the sun started to wake up, Cory drove down those roads and turned onto the dirt driveway. The land had stayed in the family, with Clay and Karen now living there with Carlos. As Cory drove toward the house, he noticed that it had a new look about it. Fresh paint, a new roof, flower boxes on the windowsills, even a wreath on the door. After Mom had died, the remaining color on this farm had faded to black and white. It had turned into a reflection of its owner,

Michael Brand.

Not far from the pretty house that Karen had surely helped make her own sat the old dilapidated red wooden barn. Time had only made it look more classic and ageless, at least in Cory's eyes. This had been his old hiding place, his refuge and sanctuary. The shadows had kept his secrets safe — at least most of them.

He parked and walked to the barn, noticing the pathetic leaky tin roof that never got fixed. It probably wouldn't have taken much, but some things in this life were just meant to stay broken.

Cory kicked open a side door and could see piles of furniture and items that belonged to his youth. The old couches and dining room table. The wooden baseball-themed pinball game they'd played to death. Pictures and boxes of mementos all surrounded by old baseballs. He picked up one of the balls and sniffed it. He liked the way it smelled and felt in his hand. It reminded him of all the things the game promised him when he was younger.

It took him a few moments to find the power breakers. Once he turned them on, the interior of the barn was aglow in cold, ghostly light. It took another couple of minutes to open the sliding doors on each side of the barn.

This was like waking up a dead man, or at least one who had been in a coma for over a decade. The smell was the same, and the shadows still hovered around like they always had. The remnants of hay underneath the vaulted roof were moldy by now. Cory could taste the dust in the air as he walked around.

In just a few moments he began to find some comfort in this place. The old bat in his hand connected with the first baseball shot off by the pitching machine. The ball wailed against the side of the barn wall. The machine stood at one side of the open doors, and Cory stood on the opposite side, trying to thread the needle.

He hit every ball the machine whipped toward him.

Being in this place made him feel six again. And ten. And sixteen.

The years were the same because his life was the same.

Every day he had woken with fear and urgency. He never stopped wondering what might happen before breakfast or before they left for school or during those long and awful summer days. He never stopped looking after Clay and never stopped preparing to hit the ball.

Cory smacked a ball straight ahead out of the barn.

Every hit had been an attempt to fight off the Devil.

Every ball had been a round fist of hurt thrown his way.

Every day and month and year spent in this place had been the same. It had felt like one long hangover. It was the party that he had missed. The joy of growing up and being young and playing ball and loving life.

As each ball flew toward him and his face and body became drenched in sweat, Cory hit harder and straighter, hoping each smack would beat down the memories inside of him.

But the memories wouldn't go away.

On the front porch of the house, Clay stood listening to the crack of the baseballs. Each hit seemed to wound him a little more, yet he couldn't go over there. He would leave Cory alone. At least for now. It was too early to try to sort out his brother's problems. The best thing Cory could do was hit those balls.

Karen joined him with a cup of coffee. He smiled in appreciation and took it.

For a long time they stood there, not saying a word, just listening to the sound of baseballs being hit one after another.

They say it's all heartache and misery, but that's because they don't know how great this feels.

Cory doesn't have a worry in the world. He feels great, and yesterday and tomorrow are nowhere to be found in this bliss of today.

He knows it's temporary, but this temporary is temporarily glorious. He feels invincible. Yesterday's heavy grays don't matter because today's bright blues blow them away. It's like the sunrise coming out of a tsunami.

He takes another drink and turns up the stereo and watches the highlights and waits for her to come back into the room.

Nobody should feel this good, and anybody who has a problem with it doesn't know how good it feels.

The day blurs away, and Cory feels great.

One hundred ninety pounds of potential.

He turns up the music just a little more. The neighbors might complain, but the cops won't do anything. If they come again — if — they'll just laugh and maybe even come in and have a drink like last time.

He's not going anywhere, and he's not going to sleep anytime soon.

The TV shows the game highlights, and he laughs as he watches his teammates staring out with blank faces. He laughs because they're all in the same bliss as he is right now. They're leaving the loss behind; tomorrow they'll be ready for another day and another chance.

A figure emerges from the darkness of the hallway, and Cory just smiles.

Life has never been better.

CHAPTER TWENTY-FOUR: STEAL

I don't need to hear this.

Cory sat in the small church on another Friday night, listening to the fiftysomething Harley dude in the torn jeans and ripped T-shirt. He knew why the guy was in recovery. From one too many Aerosmith concerts. He needed recovery from the Steven Tyler syndrome, which usually started when guys close to retirement still looked like rockers. Aging rockers.

Here we go with the same old sad story.

"My name is Rick, and I'm a Christian who celebrates recovery from cocaine addiction. Been clean for three years now."

Cory knew the drill and said "Hello, Rick" with the rest of the crowd.

I guess by "clean" he's not referring to his beard.

"I came to CR not for recovery from crack, but so my wife and my family would get off my back."

There was some low-key laughter that Cory couldn't help joining in.

Sounds familiar.

Rick held the pages in front of him like a man reading his last wish before being sent to the electric chair.

"I started my first step study because I heard that this is where the serious recovery work is done — or that's what I told everyone."

Nobody needs homework, especially not crackheads.

Cory glanced around the room and noticed the variety of people. There were a couple of businessmen in golf shirts, a grizzly old veteran, a couple of hippies with long hair, some alternative young kids, even a Grandma Sally. Cory was in the back row so nobody would notice him checking the baseball scores while Rick spoke.

"I came every week, did all the lessons, and to my surprise, I began dealing with my past and started to understand why I used."

As Rick was in midsentence, Cory noticed a Grizzlies score and exclaimed, "No!" He didn't even realize he'd spoken aloud until people turned to look at him. He just smiled and hid the iPhone back in his hand. He couldn't believe the double-digit loss the team had suffered the night before.

"When I got to step nine, make direct amends to people you have harmed, I thought: make amends face-to-face? I was like, 'I don't think so.' So I skipped over that step."

Cory smiled. *Yeah, I'd do that too. Too many people to face, not enough amends to go around.*

He kept checking the scores.

"After ushering for two years, I became the head usher here at Celebrate Recovery. However, the temptation proved to be more than I could handle, and I started taking money from the offering each week."

Wait, you did what?

Cory forgot about his phone and looked at Rick, then at the faces looking up at Rick as he spoke. He expected to see looks of condemnation, but the crowd hadn't changed a bit.

"During this time I was in a second step study, and I wanted to finally make the amends I needed to make in my life. Which meant I had to confess what I had been doing to the ministry leaders."

Ouch. That's gotta hurt.

Cory felt bad for the guy. I mean, yeah, he was stealing out of a church plate, so that was bad, but still . . .

"When I met with them I expected to be

relieved of my guilt, but I received much more . . ."

This guy — this biker dude with long hair and a leather vest and tats on his arms — suddenly broke down and started to cry. Then he looked at the people in the front row, J. T. being one of them, and he smiled as he wiped his tears away.

So how does this story end? And why's he smiling?

Rick cleared his throat and wiped more tears away. "I experienced God's love and forgiveness," he said in a choked, humbled voice.

Rick wasn't the only one wiping tears away from his eyes. Cory noticed several other people doing the same. Some wore huge supportive smiles. Some even clapped.

Cory looked back at Rick, who obviously wasn't finished.

"To complete this step, I need to make amends with you, because it is your ministry too. I stole from you." Rick stared at all of them with a childlike look on his face, tears swelling up in his eyes. "Will you please forgive me?"

The sanctuary was suddenly full of people on their feet and clapping, many of them saying yes loudly over the sound of the applause.

Rick wept and tried to hide his face with a hand. For a moment, he tried to compose himself in front of everybody.

Cory couldn't stop watching in fascination.

This is wild.

"The truth is God forgave me long before I came to CR. But I still felt broken, and I didn't know how to get healed. Then I got here and learned verses like James 5:16 that told me if I confessed my sins to somebody, I could be healed. And yeah — I can vouch for that one."

The crowd, still standing, chuckled and applauded. Rick continued to read from his notes.

"I still mess up, but I'm not who I was. I'm changing. I'm getting healed. Thank you for letting me share."

As Rick moved away from the podium and the crowd applauded him again, Cory saw J. T. and another man shake Rick's hand and then embrace him.

Cory stood up and applauded too.

Guy's got a lot of guts.

He knew he could never in a million years go up before everybody and openly confess everything. Not like that. No way.

So maybe this whole Celebrate Recovery thing wasn't completely useless. At least it was helping people like Rick, which was good. It didn't change a thing about why he was there, but he could admit that the program was working for some. It was impossible to be cynical about that.

He never thought he'd be this surprised at something in the sanctuary of a small church in Okmulgee. But — well — if there was indeed a God above, maybe this was His sense of humor at work.

For a moment, a singular second, the cheers and the rush and the wildness all fade away.

Cory sees himself in the barn. Not hitting at balls and not picking them up, but talking with his brother with fistfuls of baseball cards.

Somewhere out there Clay is watching.

And Cory wants to make it count for his little brother.

It's just a random, ridiculous thought in this game six. A win, and they've made it to the World Series. A loss, and it all means nothing.

Cory swings, knowing he'll connect, knowing he's going to win the game.

But that's as romantic as that image of Clay and Cory playing with those cards.

Cory strikes out and suddenly sees the whole world around him wave a big fat bye-bye.

CHAPTER TWENTY-FIVE:
HOME PLATE

The soft glow of the superhero night-light in Tyler's room lit up his peaceful face. Emma glanced in on her son and saw him curled up in his bed, a picture frame lying against his arms and chest. She carefully walked into the messy room and slipped the frame from his hands, then made sure his covers were tucked in around him.

Emma knew the photo well, yet she studied it in the muted light. The family picture had been taken before James's third deployment to Afghanistan. Tyler had been eight at the time, and his father was the biggest hero in his life.

He still is.

Emma felt that familiar wave of sadness and regret, the kind that usually came at moments like this, when Tyler was asleep and the house was silent. She put the photo back on the small table next to his bed, then closed her eyes for a moment as she faced

Tyler's way.

"Watch over this child, Lord. Continue to give him peace. Continue to give *us* peace. Help us to know that James is in a better place, that he's watching over us. Help us — help Tyler — to be able to let him go. Somehow, Lord. In some way."

She slipped out of the bedroom and walked back down to the empty family room. Thoughts of James followed her.

James had been God's unexpected gift to Emma and Tyler. A gift she didn't even know she was looking for or needed. For her, there had always been the great Cory Brand. He was always in the picture, and she couldn't imagine life without him. But two monumental things changed that.

First, Tyler came into the picture.

Timing in life is everything, a friend once told her. Emma knew this was true.

Once Cory made his decision, Emma made her own. She disappeared. In some ways, her journey wasn't much different from his. They both left Okmulgee behind.

Cory found his perfect match in professional baseball, while Emma ended up meeting a tall, dark, and handsome army private named James Hargrove. The last thing Emma had wanted was another alpha male in her life, especially considering she was pregnant and alone and wasn't sure what she was going to do.

James didn't come along on a white horse and rescue her. No. In James she found someone who was willing to walk alongside her for a while, and as he did she fell in love with him.

Emma wasn't in the mood for television tonight. It would either bore or depress her. She looked at the magazines on the table and then stared at the latest Vivian Brown novel she was halfway through. The book was beginning to depress her too, since it was a love story.

She and Tyler were doing fine; they were making it. But every single day she thought of James, and she knew Tyler did too.

So why, God? Why now? Why now of all times did Cory have to come back into the picture?

If this were a Hallmark movie, the two of them would keep running into each other — at the store or the supermarket — and slowly but surely they'd get back together. This, however, was definitely not a Hallmark movie. Not when the male lead was off getting hammered and embarrassing himself by knocking over batboys and cops who coached Little League.

Plus, she wasn't about to let that happen.

She wasn't worried about falling for Cory Brand. That train had left the station years ago. She had lost him once, and in his place had come this amazing man who ended up loving both Emma and Tyler unconditionally.

Sure, she would have loved to find a man who worked a regular nine-to-five job and coached Little League and went to all his son's games and was a deacon in the church. But life wasn't about filling out a questionnaire and submitting it with all the little boxes checked. She wasn't exactly the picture of the perfect catch either.

Emma wondered what Cory was doing now. If she had to be honest, she was a little worried about him.

Yet that didn't change the fact that she was more worried about Tyler realizing the truth about him.

It was just a label, a label that didn't mean anything. It was like calling Cory a coach. He wasn't a real coach any more than he was Tyler's "real" father.

She hoped he would realize this soon and end the charade and leave them alone. It would be easier that way. Easier for everybody.

Not far away, in the holding cell of a motel

room with a baseball game on in the background, Cory stared at a picture of a family he could have had. It was a recent picture of Emma and Tyler that he'd gotten from Clay. They were smiling and happy and content.

You could've been a part of this picture, buddy.

He still didn't know if he even *wanted* to be a part of that picture. He didn't know what he wanted, to be honest.

The mini-fridge caught his attention.

Cory thought of the guy who'd shared his story at CR that night. Rick. What a story, and what guts to admit all that in front of everybody.

But I'm not stealing from a church. I'm just biding my time in this little town before I go my merry way.

Emma was sweet and she had a sweet life with Tyler and that was all terribly sweet. Cory didn't have any place in that sweet snapshot. He would just make everything sour and bitter like he always had.

He put the picture on the table next to him and then sat up on the edge of the bed.

That itching urge filled him again. He needed something to make it go away. Not a deep heartache of not being with Emma and Tyler. That didn't exist. Nor did he need something to take away some deep sadness or longing or regret inside of him. But the spiraling thoughts that left an empty hole in the middle were there and had always been there. This pressure to do something and get rid of those thoughts. To make those tornadoes inside of his heart and mind simmer down.

He was bored and restless and wanted to get drunk.

Cory wasn't some guy stealing in order to sniff coke. He was just . . . bored and feeling useless and wanting to get rid of the blah feeling inside. Emma and Tyler couldn't make that go away. But the magical little mini-fridge — that was a different story.

You don't have to do this.

He heard the voice inside and wasn't sure if it belonged to J. T. or Rick or his guardian angel Pajersky.

You can be strong.

Cory sat still and stared at the fridge.

If somebody could see him now . . .

But they couldn't, and that was the point. Nobody was watching him. The lights and the cameras and the applause weren't there.

It was a very lonely place to be.

There has to be more than this.

There has to be something more.

The ads, the stupid ads, invite the foolhardy to come and experience it all. The money and the fame and the ride and the women and the life.

He doesn't want this life anymore. It's a dirty grimy floor that hasn't been scrubbed in a long time. The late nights have gotten later and the needs have gotten heavier and now all he wants and needs never seems to be there.

The smiling face of the blonde greeting him in the morning feels like the hotel bill slipped underneath his door. Just another payment needing to be made. Not necessarily in monetary terms but in some way. Emotionally. Physically.

Cory knows there has to be something more.

The images and pictures portrayed on the screen of wherever he might be seem wrong. He sees that guy and hears what they say, but he doesn't like thinking that they're showing and talking about him. Good or bad. It's a caricature of a guy he once knew. This empty hole inside needs filling, and he keeps looking. He keeps longing. He keeps lying to himself that it's just another night and just another moment and just another need.

Then he takes a little more.

But it's not enough.

So he takes a little more.

But it's never, ever enough.

CHAPTER TWENTY-SIX: AT BAT

Morning greeted Cory like a bird's nest stuck in his head. It took a while to open his crusty eyes and even longer to swallow, since his mouth felt like a hundred cotton balls were squashed inside.

Cory stood and stared at the damage from last night. Then he saw a portrait of himself in the mirror and swore.

Good job, buddy. Way to go.

An empty bottle of vodka along with a dozen bottles of beer littered the tables and floor. Another couple of wine bottles were opened and partially empty. He didn't remember drinking half of the stuff in this room. But there wasn't much to remember. It would have been the same sad scene from a hundred other nights.

Well, maybe the scene wouldn't have been *this* sad.

Cory looked out the window and saw another beautiful day waiting for him.

He didn't think about the mess around him for long. He was going to take a shower and shave and get ready for today. The Bulldogs had a special surprise in store. So things got a little out of hand last night. It was fine. No harm, no foul.

Athletes loved clichés because they kept everything on the surface.

He's got to step up now.

And yeah, sure, Cory was going to step up eventually.

He's going to give 110 percent.

Because lately, he'd been giving about 20 percent and that had been working just fine for him.

It's time to take it to the next level . . .

Cory could list off clichés all day long. They didn't mean anything. Just like saying he wasn't going to open that fridge last night. He knew he would.

It took him a moment to find another beer. He cracked it open and drained it. It got rid of the dry chalk mouth and made his head feel a bit straighter.

Just one before the shower. Then maybe a few more before leaving. But he knew he didn't have a problem and could stop anytime.

Then he'd step up to the plate and answer the bell and not pull any punches and finally knock it out of the park.

Yeah, all that. Whatever it meant.

It was the Bulldogs' first game since the debacle a couple of days ago with Coach Cory getting arrested. Now everybody was on the field except Cory, who hadn't called or shown up anywhere. It made Emma nervous.

She had asked Karen and Clay if they knew where he was, but neither of them had any idea. The looks they gave her made Emma even more nervous.

The Jets were out on the field practicing. Emma was beginning to think she'd have to coach this game alone. Clay could stand off by the sidelines and shout out orders, but he still wasn't very mobile, with his arm in a sling and his ribs ginger from the crash.

The stands were full again. Everybody had come out hoping they'd see Cory Brand and witness something awesome and terrifying like the other day. A commotion near the parking lot got everybody's attention. The Bulldogs were gathering around a beat-up truck.

At least he made it before the first pitch.

Cory was passing something out to the kids. New gear. They were shouting and laughing and putting on new caps and shirts as Emma approached.

"What do you think of the new look?" he asked the team.

Stanton was already wearing the new shirt and cap proudly. "We're *way* cooler than the Roughnecks now."

Emma helped Wick slip his skinny arms into his shirt, then looked around at the joy on the kids' faces. "Hey, team, what do you say? Thank you, Coach Cory."

The Bulldogs all joined in unison to echo their thanks.

Tyler came up to her and displayed his shirt and cap in a *check-me-out* manner. Emma caught Cory smiling and watching the two of them. She couldn't help but admire his attempts at bribery.

Emma only wondered who it was for: the team or Tyler. The next couple of hours reminded Emma why she had once loved this baseball player.

It started with the pregame practice, with Emma lining up and throwing perfect pitches toward Cory, who stood behind the plate, advising each player how to stand and what to do.

He was gentle and patient with these kids. Yes, the same guy who exploded on this very field just days ago was totally natural around the young players. He showed some of the less-talented kids like Wick and Wellsey how to do basics, like scooping up a grounder. Even when it seemed virtually impossible that either kid would be able to get it, Cory still kept trying, with seemingly endless patience.

In the third inning the two of them worked as a perfect team when Cory sent a runner rounding third toward home, with the ball following him to the plate. On cue, Emma sent the hitter from first to second. They pointed to each other like fellow coaches and friends and one-time long loves.

One inning later, as the Bulldogs headed out of the dugout to go back onto the field and Emma followed, Cory gave her an easy and natural high five.

During the fifth inning, as Cory was desperately trying to get Kendricks's attention on the field, Emma noticed and let out a high-pitched whistle that people in nearby states could hear. Kendricks turned toward them. Cory laughed and gave Emma a look that asked, *Where did you learn to do that?*

Near the end of the game, the Bulldogs had a man on second with two outs. It was Tyler's turn to bat again, and so far he hadn't had a very great day. His biological parents were somehow performing better than he was. As he settled into his stance, far out of the batter's box, Cory noticed what was happening and called for a time-out.

Tyler went over to where Cory stood between home and third. Emma watched from first base, knowing that Cory was surely trying to encourage him to step up to the plate.

As Tyler glanced up at him, face full of nerves and adrenaline, Cory acted like it was just the two of them standing in an empty field with time to kill.

"Tyler. Look at me. How many years have you played ball?"

"Five."

"How many balls do you think you hit before one got you in the face?"

"I dunno." Tyler was white and breathing heavily.

"Ten, twenty?"

"For sure."

"Fifty? Sixty?"

"Probably."

Cory nodded, still acting casual and carefree. "What are the odds that you're going to get hit today?"

Tyler shrugged.

"Probably not gonna happen," Cory said.

"Probably not," Tyler said, thinking about it.

"All right. So get in there and step up to the plate. Like really and truly *step* up to the plate." Cory leaned down and looked his son in the eye. "Nothing good happens when you hang back."

"Okay."

Tyler understood. Cory could see it in the kid's eyes. There was heart and passion and a fierce desire.

Cory stood back up and tapped Tyler in the helmet. "Now, hit the ball, knock Carlos in, and let's win this game."

They each returned to their respective bases. When Tyler stepped up to home plate and assumed the proper stance, Cory saw Emma's surprised look.

The first pitch was thrown a bit too close, and Tyler really had to step back or get hit. Cory clapped in affirmation.

"You can do it, Tyler," he said. "Stay in there."

Cory wanted this more than he had wanted that last hit in game six of the championship game.

He swallowed and stared and waited for the pitch.

Come on, Tyler, come on.

The pitch came, and Tyler hit it dead on.

The look on his face was everything Cory could have wanted and more. He beamed and looked a bit surprised as he tossed the bat down and took off toward first base. Carlos was running, and Cory waved him on toward home.

Soon they were all jumping and cheering and celebrating the victory.

Mother and son were over by first, hugging and giving each other high fives. The rest of the team cleared the dugout and celebrated with them. The bleachers were joyous, and the smiles were everywhere.

For a moment, Cory looked at this scene and felt something he hadn't felt in a very long time.

Pride.

The name blasted by the announcer on the speakers with the true high-definition sound.

Cory Brand

The bright neon name aglow with sparkles and diamonds and lightning.

Cory Brand

The name in the scrolling news on ESPN.

Cory Brand

The name followed by the number and the stats.

Cory Brand

A persona. An actor. A model. A machine.

Cory Brand

The boy wouldn't recognize you, and the man doesn't want to remember who you once were.

Cory Brand

The bright lights and big city know the name and know it well.

CHAPTER TWENTY-SEVEN: CURVEBALL

It felt natural, walking to the parking lot alongside Tyler, Carlos, and Emma.

For a few moments Cory forgot that this was not his home and these people were not his family. Listening to Tyler and Carlos swap stories about the game was priceless.

As they neared Emma's truck, a honk from down the row got their attention.

"Carlos," Karen shouted from inside their SUV. "Let's go."

Clay was sitting in the passenger seat next to her. Both of them had avoided Cory, which he understood and didn't take offense to. He wanted to be spared the high and mighty treatment from the couple who had it all figured out, so it was fine with him that they were keeping their distance.

Now, instead of bringing the cops to arrest him, Cory had brought the Bulldogs a win.

"Awesome game," the animated Carlos

said. "See ya later."

They told him good-bye and watched him rush off with his gear in hand. Emma tossed a couple of bats and Tyler's hat in the back of her truck as Tyler held off and faced Cory.

"Thanks for helping me today," Tyler said. "I couldn't have done it without you."

Emma watched them, appearing surprised at Tyler's admission.

"Hey, the team couldn't have won it without you," Cory said. "You were awesome out there."

Cory got an affirming smile from Emma just before she climbed into the truck. Tyler followed her, closing his door and rolling down the window.

"Talk to you later, Coach."

The last word seemed to pull Cory back like a fishhook.

It's too early to watch these two leave. Way too early.

He saw Emma's pretty face leaning over and looking at him through the window. "Good game, Coach."

"Yeah, good game. We made quite a team out there, huh?"

She gave him the polite, safe smile, not saying anything.

"Hey, you guys want to grab some pizza?"

"No."

Emma's reply was out almost before Cory could finish his sentence.

"Come on, Mom."

"No, but, uh, sorry. It's just — we have this thing."

Cory reverted back to his high school ways, giving Emma a sad face that was partially to try to be funny but also to show how he felt.

Emma, however, looked like she was a long way away from high school. Her serious eyes and tight lips didn't budge as she shook her head. Soon she was backing out of the parking lot with a disappointed Tyler in the passenger seat.

Sorry, kid. I tried.

"Bye," Tyler called.

"Have fun at your 'thing,' " Cory joked.

He watched the truck drive off, along with a few of the other vehicles leaving the park. Then he glanced over and studied the saddest, most pathetic truck still in existence.

Yep, that about sums it up.

He didn't want to be left alone, not tonight. Not after the victory and the game. It would be a total letdown.

It's not like I'm going to try anything with her. I just want to hang out with her and with our son.

But maybe that was the point. He was

already thinking of Tyler as "their son," which Emma would probably find offensive.

He was almost to his truck when a familiar voice called out his name. Cory turned and saw J. T. walking toward him.

"Got plans tonight?"

Cory raised his eyebrows and nodded. "Yeah, ESPN. Then ESPN. And then, after that, maybe I'll try a little more ESPN."

J. T., who had missed his calling in life to be a reverend or a priest, simply gave him that patient grin. Silence always unnerved Cory, especially since most people he met couldn't shut up when they were around him.

Cory stated the obvious. "No, I don't have plans."

"You want plans?"

I want to wake up without feeling like the Budweiser Clydesdales have been walking over my head.

"Sure."

"There's a Wild West Chili Festival," J. T. said.

Oh no.

"A festival."

"I'll come by your motel around six."

"Sounds absolutely great."

J. T. couldn't miss his sarcasm, but he didn't bother responding. He walked over to his own truck, where his wife was waiting.

Somehow his grand plan of pizza with Emma and Tyler had morphed into a chili festival. One where he couldn't drink 'cause he'd be with Mr. J. T. Celebrate-Being-a-Teetotaler.

Cory was still wet from stepping out of the shower and had started to shave when Helene decided to check on him. He wanted to hurry up and get out of this room, because if he didn't, he'd start doing some spring-cleaning again on the fridge. The game — not just the game, but the win — had rejuvenated him and made him feel like the old Cory.

He pressed speaker on the phone so he could keep shaving.

"In an effort to earn the money I soak you for, I've scored you a national television interview this Sunday."

"Hello, Helene," he said. "Nice of you to call."

"We need to get you back in the public eye looking clean and sober, and get people to love you again."

"Oh, please. They've always loved me."

"That's 'cause I *remind* them how much they love you."

Ah, Helene. Always working the angles and reminding me why I keep her.

"What would I do without you?" he joked.

"Well — I'd rather not say." She didn't sound like she was joking.

"Okay, book it. Let's get me 'seen.' "

She didn't stay on the phone or end it with a *Sleep tight and don't let the bedbugs bite* or anything like that. She was gone in a blink, just like always.

After finishing shaving, Cory felt his mouth water and thought of the mini-fridge.

My whole life these days revolves around a three-foot-tall cooler.

He grabbed the bottle of vodka and studied it, then bit his lip and sighed and stashed the bottle back in the fridge.

He could wait. He had to wait. He could show J. T. that he was just fine and that he didn't need to drink.

Cory knew it wasn't just about showing J. T. anything. It was more like staying out of the guy's way. The stuff he'd already been exposed to — the stories like the one he heard the other night from Rick — was great and powerful and everything, but it wasn't for him. Cory didn't need J. T. and didn't need Rick, and he certainly didn't need to celebrate any kind of recovery because he didn't *need* to recover.

The only celebrating he wanted to do was to celebrate leaving this place and getting back on the field in Denver.

He just hoped that day would be coming soon.

Cory had forgotten that festivals like this still existed in small towns across the country. In fact, he'd managed to mostly forget about small towns like Okmulgee.

They'd never done anything like this when he was young. Concession stands covered the sidewalks and streets downtown. The park where Cory walked with J. T. and his family had a line of glowing neon rides in all shapes and colors, including a small Ferris wheel and one of those mock flying airplane rides that would make you barf the hot dogs and cotton candy you ate just minutes earlier. Kids wearing fresh face paint wandered around carrying balloon animals. Ticket counters were spread throughout, to force you to purchase a fifty-pack just to make it through the night.

J. T.'s rotund wife, Doris, looked like Mrs. Claus with her permanent smile. Their son was four years old and wanted to wander around everywhere. They made a cute family and were kind enough to chaperone Cory as various people came up to congratulate him on the game or simply take his picture on their phone or shake his hand.

"We don't get celebrities around here much," J. T. said.

"Who are you talking about? Did Brad Pitt show up?" Cory often said stuff like this when people called him a celebrity.

"Hey — hometown hero."

Cory gave him a knowing look just as a trio of teenage girls came up to him, laughing as if it was a dare and asking him to pose for a picture.

Yeah, I'm a hometown something, but not sure I'd call it a hero. More like hometown screwup.

A tall, lean figure in a floaty floral dress and stylish cowboy boots drifted by over toward the street. Cory couldn't help noticing the striking brunette, then smiled broadly when he saw it was Emma. No more jeans and a Bulldogs jersey. Her hair was loose and flowing, and she looked nothing and everything like the girl he'd fallen in love with years ago.

"Hey — excuse me for a moment," Cory said to J. T. as he walked over to a concession stand and purchased a couple cans of soda.

He greeted Emma with a smile and a complimentary drink. "So, this is your 'thing'?"

Emma waved her hands in a *You got me* manner. She also looked a bit embarrassed to be caught. He let her choose between a Diet Coke and a Sprite.

"Not very hospitable of you, Emma Johnson, to let a poor stranded fool miss the Wild West Chili Festival."

"Fool, yes. Stranded? Never."

The sounds of the crowd around co-cooned them like a warm blanket. They shared a glance — yes, it was a glance, and they shared it — and remained silent for a moment.

"Have you had your Wild West Chili yet?" Cory asked.

"Not yet," Emma said. "They haven't told me just how wild the chili really is."

He pointed to a nearby park bench and then sat down. He was going to feel like a real moron if Emma didn't sit next to him. Thankfully, she didn't resist. She sat — keeping a healthy distance, of course.

"You must be missing life in the fast lane," Emma said.

A couple passed by, holding hands, walking behind their two little girls. Cory nodded to her question.

"Well, yes and no. I mean, beating the Jets was definitely a new kind of rush for me."

The look on her face said more than she could have actually articulated. Perhaps he should've used a different word than *rush,* but it was too late.

"You were right about Tyler," Emma said. "He needed to be pushed. I just get too . . . I don't know . . ."

"You're a great mom."

Emma didn't respond. Cory didn't want to sit there second-guessing himself, worrying about what he should or shouldn't say.

"Tyler's the best," he added.

"Yes, he is."

The tone was still there in her voice. He knew she was just being a protective mother. He didn't blame her. He'd probably be the same, considering everything.

"You're doing an awesome job."

He knew how the compliment might have sounded. Just another nice sweet toss by Mr. Charming. But Cory meant it and knew he couldn't do anything to prove he meant it. Emma looked uncomfortable, not at all swept up into the whirlwind of Cory Brand.

"Thanks," she said in a subdued tone.

A scampering of feet disrupted the silence between them. Tyler and Carlos showed up out of nowhere, all nervous smiles and sugar-induced energy. Tyler tried to play it cool as he got Cory's attention.

"Hey, uh, Coach."

"We found your rookie card," Carlos blurted out.

"Yeah, and uh, would you mind signing it?"

Cory took the card and the Sharpie from Tyler. For a second he glanced at the front.

"Remember this guy?" Cory asked Emma as he showed her the picture of the cocky twenty-three-year-old kid in his first year as a Grizzly.

"I've tried to forget about him," Emma said with a teasing smile.

Cory signed the back of the card as he had a thousand others before. "Didn't know you two collected baseball cards."

"Oh, yeah, all the time," Carlos said.

Cory handed Tyler the card. When the kid read it, his face lit up like a sparkler.

"You know," Cory told them, "I got some good ones out at the barn."

Both of the boys looked hooked. Cory still found himself thinking about those cards, tucked away in the box.

"Got a '93 Derek Jeter in there, a '73 all-star Carlton Fisk, worth a bit of dough, some older —"

"I've got a Jeter and Fisk too," Tyler shouted.

"Ah, we gotta get together and compare."

"That would be awesome."

Cory had an idea. "Maybe when we leave here, we can all go to the barn and take a look."

Tyler gave his mother the same look he had in the truck not long ago. This time she gave a nod and a smile.

"Okay. Sure."

Tyler and Carlos looked almost as thrilled as Cory felt. Tyler put his arm around Emma and then showed her the card Cory had just signed. He hadn't expected Emma to read it, not so soon. She looked down at it, then gave him a nervous glance.

Cory had signed the card *Proud of you — Coach Cory.*

A voice in the background announced a tug-of-war tournament starting in ten minutes. Carlos and Tyler instantly forgot about the baseball cards and the barn and screamed about entering the contest. They ran off and left Cory and Emma alone again.

Before the silence could get awkward, Cory raised his can of soda. "To the best day I've had in a long time."

They clicked cans, and Emma finally seemed to be easing up around him. She took a sip and said, "I'm glad you found our 'thing' tonight."

"Here you go."

The young kid with the freckles and the bright blue eyes hands him a Sharpie. Cory's been here before, but he was the kid asking for an autograph.

For a moment he looks at the card with his face on it. Normally he just whips through a long line full of fans with these cards without even thinking twice about it.

He stops for a moment and thinks of Clay.

It's been too long, and he's been too far away.

Someone tells him to hurry up while someone else urges the boy aside.

Cory signs the card and then gives the kid a signed shirt. "Take it easy," he says.

"Thanks."

For a moment Cory wonders which town he's at. Then he wonders if it really matters.

He's been long gone.

And he's just another face on a card with a name and a number.

CHAPTER TWENTY-EIGHT:
KNUCKLEBALL

Cory hadn't even thought of the baseball cards when he was in the barn the other day. He'd just wanted to find the old baseball machine and hit as many balls as he could. Tyler and Carlos watched as he dug around and moved boxes and furniture.

One box caught his attention. It held what looked like the contents of a desk, papers and newspaper clippings and documents and photos all lumped together. Cory wondered if Clay even knew this stuff was out here, this pile of random memories from their youth.

Maybe he's trying to forget about our miserable childhood, just like me.

Cory pulled out a picture of a tall, fit guy leaning on his bat and dressed in an AA baseball uniform.

"Who's that?" Carlos asked.

"My dad."

"Your dad played ball?" Tyler sounded

surprised.

"He was a great player, but he never got past AA."

Just another disappointment in a disappointing life. Cory didn't know that young guy in the picture. He'd just known the bitter man who needed someone to take out his anger on.

There was a box marked *Baseball Stuff* that Cory pulled out of the corner. He knew he'd find his cards inside this box. But five minutes later, they were still nowhere to be found. Inside he'd pulled out trophies and certificates and all these mementos from his childhood. Tyler and Cory were impressed, but Cory wasn't interested in any of that stuff.

He wanted those cards.

"They can't be gone."

A helpless feeling raced through him. Anger at not finding them and not being able to figure out where they were. He pulled out another box and then another, tossing the contents aside as he scavenged through box after box.

No way they're not here.

Suddenly there was nothing he wanted more in this world than those cards.

They weren't just cards. They were maybe one of the only things about his past that he had ever loved and ever owned. Maybe the one thing that solely belonged to him and his brother and no one else.

His heart raced, and he wiped sweat from his forehead as he moved another box, trying to figure out where the cards might be. He forgot about the boys behind him. He forgot about Emma and Karen and Clay, who were in the house. He forgot about everything except the cards that he suddenly believed had been taken from him.

Cory turned and walked back out of the storage area, looking at the line of boxes he'd already gone through.

"What's wrong?" Carlos asked.

They wouldn't get it; of course they couldn't in a million years understand. They collected baseball cards for fun. Cory had collected them to keep some kind of morsel of hope alive in the midst of a really miserable childhood.

For a moment, he saw the picture again of Michael Brand.

You wretched piece of work.

That's when it clicked. Cory cursed and couldn't care less that he was doing it in front of the boys.

"He must have sold them all," Cory said in disgust. "Of course he did."

It was one last *see-you-later-Cory* from his father.

One last kick in the stomach from the old man.

Cory blasted a box with his foot and sent it flying. He swore again, lashing out at the man who had stolen his childhood.

Emma and Karen had been sitting on the porch, taking in the stillness of the country-side and enjoying glasses of iced tea. Emma had always felt welcome at the Brand house. Clay and Karen were among the only ones in Okmulgee who knew the truth about Tyler, and they'd always tried to make the two of them feel like family.

"Have you decided if you're going to tell him?"

It was as if Karen sometimes could read her mind, although the question was an obvious one and had been ever since Cory had stepped foot into town.

"I don't know." Emma sighed and took a sip from the glass. "I'm hoping I don't have to."

"At some point he should probably know."

"I know. I'm just waiting . . . until he's about forty years old."

Karen laughed and started to say something about Carlos when she suddenly stopped. "What was that?"

They heard a crashing sound. Then shouting.

"Is it the boys?" Karen asked, standing up.

Emma stood next to her and suddenly knew.

The brief firefly of hope had suddenly been extinguished.

"It's Cory," she said.

The two women left the porch and headed to the barn to see what was happening.

"I'll handle it," Karen said. "You let me go in there first, okay?"

Emma nodded. She wanted to think that Cory wouldn't hurt the boys, but she didn't know what he was capable of. Which was *exactly* why she hadn't told Tyler the truth and was afraid she might never be able to.

Cory glared at the opened boxes. Nearby, Tyler and Carlos watched him, unsure of what he was doing or why he had suddenly become so enraged.

"It's a wooden box — with a metal latch. All the valuable cards are in there."

For a moment, Tyler looked like he knew what Cory was talking about.

"What?" Cory demanded. "You've seen it? It used to be in here."

"No. I just thought — never mind."

Cory looked again through the box that had contained the baseball stuff. Then he picked it up and flung it against the wall. It landed on its side, and the contents spilled out. He cursed again, kicking the side of the box.

He had been hoping to surprise the kids — to surprise Tyler — by showing off the box. But as usual, there was a hitch in his plans.

He could see his old man laughing, hear the mocking voice bouncing all around these walls.

You're a failure just like me, Cory. Couldn't handle it in the big bad world, so they sent you back home, and now you're fussing like a baby because you can't find your stupid cards.

Cory wasn't going to accept *no*. There was just no way. He began tearing through another box and tossing out items when he heard a voice behind him.

"Take it easy, Cory."

It was Karen. He shook his head. She had no idea what he was dealing with. He swore and told her he wanted to show them the cards.

"It's all right, we'll find —"

Cory interrupted her with another curse at his father. The old man. That wretched man who was now a thief as well.

Karen put her arms around Tyler and Carlos. "Boys, why don't you go inside? We'll let you know if we find them."

Cory sat down and let out a sigh as the boys just stared at him.

When you grow up you'll get it. You'll understand that this world's a miserable place and you gotta fight for what's yours because the world keeps sucking you dry.

But the expressions on their faces startled him.

They were afraid.

Hey, I'm not the bad guy here, boys.

"Look — they don't have to leave," he told Karen. "I'm fine."

"Right."

Karen walked the boys out of the barn. Cory picked up where he'd left off. That wooden box had to be here somewhere. Surely Clay didn't have it — Carlos would know and would have said something. No, it had to be tucked away in here somewhere.

Another box only had old clothes in it. He hurled it away, wiping his face of sweat and feeling like he could start clawing his flesh, he felt so angry.

"For crying out loud, *what* is your problem?"

Karen had come back, without the boys.

He didn't want to get into it with his sister-in-law.

"Cory — no one's touched your precious stuff for years."

"Dad did. He always messed everything up. He ruined absolutely everything."

Karen walked a few steps and touched him on his arm. "Cory, stop."

He jerked back, not wanting her to talk to him or touch him or even be two feet away from him. "Just stay out of this."

While Karen looked like she could be Emma's sister, she had always had more of an edge about her. In her glance and tone and the way she held herself. Cory sometimes wondered if that was what had attracted Clay to her, this cutting edge that sweet and amiable Clay just didn't have.

"You can't keep playing the victim," Karen said. "Believe me . . . it doesn't work."

How dare she have the guts to say that to my face.

"What do you know about my life?" he hurled back at her. "Or anything for that matter? You're a small-town, sheltered Sunday school teacher, so spare me the lecture, because until you've lived through something tougher than your sink backing up, I don't want to hear it."

If she weren't a girl he'd probably reach

over and punch her in the nose.

Cory gritted his teeth and stared at the mess all around him. He heard a shuffling and glanced up to see Emma.

She'd heard the whole conversation.

You'll never change, Cory, not in a million years.

"Let's go," Emma said to Karen.

The two of them walked out of the barn, leaving Cory in a familiar place.

The kid standing in the barn all by himself after being chastised.

They don't have a clue and never will.

The pretty, innocent face belongs to a pretty but not so innocent blonde, who smiles and waves at him like any fan leaving the stadium after Cory wins the game for the Grizzlies.

He gives her a farewell grin and watches her leave his hotel room.

It's four in the morning, and he pours himself another drink and turns on ESPN to watch highlights of himself. Again.

The surreal part of this is that nothing's surreal about this at all. This is his life. No fear and no shame and no feeling.

He drinks and feels the familiar restlessness. Coming back down is never fun.

Chapter Twenty-Nine:
Designated Hitter

"Come on — get in the car." Clay had already asked him twice, and Cory was acting like a baby by refusing.

"I'm not gonna listen to ten minutes of lecturing, if that's what you have in mind."

Emma had already taken a bewildered Tyler home, and Karen had put Carlos to bed. Clay had shown up to see the aftereffects of another Cory Brand meltdown.

"I'm not going to say anything. What else can I say?"

"I'm sure you'll think of something."

Cory got in the car, and Clay followed. He didn't want to let Cory go walking into the night again, as he had when they'd left the police station. Clay had felt guilty about that but had known he needed to do *something* to try to get through to his brother.

I've already tried pretty much everything.

The SUV rumbled into the night as Cory sat in silence next to him. For a few minutes

Clay kept his word and didn't say anything. But all the thoughts in his head nagged at him like a dog scratching at the door to get out. Eventually he couldn't help but open the door.

"Man, what's going on?"

"Here we go," Cory said in disgust.

"I'm just asking."

"Why? So you can try and fix your broken brother?"

"I want to help."

"Oh, okay, that's right. How noble of you."

"I'm not trying to be anything here," Clay said. "I'm just — I want to know what I can do."

"You can just keep living your pretty little life that's all fixed up and clean like you got the farmhouse looking. You just need a picket fence to go with that nice snapshot you're going to send out at Christmastime."

"That's unfair."

"Is it? You've been on my case for ten years to come back home. To come back to all *this*. So here we are. I'm back. But you don't want *me* in your life, little brother. You want some fairy tale. Now that you have a son, you want to have Uncle Cory throwing a ball in the backyard, right? Post pics on Facebook and show the world what a tight-knit, loving little family we are."

Cory looked out his dark window and cursed.

"What is wrong with you?"

"Well, you can't blame the drinking tonight, Clay."

"You're some walking, talking time bomb."

"You don't get it," Cory said.

"What don't I get? Tell me. Help me understand."

Cory swore again and appeared to be in no mood to help Clay understand. They rode in silence until they got to the motel. Clay had offered to have Cory spend the night, but Cory had refused. Once again.

Putting the SUV in park, Clay left the engine running. He turned and faced Cory.

"Look — I'm sorry if I'm trying too hard or doing the wrong thing. It's just . . . I'm the only family you have now."

"Yeah, I've kinda noticed that."

"I know I don't fully understand," Clay said, trying to find the right words this time, trying to leave things on a hopeful note. "But I'm really trying to."

His brother's face didn't try to hide anything. The signature smile was nowhere to be found. Cory didn't have to hide behind it. Not with Clay.

"You don't have to try and figure out

anything, because there's nothing to figure out," Cory said. "I'm a lost cause. You just gotta let it go."

Before Clay could say another word, Cory was out of the car and walking to his motel room.

Clay had said and done everything he could. But once again, it hadn't been enough.

His shoes crackle over broken glass. Not one glass, but all of them. His kitchen cupboards are open, and the shelves are empty. Dents and cuts in the wall show the scars of her anger.

Cory doesn't bother to start cleaning up. He just examines all the debris, the tiny shards of glass everywhere.

Nicole is long gone and will never be back. This is her going-away present. Not that he especially loved all those glasses she broke, but it's the message.

This is your life you're stepping over, Cory thinks.

He can't avoid the shards of glass.

These are the pieces that have been blasted and can never be put back together again.

He'll get this mess cleaned up and find a new selection of glassware and move on. Nicole will be out of his life, and by that time Rene probably will be too. He's not too worried about it. It doesn't annoy him. It just makes his head hurt.

He hears her last words, at least the ones he could make out.

"All you care about is yourself, that's all, and you're going to die with that smug smile still on your face."

For a second he thinks about Okmulgee and Clay and Emma. Just for a moment.

Then he knows Nicole is probably right.

He finds the keys to his car and gets out of here before all the shattered pieces start cutting into him and reminding him. Before they begin to start hurting.

CHAPTER THIRTY:
RELIEF PITCHER

It was a little after lunch when the doorbell rang. Emma immediately suspected who it might be. It wasn't like she and Tyler got a lot of guests.

She glanced out the window and saw the old truck. Sure enough. Emma braced herself, not knowing what condition he'd be in or what he wanted with them. When she opened the door, the first thing her eyes found was a tiny puppy bouncing around in the middle of her porch.

"What's this?" she asked.

Cory smiled and raised his eyebrows. "Sort of impulsive, I know. But I wanted to give him to Tyler."

"What?"

She wanted to shut down time and hold off so that Tyler couldn't see what was outside. Too late.

"Is that a *dog*?"

Tyler rushed out past her to the porch.

Cory scooped up the puppy and handed him to Tyler. White paws that looked like gloves moved frantically, as if they were waving at him. Another white spot covered half the pup's perky nose.

"For you," Cory said.

"No," Emma said, just as Tyler shouted, "Whoa! He's *mine*?"

"No," Emma said, repeating the word over and over.

Tyler held the Lab-beagle mix up to his face and was embraced by little kisses. Ignoring Emma and Cory, he carried the puppy onto the lawn to play.

"I got all the stuff you need for him," Cory said. "Leash, food, a training crate. You name it."

You're out of your mind.

She couldn't believe it. Of all the things Cory had done so far around here, this was the most insane and infantile.

"What are you doing? You can't just come over and give *my* son a dog."

The man who had been freaking out last night in the middle of a barn because of some silly lost baseball cards now looked like the picture of cool. He grinned.

"Well, I wanted to apologize to him for getting upset last night."

"And you do that by heaping a ridiculous

responsibility on him — and me?"

"Mom, I want him."

Emma had known the moment the doorbell sounded that this was going to be yet more Cory Brand trouble.

"Tyler, we are not keeping that dog."

There was no way. She had enough to deal with — *they* had enough to deal with. Getting a puppy was out of the question.

Tyler held the dog and gave her a sad and dejected look. "Figures. You always say no."

"Tyler, give Cory the puppy."

Eventually Tyler stormed back inside and up the stairs, slamming his door shut so they could know exactly how he felt.

"Come on," Cory said, as if he had everything figured out. "A dog would be good for him."

She wanted to take her hands and strangle this idiot in front of her. He had no clue.

Don't say or do anything you'll regret. Keep control.

"You don't get to have a say in what is or isn't good for him," she said, only inches away from his face.

That wounded look filled Cory's face, but it no longer worked on her. It used to when she was a girl, but she'd grown up and gotten over it. The same way she knew that Tyler's wounded face didn't mean she couldn't discipline or decide things for him.

Cory's just like Tyler. He's still a silly little boy.

"This whole thing is —"

Insane. Infuriating. Insipid. Ignorant. Irritating.

She couldn't come up with one single word to cover it all.

"— *so* not okay," she finally finished. She regained control and shook her head, facing Cory. "I gotta go. Take the dog with you."

Emma shut the front door without waiting to hear a response or see how dejected Cory would look. She had seen and heard it all from this man and wasn't willing to put up with it anymore.

It's May 16. Cory tries to forget, but once he sees the date on his computer it's impossible.

Emma's birthday.

It's been a little over five years since he saw her.

He doesn't understand how one day two people can be talking about love and marriage and a future together and then the next just . . .

Gone. Like you.

It's early, and he doesn't have a game today and he knows it will be impossible not to think of her.

For a moment, he imagines what life must be like for the happy little trio. Then he wonders what Tyler looks like. If he looks like his father.

Cory spots his cell phone. He thinks of maybe — just dropping a line or maybe an email or something . . .

But of course he doesn't.

He turns the music up loud, and then he makes plans and heads off to work out.

You can leave people behind, but you can't leave memories.

Wherever Cory goes, they follow him. Sometimes quietly and in the dark, but they're always there. At every game and in every bar and in every hotel room and on every plane.

Happy birthday, Em.

CHAPTER THIRTY-ONE: FASTBALL

Cory entered the sanctuary and slipped into the last pew. The room was nearly full, but he was glad to be the only one in the back row. He thought with mild humor that he'd spent more time in church since coming back to Okmulgee than he had in the previous decade. For a moment he checked out the others in the room, then noticed someone who looked a lot like Clay sitting in the front row.

It *was* Clay.

He wondered if Clay was waiting on him to arrive. But they hadn't talked about it, and Cory sure didn't want his hand held during a Celebrate Recovery meeting.

Then he noticed Karen and Emma sitting next to Clay.

What are they doing? It's not like I'm speaking.

As J. T. introduced himself and welcomed everybody, Cory thought about leaving. He didn't want his family here spying on him or whatever it was they were doing.

And then J. T. asked Karen to come to the podium.

Are these testimonies from women who've been traumatized by their famous brothers-in-law?

The confident and angry woman Cory was used to seeing wasn't standing there behind the podium. It was someone whose voice shook and whose hands trembled as she stood there facing everybody.

"My name is Karen, and I'm a grateful believer in Jesus."

That I already know, Cory thought as everybody else welcomed her.

"I celebrate recovery from sexual abuse by my father from the time I turned eight until I was sixteen."

The room suddenly felt like it was spinning around him. He felt confused and on the end of a really bad joke. He looked at Clay to see if his brother was equally as confused and shocked, but Clay just sat there giving his wife an assuring smile.

She's not kidding.

"While going through these experiences I felt alone with no one to reach out to, not one person to tell."

Cory let out a ten-year-long breath and

then closed his eyes.

He didn't want to hear this. This wasn't happening, not here, not now. This wasn't some crackhead or porn addict speaking out. This was Karen. *Clay's* Karen. *Their* Karen.

"My whole life I had carried a burden of pain and shame from my past. And even though I had been a Christian for years, I hid my pain and shame from everyone I knew."

Cory opened his eyes again and could see Clay giving Karen an encouraging nod. She smiled, and Cory felt something toward her he had never felt. He saw her in a whole new way. She wasn't that cute and annoying girl that Clay had fallen crazy in love with, the one who didn't like Cory's actions and always seemed so defensive. She wasn't the prude anymore or the uptight and sour woman he thought her to be.

"When I learned as an adult that I would not be able to bear children of my own, this was the final blow. I felt completely abandoned by God."

Heavy eyes full of tears looked up from the paper in front of her. Karen paused and swallowed.

"When I attended Celebrate Recovery, I wasn't prepared to experience the freedom and relief I would gain by sharing my deep hurt with God and others."

The sanctuary full of people seemed to disappear. Cory was sitting in an empty pew in an empty church listening to his sister-in-law tell her story. To him and only to him. This wasn't an act; this wasn't for show or publicity's sake. This was real. He was the only one here, and she had his full attention.

And maybe she could have had it years ago if I hadn't been off being Cory Brand.

"I love that I don't have to hide who I am here. I can go to my step study and share openly without fear of being judged. I can be completely honest with everyone around me. I'm just me. Banged up and imperfect."

The thought of Karen being banged up and imperfect was crazy. It was incredible. And if Cory weren't sitting here listening to her talk, he wouldn't have believed it himself.

All this time . . .

"Because of the work of Jesus, I'm no longer living my life in the pain of the abuse and disappointments in my past. Thank you for letting me share."

Everyone stood to applaud Karen, and so did Cory. But he had to leave. He couldn't take any more. He didn't want to face Karen and Clay and Emma. He couldn't. He didn't have anything to say to them. There was nothing he could say to make up for or change or erase the harsh reality breaking down around him.

Nothing.

I'm through feeling like this.

So he tells himself.

Tired of feeling like this.

So he tells himself again.

Tired of the sluggish, sickish way his body and skin feel. Tired of forcing himself to get through the aches and the pain. Tired of another day of knowing what came the night before.

Yet the pain goes away, and Cory remains the same.

Another afternoon comes, and the desire with it. He forgets again and ignores it again and decides once again that he doesn't care about feeling tired. Because he wants the rush. He wants to feel whole again and wants to feel right.

So he takes that first drink and knows he'll be better.

I'll stop someday, when life isn't so stressful.

So he tells himself.

CHAPTER THIRTY-TWO:
DOUBLEHEADER

"Go on. Get."

He brushed the puppy away, but the little thing kept wanting to lick his hands and bounce around in his lap. Cory had thought it was a great idea when he woke up this morning. Now, after sitting in his motel room for an hour, watching some baseball and getting nice and drunk, he was beginning to realize how stupid the idea had been.

Now I'm stuck with Stubby here.

He wasn't exactly sure what breed the dog was. It definitely had some beagle and Lab. Maybe some corgi or shepherd as well. For a few moments, Cory thought of interesting name combos the mixtures produced. A lorgi or a bepherd or a corgle.

When it was obvious that the pup wasn't going to stop harassing him, Cory picked it up and brought its face up to his.

"You look about as sad as I am," Cory said. "Maybe you do belong to me."

The puppy began to lick his mouth. Obviously the dog liked the taste of vodka too.

"I'm gonna name you Bull. Because that's what this whole situation is."

He sat Bull in his lap, and the puppy turned on its back, then jumped on the side of the bed next to him and began rolling over. Cory wondered if the dog might accidentally pee on the comforter, then thought it didn't really matter. Nobody would be too bothered. Especially not him.

He drained the small bottle of Absolut Citron and tried not to think too hard about the day.

Karen's words kept coming back to him. He could see her face and hear her tone.

I'm just me. Banged up and imperfect.

Cory went to get something else from his all-you-can-drink mini-fridge. Every day he'd find something different, like the kid was having fun picking out a variety of alcohol for him. He'd drink the vodka so the kid would get more. Just different brands and flavors.

He cracked open a bottle of beer and then sat on the edge of the bed, watching his team looking awful in the seventh inning. He should be out there with them. He should be anywhere but here.

The puppy's nose nudged his back. He

turned around and took Bull in one hand.

"Maybe you and I can pack up the Ford and then just drive off to Mexico. How's that sound? Find a little hut and just live on the beach for a few weeks. Or years."

Bull wiggled free of his grip and bolted back over the bedspread. He seemed perfectly delighted with the idea.

Cory knew he wasn't going anywhere. All these people and lives he thought he had figured out — he didn't have a clue. About any of them. Not Emma or Tyler or Clay or Karen or any of them.

The question was whether he wanted to start getting to know them. To start getting to *really* know them. If they'd even let him.

Maybe it was way too late even to try.

Emma was young and stupid once and had believed that love could conquer everything. She hadn't thought of the future, only of being with him.

Even after realizing she was pregnant, she still believed. She still hoped.

That was the difference between the twenty-two-year-old version of herself and thirty-three-year-old Emma. She wasn't a fool anymore. She couldn't allow herself to be. Not with this young man growing up right in front of her.

It had been both an inspiring and a heavy night, attending the Celebrate Recovery meeting with Karen and Clay. It hadn't been the first time, but she had gone hoping to see Cory. Hoping that perhaps Karen's words might get through to him. She wasn't going to try to talk to him about anything. That wasn't her place. All she wanted was to be seen there, to show that she supported her friend. To show what family was all about.

She looked in on Tyler and saw his light on, so she slipped into his room to turn it off. She noticed the baseball card resting just next to his opened hand.

It was Cory as a rookie, the future so bright and endless. She read the note on the back again.

Proud of you — Coach Cory

For a moment Emma sat on the edge of Tyler's bed, thinking about this man she didn't know, picturing this man that part of her still loved.

Love doesn't go away. Sometimes it's put in a wooden box and hidden away like other valuable things belonging to you. Sometimes it's lost and forgotten about and never to be found again. But it doesn't go away.

Not when love can create something so beautiful and remarkable and amazing.

Emma smiled as she looked at Tyler, then stood up and kissed the sleeping boy on the forehead.

You're not a cowboy and you don't ride on a steel horse and you're definitely not wanted dead or alive. You're a guy who plays ball. It's not heroic. You hit balls and catch them. And yeah, there's more to it, a lot more in fact, but the world simply sees that. The hitting and catching.

There's no more drama than that.

The cities and the faces and the moments don't need a soundtrack, don't fit into some epic adventure.

You're just that same stupid kid from Okmulgee and always will be.

CHAPTER THIRTY-THREE:
SAFE

When he whipped the pickup truck into the parking space at the baseball field, Cory realized he was moving a bit too fast. He rammed on the brakes. Something underneath his seat hit the back of his foot. When he turned off the motor and got out, he realized it was his phone.

It had been a day since he'd lost it. The last few days had all started to feel the same. One bad nightmare. A blanket of haze. Besides coaching the team, nothing else happened. The same repeats of late nights in his motel room. The same groggy mornings with him vowing to stop this party and get on with his life. The same inspiring moments filled with watching the kids playing ball. The same emptiness as he watched them all leave him behind.

Today was another big game with the Roughnecks. As usual, the parking lot and stands were full. Cory turned on his phone and grabbed his gear, then heard the incoming call.

"Hey, Helene," he said after seeing her name.

"Why aren't you in a limo right now? Why aren't you on your way to Tulsa? Any of this ringing a bell?"

He cursed as he realized what she was talking about. "Listen, I can't leave now. You'll just have to reschedule."

"Cory, I'm gonna blow an artery if you just said what I think you just said."

"I'm not kidding," he said. "I'm not missing this game. Reschedule it."

"You're not missing this interview. They moved a kid up from the Springs, and this kid is *good,* Cory. And guess what? He's not a pain in the butt. You will not say no."

"No."

Cory had seen and heard it all from Helene, and he was tired of it. She wasn't down here shacked up in a dingy motel room. She didn't know the first thing about putting family first.

"I'm not missing my son's game."

"Your *son?* Is this some kind of party line from *Green Acres?*"

"I have a son, Helene. He's on the Little League team. I'm his coach." Cory could see Emma walking up to him. "Gotta go."

"Everything okay?" Emma said after he hung up on Helene. She had a look of concern on her face.

She's coming over here because she's afraid something bad's going to happen.

"Yeah, everything's fine. I just forgot I had this TV interview scheduled."

"You should go."

"No, I already told my agent to forget it. It's too late. It's done."

"Are you sure?" Emma asked. "If you need to go, it'll be fine. We'll be okay without you."

Cory got the bag of bats from the back of the truck and then grabbed his duffel bag. "It's fine."

They walked over to the field. As Cory was putting his gear in the dugout, a black limo arrived. It must have been waiting at his motel.

Helene didn't waste a minute.

A text came through his phone.

GET IN THE CAR.

Helene didn't like taking no for an answer. That's exactly why he had her for an agent. That's why she was one of the best in the business.

Emma still looked worried. "Doesn't look too late to me. Seriously, just go."

Her continued efforts to get him off the

field only made Cory more adamant about staying.

"It's your career," Emma continued. "Go. Believe it or not, we *will* survive."

I just love having all these women in my life who believe in me so much.

"I'm not leaving." He picked up his glove and went out to the field to begin pregame warm-ups with the kids. "We got a game to play."

Cory glanced back at the limo waiting in the parking lot.

It looked almost as out of place around this field as he did.

The game had an ominous start. A long hit to right field left Wellsey squinting in the sun, trying in vain to hold up his mitt to even attempt a catch. The ball clipped him in the head, sending both Wellsey and his outstretched mitt down.

After Cory ran out to make sure the kid was okay, he couldn't help thinking that at least this time it wasn't *his* fault that someone was laid out on the field.

The Roughnecks took the lead in the first inning, but the Bulldogs came back when Carlos managed to get on base and then made it home after a couple of errors by the cocky Roughnecks.

After Coach Pajersky's son hit a home run in the fourth, Tyler went up to the plate. His stance was fine, but Cory knew he was trying to blast the ball just like Caleb Pajersky had. Stanton was already at second base. Cory tried to give Tyler a signal to just try to make it on base, then he called time.

"Don't try to make it over the fence," Cory told him. "Just get the ball over the second basemen."

"Really?"

"Yeah. There's a hundred percent chance he won't catch it. No way. Knock it out there, and you'll get Stanton home."

Tyler swung too hard and too fast at the next pitch, then connected with the following one. It didn't quite go over the second basemen, but it still made it out in right field, bringing home Stanton and tying the game.

As he stood on first base, Tyler glanced over at Cory, who gave him a wink and a grin.

It was the last inning, and Kendricks was up to bat when Cory called for another time to talk to the batter.

The Bulldogs actually looked better than the Roughnecks, and not just because of their new uniforms. Everything was clicking. Cory was trying his best to help them in every way he could, and that included ignoring the waiting limo and Coach Pajersky.

He walked over to Kendricks. He was keeping his eye on Wick, who was on third. *We can actually win this sucker.*

"What's up, Coach?" Kendricks asked.

He was growing to love the sound of that name. "Nice day out, huh?"

"Yeah." She waited to hear what he wanted.

"Nice breeze," he said. "How's your family?"

"Fine?" Now Kendricks was confused. Everybody was watching them while Cory asked these silly questions.

"Pitcher's nervous, and the second baseman's got a weak arm. We're going to shake things up."

Cory gave her a wink and could see she finally knew what he was talking about.

"Got it," she said as she returned to bat.

As he walked back over to third base, he noticed the limo pulling away.

Helene was going to be irate. His publicity opportunity was gone.

It didn't matter. He had a game to win.

Emma found it a bit amusing how freaked

out Coach Pajersky looked. Normally he treated games against the Bulldogs as practice sessions. But with the score tied in the bottom of the ninth and a runner on second and two outs to go, the man didn't just look rattled. He was incensed, his body and face rigid and angry.

"One out," he yelled at his team. Pajersky never talked without yelling. "Hold the runner. C'mon."

Emma stood near first base and glanced at the rest of her team. The mood in the dugout was a little different. Stanton made a farting sound with his mouth, making the rest of the kids giggle.

"Stanton," she called out. "Was that you?"

"I'm trying to fart in a run."

She didn't want to laugh, but she couldn't help the smile spreading on her face. That was like a green light to the kids, who all cracked up.

The levity only seemed to infuriate Pajersky even more.

Emma noticed Cory giving some signals to Wick. The kid gave a slight nod, his eyes wide behind their glasses. Then Kendricks followed suit and gave a nod.

These kids know what to do.

The pitch was solid, and Kendricks edged her bat into the perfect position to fire off the bunt. It seemed to surprise the pitcher, since he didn't start going for it at first.

"Hold the runner!" Pajersky hollered.

The pitcher turned to Wick, who froze a few steps away from third. Kendricks kept running past Emma and past first, as Caleb suddenly noticed her and heard the shouts of his team to chase her down for the out.

Pajersky's warning wail was ignored as the pitcher tossed the ball to the second baseman, who began to run toward Kendricks. Wick was sprinting wildly toward home as the second baseman tagged Kendricks.

The second baseman threw the ball toward home. Wick kept running. Then began to slide.

Come on, get in there.

Wick slid right into the catcher, and the umpire's voice roared across the Little League field.

"Safe."

For a moment Wick looked unconscious, then he slowly stood up and dusted himself off.

Emma saw Cory raising his fist in celebration as he jogged toward home plate, where the Bulldogs were all surrounding Wick and congratulating him.

Wick tried to shrug it off, but everybody knew better. They were laughing and jumping and showing off for the Roughnecks. Coach Pajersky was already heading off the field, obviously not bothering to congratulate the winners.

Emma stood on one side of the jubilant celebration as Cory stood on the other. Cory gave her that never-changing smile.

This time, she gave one back.

It was a nice moment, and she knew it was because of that grinning grown-up boy staring her down.

Come on home, she says.

I can't now.

That's what you always say, she says.

I can't help it.

Yes, you can. I'm not stupid, you know.

Only stupid thing you've ever done was to marry Dad.

Stop it, Cory.

Just sayin'.

I really want to see you.

You will, and when you do you won't believe how buff I am.

I just want to see you, she says.

Very soon okay I gotta go.

I love you.

Love you too, he says to her.

The last words he ever says to her.

The words he replays in his mind on the ride home after getting the message from Clay that she's gone.

Just like that.

Chapter Thirty-Four:
Strike Out

It was the same old story.

It was like he was ten years old again, having a great day and a wonderful celebration and then waking up to find something miserable spilling all over him.

Back then it was Dad showing up drunk and making whatever joy Cory had experienced in the day dry up. It was still the same. Something inevitably happened to drain the joy from Cory's life.

There had been plenty of high fives and handshakes and shoulder taps and love flowing as the parents and spectators filed off the field. *This* was the story everybody had hoped for. Coach Brand coming to save the day. The Bulldogs beating their archrival. Pajersky sent off without congratulating any of them.

Cory was following Emma and Tyler to the parking lot when Stanton ran up to them with a face of disbelief.

"Coach. You got robbed. It's not an all-star team if you're not on it."

Cory had forgotten all about the all-stars.

"Whoa, buddy. What are you talking about?"

"How's the league gonna win without you on the team?"

Stanton's father called his name and he ran off, leaving Cory to process the news.

Normally this sort of thing came from Helene. But, well, he was ignoring Helene. Just like he was ignoring the Grizzlies and the rest of the league.

But life goes on without you. It always will. Nobody's gonna wait.

Tyler and Emma waited for him to say something.

"You all right?" Emma asked.

"Yeah, yeah," he said in a casual tone. "Just forgot that was coming out today."

Maybe I didn't want to remember.

He didn't want them to see the surprise and hurt he was feeling. He just wanted to leave this scene and deal with the news on his own.

"Bye, Coach," Tyler said.

He nodded. "Good game, Tyler."

Eight consecutive years of making the all-star team, and now this.

He turned, not wanting to see his disappointment reflected in their faces. Not wanting to risk getting an invitation from Emma tonight.

It didn't matter what good thing might happen in life. Somehow, the Brands had a way of wrecking anything wonderful that might come their way.

"Mom?"

Tyler's voice had that tone, the one that inevitably meant hard questions were coming.

"Yeah?"

"Do you like Coach Cory?"

She glanced at the red light and wasn't sure what to say. They were only minutes away from the house. To adequately answer Tyler's question, she would need a good hour or two.

"Of course I do," she said in her best mommy voice.

"Then why don't you like having him around?"

"What do you mean I don't like having him around?"

"Anytime he wants to hang out you say no. We always have to leave after games. It's like you don't like him."

Oh, Ty.

"It's not that."

Emma didn't know what to say. This was a complicated conversation to have with anybody, including herself. She still didn't know exactly how she felt about Cory. He'd left over ten years ago, and a lot had happened since.

But love doesn't necessarily fade, does it?

"Is it 'cause he gets angry?" Tyler asked.

"No," she said instinctively, then quickly added, "Well, partially. It's complicated."

"Why?"

She was never ready for conversations like this. Like when Tyler asked about his father's death and why God would allow something like that. Parents didn't always have the answers, and single parents like Emma *certainly* didn't have the answers.

I'm trying to figure this out as I go.

"Do you remember Daddy's friend Isaac? The one who visited us that time? He served with your father in Afghanistan?"

"The sad guy?"

"He wasn't sad, Tyler. He was just — he suffered a lot."

She thought of the army sergeant who had come to pay his respects. She could tell something was not right with him. It wasn't anything he said or did, but just the way he looked and spoke. She could see the dark shadows of depression in his eyes and hear the sadness in his tone.

"Some people — they have things they have to overcome in life. Some deal with things like war and death in different ways."

"But Cory's not like the army man. Cory's fun."

Not all the time.

Emma pulled into their neighborhood.

"I'm not talking about Cory not being fun. He just — his father wasn't a very good man. Cory had a tough time when he was your age."

"And that's why you don't like him?"

"Tyler, I never said I don't like him."

"Yeah, I know. It's complicated."

Emma knew that losing James had left a gaping hole in Tyler's life. In both of their lives. It was natural for Tyler to gravitate toward the fun-loving and funny Cory Brand, who just happened to be one of the most popular major-league baseball players out there.

That would be complicated enough.

But, oh yeah, Tyler, by the way, he's also technically your father.

They arrived home, and Tyler seemed content to forget the conversation and turn on the television. But her son's words stayed with Emma. She wondered if she had been too harsh with Cory.

*God only knows what kind of mess he's go-
ing to get into tonight.*

A couple of hours later, Emma found
herself back in her truck, heading out to
check on Cory. She didn't want to have to
explain it to anybody, including herself. She
was worried about a guy she once loved and
maybe deep down still loved in some weird
way. This was a troubled man who didn't
have many real friends and probably didn't
trust anybody. But she knew there was only
one Emma in his life. Regardless of all of
the other women who had come across
Cory's path, none of them had their shared
history. And none of them had someone like
Tyler.

At least not that I know of.

She had asked her aunt to come by and
stay at the house while she was gone. Aunt
Becky was one of the few relatives on Emma's side who was still around. Emma
could call her at nine at night and know
Becky would help out.

Emma wasn't sure what she was going to
say or do when she knocked on Cory's door
at the motel. But it didn't matter, because
when she turned into the parking lot, his
pickup truck wasn't anywhere to be seen.

An idea came to mind. She knew Cory.

People didn't change *that* much in ten years or even forty.

Emma had always known she couldn't hold Cory back. He had to get out of this place. He had to see the world.

He had to get away from the pain of those first eighteen years.

She drove back to the field. Sure enough, there was a truck in the outfield with its lights on. A figure stood in the back of the truck.

What is he doing?

As she slowed down to park, Emma rolled down the window. The night was cool and still. She could hear the sound of a baseball game being blasted from the truck's speakers. Every few moments she heard the thwack of a bat connecting with a ball. Then she heard him yell something.

Emma thought about leaving, knowing that this could be messy. She knew the state he was probably in.

She sighed, then climbed out of the truck and began walking toward him.

As she approached, she heard the sound of something else being hit. Not a baseball. What was he hitting?

"Foul." Cory's wail could probably be heard for five miles.

He threw something up and swung at it,

sending it exploding with a plume of liquid. A beer can. Cory staggered a bit at the back of the pickup, leaning over to reach for something. He tossed up another beer and then tore into it, sending it spinning wildly forward as it erupted in a foamy mess.

"Way back, way back, it's going, it's gone."

Emma stopped about twenty feet from the truck, hoping not to get hit or sprayed with beer. She called out his name several times, then shouted it over the sound of the radio.

At first Cory looked stunned to see her, then he looked embarrassed. He dropped the bat like a kid caught doing something he shouldn't.

He's still that boy I met and couldn't run away from, and he always will be.

"What are you doing?" Emma asked as Cory moved to the back of the pickup and sat on the edge.

She stepped over a couple of burst beer cans and then noticed the truck bed was littered with empty cans.

"Hey," Cory said in a tired, drunken voice.

His eyes looked glazed, and she could tell he was bombed. She saw an empty case of beer in the pickup and another half-empty case on the other side of the truck bed.

"Nice," she said, not even trying to hide her disdain. "Okay. Well, I wondered if you were doing all right after the all-star news. But I see that you — are the same as always."

She couldn't talk to him in this state. She wasn't sure what exactly she was doing here. She wasn't his caretaker or his lover or even his friend. She turned and began to walk back to her truck.

"Come on," Cory shouted behind her. "Don't leave me here. It was the all-star thing. I didn't get the votes."

"Yeah, I know," she said, not even bothering to look back.

"Emma, come on. Give a guy a break. I was upset. My career's not looking so hot. I mean — I don't even know what I'm doing here in this town."

Emma turned around and looked at the pitiful sight sitting on the back of the truck. "Well, I'm sure it's very disappointing. But then, adults cope with disappointment all the time. Want to ask me how I know?"

"Yeah, yeah," Cory said, not looking at her. "I disappointed you."

She knew Cory was used to giving apologies. It was just a line from a man who was used to giving lines.

"I didn't just leave to play baseball, you know?" Cory was now looking at her, a dejected look filling his face. "The thought of being a dad scared the life out of me."

And you think it didn't terrify me?

If she were closer she might have slapped him on his pretty face. She couldn't say a word.

"But I've changed, Emma."

This line — no, not just a line, but a lie — snapped her out of her silent anger and made her want to tear into him. He actually sounded like he believed what he was saying.

She laughed in contempt. "Clearly you've changed."

Cory wasn't about to back down. Not now. The cool and calm Cory who made everybody laugh and love him was gone. This was the drunk Cory, the one who would do whatever it took to have his needs met.

It was the same when he was sixteen or twenty.

"I've been thinking," Cory said. "I want us to be a family. I never feel like the kind of man I do when I'm with —"

"Stop talking."

He had the gall — the drunken delirious audacity to actually suggest —

She began walking away again, and she could hear him get off the truck and start rushing toward her. Then she heard him

342

stumble and let out a moan in pain. Emma looked around. What a mess of a man Cory had become.

"Better be careful," she said.

"Emma, stop. Listen to me — *I've changed.* I want to be Tyler's dad."

She looked at him and wanted to make sure he heard what she was about to say. She wanted to make it crystal clear, to know that Cory *got* what she was going to tell him.

For ten years she had wondered if this conversation would ever happen. She was ready.

"Really? *Really?* You want to be his dad? You were too scared to be his dad ten years ago, but now you have somehow summoned your courage and you think you're ready to be Tyler's father?"

"Yes. I —"

"Oh, no." Emma took a few steps closer so he could see her and hear her clearly. "It takes courage to be a parent, Cory. It's sheer bravery to love a child — to care for him, be there for him, to love him when he pushes you away. It takes courage to put your dreams on hold, to juggle your own heartache and disappointments while you . . . pray for the wisdom to navigate the endless decisions — and activities."

Emma was seething and couldn't hold back. Not now, not with Cory in this condition, not after what he was suggesting.

"What's too much, what's not enough," she continued. "And split-second choices, never knowing which ones are going to affect the rest of his life and which don't really matter. And just when you think you might be getting the hang of it, you lose your husband. So you now get to make every choice alone — again. So while suffocating in grief you have no choice but to pull it together so you can care for the most precious, most amazing person you have ever known."

Cory didn't say a word. He just stood there, his face full of hurt and guilt.

"Yeah, parenting is not for the faint of heart, Cory. It's not for the scared or the self-absorbed."

Emma glanced around to see if they were still alone. "You ran once," she said. "You'll run again. People don't change."

"It was a mistake," Cory yelled at her. "A huge mistake. The old man said I'd only end up resenting you and the baby the way he resented me."

Emma paused.

No father — no parent — would be that cruel.

"He told me I'd just screw up the baby, and I believed him. *I believed him.*" Cory wiped his mouth. Were those tears in his eyes?

Of all the things she'd expected to hear — excuses and apologies and admissions — Emma had never expected this.

"So your only choice was to write us off." Her voice now was weak and soft.

"That's not true. I never wrote you off. I was coming back, but by the time I got my guts up to call you, you were married."

She had never heard this.

It doesn't matter.

This was all new to her and —

It doesn't matter. It doesn't change a thing.

It wasn't enough. It would never be enough.

She glanced at him and hoped he fully saw her staring at him.

"Whatever is broken in you, Cory . . . whatever your dad did or didn't do, I can't fix it. And neither can Tyler. And that hurt in you will hurt Tyler. It already has."

Cory looked defeated. Crushed. "He needs a dad."

"He had a dad. He died. James was there for us when you left. And that amazing, unselfish man is the only father Tyler has ever known. And for now, that's how it stays."

She was done here. She had said enough — probably way too much — and it was time to leave. Emma turned around for the third time and began walking. This time, Cory didn't call or run after her.

As she walked under a dark sky full of a thousand shimmering stars, she began to cry.

Tears could be stored up and poured out at any perfectly awful moment. She didn't realize she still felt this way inside. Yet speaking those words to Cory — they broke her heart again.

The world feels a little better when you have a little help.

He's no different from all the others who have felt the same way.

Centuries of people who have needed a little help. Just a little help to get through those dog days.

People who end up realizing that others don't understand and don't get it and don't fathom all the things on your plate.

You stand here every day, and the world watches.

You need a little help 'cause God knows nobody's gonna give you any.

You take a little, and it's okay.

You take a little more, and you think it's all right.

The world is crazy busy and you have to make sure you cope and you are finally able to rise above the noise.

With a little help.

Just a little.

And a little more.

And a little more.

Because that's what you need.

And there's nothing wrong with it. Because everybody's doing it and everybody's done it and everybody will keep doing it.

Nobody understands your life.

A little help isn't going to hurt anybody.

So you pour the bottle and find the help and pour a little more and keep hoping to find that help. Over and over and over again.

CHAPTER THIRTY-FIVE:
BASES EMPTY

There'd been hundreds of mornings that felt like this. Maybe even a thousand.

It wasn't just feeling hungover. Cory didn't really get hungover in the traditional sense, like a teenager might after downing his father's whiskey. He couldn't remember the last time he'd gone a couple of days without drinking. It wasn't just about feeling sluggish and scrambled. It was that empty feeling, like something wasn't right and shouldn't be this way. The hole inside of him stayed there until he could fill it again.

That's what he did, over and over and over again, regardless of where he was or what he was doing. Playing ball, dating models, filming an ad, working out at the gym, taking a vacation. Or in this case, coaching Little League and trying to celebrate some recovery.

The same old story followed him every

time. A shadow that once resembled him, looking smaller each day. Soon there wouldn't be a shadow left.

He remembered everything Emma said. Whatever happened in his life, he would know that it was too late. Too late for him to suddenly turn into some magical prince and save the princess. The storybook ending had been out of reach for some time.

The first thing he saw when he climbed out of bed was the minifridge. He was beginning to hate seeing that thing. Every night it looked like the smile of his best buddy. Every morning it resembled the disappointed face of — well, of everybody in his life.

Wearing only boxers and a T-shirt, Cory unplugged the half-full fridge and pushed it outside the door. Chad could have the rest of the contents. Cory was finished.

He needed to get his act together. He had only been here for two long and endless weeks, and there were six more to go.

I might die in this sad little motel room if I don't watch out.

The restless feeling stayed with him. He knew he had to do something about it. Go find a place to work out or go jogging. He could sweat off all the beer he'd had last night.

Then he thought of something better.

The swing never got old.

The batting machine launched the ball, and Cory hit it with perfect form. He would've felt a little better with a few beers in his system to get rid of that unsteady feeling. But it was time for him to try, and he could do anything he wanted to. Well, pretty much anything.

He was in the old barn hitting away, just like he used to do during high school. It was always better practicing with this machine than taking wild pitches from his father. Cory had knocked on the door of the farmhouse, but nobody was home. That was fine by him.

With each ball coming his way, Cory hit harder.

The bat hitting the ball wasn't just practice. It was a connection. It helped fill the vacancy inside. Little by little.

There weren't enough balls in the world to completely fill that hole. But it helped. Just a bit.

Whatever is broken in you . . .

Emma's voice interrupted his father's orders.

He swung faster. Gripped the bat tighter. Smacked the ball harder.

I can't fix it.

Nobody can, Emma. Nobody.

"I thought meth could just be like a fun thing. And I could stop anytime. I wasn't a tweaker or nothing."

Cory sat in the circle of men inside the small room in the church. This was what J. T. referred to as the men's step study. Each of them, including Cory, held a workbook in his hands. The kid talking was skinny and scraggly with piercings and an old cap over his head. He looked like the oldest twentysomething Cory had ever seen.

"But coming down was hard. And then I had to have it. Stole money from my grandma's purse to get it. I couldn't stop. I wanted to numb out. I forced myself to start answering these dang questions."

He smiled as he pointed to his workbook. Cory listened to the young guy and knew what he was talking about.

"Doing these books, I found out why I used."

Cory glanced at the white space in his book. He hadn't even opened it except at these meetings. He didn't want to feel like he was back in school again.

"I still struggle," the guy said. "But I don't feel hopeless. It's getting better. I'm changing. I feel myself changing."

He thanked everybody for letting him share. Cory knew that this kid wasn't talking just to talk. He probably didn't want to be there, just like Cory. But he wasn't making this up either.

Cory scanned the question at the top of the page.

How do you handle pain and disappointment?

Cory thought about how he'd ended up here. Knocking over Carlos and giving him a bloody nose. The incident with Pajersky. The whole meltdown over the baseball cards.

And yeah, then there's the all-star snub.

Cory knew how he handled pain and disappointment. He lashed out, then tried to find a way to numb back up.

He could answer these questions. But what then? That didn't mean he would magically be fixed.

If you bother reading through the booklet maybe you'll see.

He still had plenty of time to do so. Plenty of time.

He stares at the picture Clay sent him.

Emma looks the same. She still looks beautiful and happy. He misses that smile of hers and those bright eyes. Eyes that told him he was going to make it, that she knew he was going to make it.

But the boy next to Emma — Cory can't believe his eyes.

He knows he probably shouldn't ask Clay to send him these pics, but he's curious.

Yet, holding this picture in his hands, he's no longer curious.

Something deep inside feels cut and bleeding.

He still can't believe they're out there somewhere, living a life that he doesn't belong in. Living a life he chose to forget.

Tyler is five, and he has his mother's smile.

A part of Cory wonders if he'll ever meet him. But he knows there's no reason to. All he'd do is make a mess of things if he ever went back home and saw Emma again.

Emma is married and has her own life and that's good. He's happy for her, for them.

A part of him knows they're far better off being far away from him. That's just the cold, brutal truth.

CHAPTER THIRTY-SIX:
CYCLE

The next time Emma saw Cory on the field, he gave her a polite nod and said a polite good afternoon and then proceeded to coach the Bulldogs. There were no high fives or shared glances. Cory kept his distance.

The camaraderie that had started to build had washed back out to sea.

Emma was cautious, knowing he could be doing this for attention, sulking like he used to so she would come back around and tend to him. But when the afternoon practice ended and the kids left and Cory said good-bye to Tyler, Emma knew he wasn't sulking.

He was just keeping his distance.

As he should be.

She saw him get in the old pickup truck and leave the parking lot. Alone.

Cory realized he was still only halfway through Celebrate Recovery's eight weeks when he tried to start taking better care of himself. This began with getting back into shape and starting to exercise.

Sometimes he would jog in the middle of the night on a back road going nowhere. The night stars reminded him of all those times when he was young, looking at these same stars and believing he could be something when he left this place behind.

Those same stars were still there, even when the bright lights of the big city and the big stadiums drowned them out.

It was the third time he'd tried calling Cory, and this time his brother answered.

"Do you want to come over for dinner?"

"No, it's okay, thanks."

Clay stared at the picture of Karen and him standing next to Carlos. It was the first official family picture they had taken.

"Cory — it's been almost four weeks since you came to Okmulgee. You've come to the barn half a dozen times, but you still haven't had dinner with us."

"I have my reasons."

"Stop being stubborn."

There was a pause, and then Cory finally said, "Okay."

"Really?"

"Yeah."

His brother sounded different. The attitude and arrogance were somehow slipping away.

"It'll be no pressure — promise. Just hanging out. Watching some of the game. If you want."

"Yeah, okay. Thanks."

"Great."

"Hey, Clay?"

"Yeah?"

"You mind if I bring a puppy over?"

"A puppy? Uh, yeah, sure."

"Cool. See you soon."

Clay stared at another picture hanging on the wall. It was a picture of his brother in his first major-league game after his first home run.

The picture still inspired him. He just wanted that guy on the wall — the wide-eyed baseball wonder who could do no wrong — to come back around.

He wanted that guy to grow up the way the rest of them had.

There's still hope he can change.

Karen had proven to Clay that hope was real and alive in this world and that anybody — *anybody* — could change.

All this talk of God, yet Cory still wondered if God was paying any attention to them.

He didn't doubt that there was a God

above. His mother's faith made him realize that there must be something in it. If she could put up with the man she'd married and still try to love and respect him because that's what God wanted her to do — well, there was something real about that.

Cory watched J. T. and knew the faith this man had was real. He didn't wear it like a logo on a hat or a shirt. He wore it like a belt buckle, hidden away but necessary 'cause it held him up.

Every day Cory thought about drinking, but a day without it became a week. The two meetings helped. So did seeing Karen and Clay. So did working out. So did coaching the Bulldogs and keeping out of Emma's hair.

Those empty Celebrate Recovery books started filling up. But he still wondered if this was for him and if he could really change and if he really needed to change.

He'd been doing it alone his whole life. God or not. Emma or not. Clay or not.

The one constant had been Cory stepping up to the plate. Every day.

This plate he was stepping up to, or at least trying to step up to, felt different somehow.

It wasn't about the crowd out there anymore. It was about him.

And he didn't know. He just didn't know.

Emma knew that God said to pray for your enemies, but she wasn't sure whether Cory was her enemy or her friend. At night, after Tyler went to bed and the stillness of the house greeted her, Emma would think about Cory. He looked lost and confused. She wanted to ask him how he was doing and how the CR meetings were going, but she couldn't.

You already said enough to him to last a lifetime.

Part of her wanted to apologize for her angry comments, or at least try to reframe them. But she knew she couldn't.

Maybe those words would make the difference. Ultimately Emma knew that only God could change a person's heart. She had learned this the hard way years ago. And she continued to learn it on a daily basis.

Cory didn't realize that every single person living and breathing was broken. Maybe they didn't carry the weight he did, and they didn't fracture themselves so much in life, but everybody was lost and in need of saving.

Everybody stumbled and failed.

But oh . . .

Oh, what joy for those whose disobedience

is forgiven, whose sins are put out of sight.
Yes, what joy for those whose record the Lord
has cleared of sin.

Emma hoped and prayed that Cory would
realize this. It wasn't *just* him. He wasn't
the only person down here suffering and
stumbling around.

His mistakes and failures had been cleared
just like everybody else's.

Cory just had to make that step and
believe that grace could come to someone
like him.

All Emma could do was keep praying he
would come to understand this. That God
would open his eyes.

Time ticked by like a pesky fly buzzing
through a room and bouncing off the walls.
So slowly. A painful, dreary kind of slow.

The kind that made you dream about
drinking.

On his sixth week in Okmulgee, Cory
decided to stop at a liquor store. He barely
made it back to the pickup before opening
the bottle of vodka and chugging it.

He just wanted the emptiness to go away.

Not drinking did nothing except make
him think about drinking.

He'd been hearing things that made sense
and seeing things that made sense, but he

still didn't share what he was really feeling.

He just closed his eyes and took another drink in the parking lot of the liquor store.

Tomorrow would be another day, and he'd stop drinking again and keep going. Keep doing what he was doing. Keep smiling and listening and keeping his distance from those like Emma who could hurt him. He knew now that anybody in this life close enough to hurt would eventually reach out and strike you down. Even angels like Emma eventually fell.

Everybody did.

The first few drinks didn't do a thing. But eventually he'd blank out and not feel anything.

That's what he needed.

Cory listens to the man detail the story about his childhood abuse and abandonment. The suffering he went through after moving from home to home. After losing both parents. After losing everything.

The man details each step taken on the downward spiral and then documents how God rescued him.

How God loves him.

But that's him, Cory thinks.

All this time, and he still feels different from this man.

Tim and Mary and Carl and Mac and Keith and Marnie might all be in the same boat, but it's different with him.

Maybe I'm unreachable, Cory thinks.

Maybe it's going to take a miracle to get to me.

His time served in this place is almost finished. Then he'll go back out and resume a life that none of these people understand. A dream of a life that just got derailed a bit.

The dream is gonna continue, and Cory's gonna be fine.

Cory Brand is always fine.

Chapter Thirty-Seven: Closer

J. T. walked up to Cory after the Tuesday night step study and handed him a folded sheet of paper. "Well, this is your eighth week."

In some ways, Cory felt like he'd been back in Okmulgee much longer than that. But he also felt like it had just been yesterday that he was cruising in the Corvette with Clay until the tractor showed up and ruined their day.

"Is it really? Wow." Cory opened the document and could see the letter written to verify he had gone through eight weeks of recovery. It was signed by J. T. himself. "Well, it looks official."

J. T. gave him a weary old grin. "Your mandated time is up, Cory, but I hope you keep coming back."

"Okay. Right. Thanks."

As Cory headed outside of the church to the still night breeze, he talked and chatted with some of the guys he'd grown to admire.

For a second he thought of the way it used to be in the fancy Grizzlies clubhouse. Eighty-five thousand luxurious square feet and not a close friend to find anywhere. Yet here in this town, surrounded by men connected by the hurts, hang-ups, and habits of their lives, Cory had found some true teammates.

I'm even beginning to think like they do.

He knew it was more than just rhetoric.

These guys were doing more than simply reciting some lines they'd learned to make themselves feel better. Cory wasn't there yet, and might never get to where they were, but he still could admire the change in their lives. Each man's story had been incredible.

So yeah. Maybe there is something to celebrate, even if I'm not where they're at.

Cory felt good. He felt excited to leave this place in a better condition and get back to playing baseball. He needed to get back to the life he knew.

A part of him felt like celebrating, but he could hold off.

He could depart knowing that he'd allowed himself to chill on the boozing and to relax and let go.

Cory didn't need a drink tonight. There'd surely be some of that ahead, when he was back out there on the road, a weary warrior doing his job. For now, he could take a break.

An hour later, as he walked to fill up his bucket of ice for the soda he was drinking in his room, his iPhone buzzed. He could see Helene's name on the screen.

Finally.

"Where have you been?" he asked. "I've left six messages. I got my walking papers tonight."

"Yeah, listen, I only have a minute," Ms. No-Nonsense-Like-Always said. "I've got bad news. You're a free agent."

Cory dropped the empty bucket and heard it bounce on the cement floor.

It had been two weeks since he'd talked with Helene. Two weeks.

"What happened?" he asked.

This is what happens when you step away from the world you know and love and once owned.

"Truth is, they haven't missed you that much the last two months. You're too much trouble."

Well, please, Helene, don't hold back on how you're feeling.

Cory cursed and looked out to the dark countryside beyond the motel. "I can't believe this."

"I've made other inquiries —"

"I can't *believe* you let this happen, Helene." Before she could say anything else, Cory hung up.

She was supposed to be doing her part while he was stuck in this town. But like everybody else he knew, she let him down.

The only person who can get things done is me. The only person I can truly trust and truly expect to figure things out and do them is me.

Me.

Cory went to his room and grabbed the keys to his truck. He was finished celebrating recovery. Now it was time to celebrate being a free agent.

The bartender at Hank's Tavern sees Cory coming and lines up a couple of shot glasses on the bar. This is when Cory knows that the rest of the world knows. That's the way things are now. You knock a batboy in the nose. You knock over a tractor in the middle of Oklahoma. You knock a know-it-all father in the middle of a game.

Everybody finds out about the knocks as soon as they happen.

Thankfully, nobody knows about a college kid knocking up his high school sweetheart just before he was drafted by the majors.

It's fine by him to keep a few things secret.

He downs both the shots and tells the bartender to give him another round.

He's got some catching up to do.

CHAPTER THIRTY-EIGHT: FORCE-OUT

Emma had feared this moment for ten years now.

Ever since she first held on to that precious little crying soul she named Tyler, Emma had dreaded telling him the truth about his biological father. Not because she was ashamed of who he was or what had happened.

But because a part of her always feared that somehow, in some way, telling Tyler might also mean losing Tyler.

That's crazy. This is crazy. Surely Tyler's fine.

But she'd checked the house twice and had called the cell phone he was supposed to have on him when he was away, and so far Tyler was nowhere to be found.

Emma had arrived home that evening from doing errands to find a newspaper on the kitchen counter. This was odd, since they didn't get a paper, and Tyler checked out news online if he was interested.

The headline had said it all: CORY BRAND PUTS FAMILY FIRST.

Underneath was a detailed article on Cory Brand's journey from all-star to disgraced major-league player in recovery. The way the writer made it sound, this was some sort of pilgrimage Cory had made back to Okmulgee, to the town he left and the love he abandoned.

It talked about Cory wanting to make things right — wanting to focus on his family.

Then it mentioned his son, Tyler.

It mentioned Tyler's name as if it were public knowledge.

Nobody knows about this. Nobody except Karen and Clay.

There was a reason Emma left this town after Cory bailed. She didn't want to be stuck around here with people knowing the truth. Everybody would have known, too.

Just like they do now.

She couldn't believe Cory could betray her. That he could betray them. That he could do something so malicious and hurtful to Tyler.

I thought he was changing. I thought there was a chance . . .

Emma cursed her own foolishness even as

she tried to think of what to do. She called Karen, who had just arrived home from the grocery store.

"Karen — do you know where Tyler is?"

Karen sounded nonchalant as she said, "I don't know — let me ask."

When Karen got back on the line, she sounded different. "I'll call you right back."

"What is it?"

"It's Carlos," Karen said. "He looks like the kid who stole from the cookie jar."

Emma wasn't going to wait around for Karen's explanation. She grabbed her keys and went out to her truck to go looking for Tyler. She checked the garage, and her assumption was right. Tyler's bike was gone.

He's gone looking for Cory.

She never thought things would end like this. She assumed that Cory would eventually disappear, go back to his fancy life and leave them behind. Then the worries and weariness she had carried around would subside.

Driving toward downtown Okmulgee with the sun fading away, Emma prayed out loud.

"God, keep Tyler safe. And if — if he ends up finding Cory — help them — let Cory just —"

She couldn't finish the words she wanted

to say. But God knew what she was thinking.

Let Cory just stay away from him.

God knew exactly what she had felt ever since Tyler was born.

Keep Cory far away from Tyler.

It was the thing she feared the most. That Cory would suddenly turn on a light switch and realize what she had known for the last decade. That this wonderful kid was the brightest spot in a dark and dreary world.

And if Cory suddenly realized that too . . . with all his money and fame and clout . . .

Keep Cory's hands off him. Keep him away, Lord. Please.

He heard the song playing in the jukebox and couldn't believe it. Then again, this was what they called karma. This was what he found in the back of bars.

The first time Cory remembered hearing this song — *really* hearing this song — was when he was driving away from Okmulgee and heading to his future. He'd never been a big Elton John fan, but he paid attention when he started talking about staying on the farm and listening to his old man in the classic "Good-bye Yellow Brick Road."

It felt fitting. Pretty much every part of his life was in the gutter. His family life.

Check. His personal relationships — whatever few he really had. Check. His career. *Thanks for letting me know, Helene!* Double check. His soul. Check.

It was going to take more than a couple of vodka and tonics to set him on his feet again. Forget the tonic and load up on the vodka, sir.

Yep. I'll be getting that replacement. And yeah, there's many of me to be found.

Some clueless, carefree kid suddenly sucked into this machinery and thrust into the limelight.

Go to work, Cory. And if you don't produce, you go back to Okeymoky or wherever you come from.

Face the heat and face the stares and face the horrifying expectations.

And do this even though you're just a kid out of college who is still sort of dumbstruck and lovestruck and headstruck.

Nobody understood except the guys who filled his shoes. And now somebody was going to fill his jersey and his lockers, too.

He pointed to the bartender and lined up another. Seven shot glasses were lined up in victory, and he'd only been here an hour and a half.

They were going to have to take him out of here on a stretcher.

Just take me out the back so it doesn't show up on YouTube tomorrow, please.

He nodded at the fine form of the bartender, who was going to get the biggest tip of his life tonight, and then he took another shot.

Smooth as water.

There was a commotion at the door, and Cory heard someone yelling and saying "him."

Then an unmistakable voice shouted out "Coach" several times.

Standing there with a big man with bigger cowboy boots was Tyler.

"Found him looking in the windows," the cowboy said to Cory.

"Tyler," Cory bellowed in a voice that even surprised him. "You shouldn't be here."

For a moment Tyler just stood there, looking frightened and clueless. Cory could feel the wave of shame and fear deep inside.

"Do you hear me?" he shouted, cursing loudly. "Get out of here."

He hadn't meant to yell so loud. Or to use that kind of language.

The boy in front of him looked crushed.

Crushed and scared.

For a moment Cory turned around, angry that the kid had come out to find him. He

375

cursed and gritted his teeth.

Of all the times and in all the places . . .

He could feel the panic and the loss of balance and his world suddenly crumbling around him. For a moment Cory didn't know what to do.

For a moment he could hear his yelling and cursing father, and he was back at the farm with his old man screaming at him.

Then he realized that the old man screaming wasn't his father.

It's me.

He turned in horror, realizing what had happened. He was only half there, but the half of him that understood was horrified. Cory turned to say something to Tyler, to apologize to the kid and try to make it up to him . . .

But Tyler was already gone.

You ain't special, a voice tells him.

Doesn't matter how many times he's been voted an all-star or how many awards he's earned or how many runs he's batted in.

That voice remains the same.

You're always gonna be a nobody.

The voice follows him off his barstool as he runs out of the bar to try to find Tyler.

It's the same old scene. Yet it's different.

Everything is different now.

This is Tyler, another voice says. *This is your son.*

This is a snapshot of a boy you could have been. A face of hope you could have had.

And you're destroying it just like your old man destroyed you.

CHAPTER THIRTY-NINE: RUNDOWN

Tyler was standing next to his bike by the time Cory got to his side.

"What are you doing here?" Cory wasn't yelling anymore, but he was talking with the firmness of an adult and a parent.

An adult and parent who's just downed about ten shots.

The boy didn't say anything. Hurt still filled his face, the kind of hurt that Cory knew about too well, the kind that wouldn't go away with a simple apology.

"Look, Tyler, you shouldn't be out this late. And you definitely shouldn't be here."

They heard the sound of a truck engine racing down the street. Headlights splashed over them, and the truck pulled to a stop.

A part of him knew what was coming.

The door opened, and a woman he hardly recognized bolted out of the truck. "Get in," she screamed at Tyler. "Now!"

She grabbed his bike and put it in the

back of the truck.

Cory wanted to stop her or at least slow her down and explain, but he knew he wasn't the most stable at this moment. He carefully thought over his words so he wouldn't slur them.

"Emma — what's going on?"

She looked at him, and he knew she could tell he was drunk. It wasn't a big secret.

I didn't bring him here, so don't go crazy over something I didn't do.

Emma shouted out Tyler's name again and tried to get him to go around the truck and get in the passenger side. She grabbed something off the front seat of the vehicle and threw it at him. It was a newspaper. A newspaper she threw in his face.

"You had no right. *No right.*"

Cory had never heard Emma sound like this. Even the time she laid into him at the baseball field, it wasn't like this. She sounded like she wanted to rip out his heart.

"Tyler, right now," she said, pointing to the truck.

He looked over at the boy and saw tears on his face.

What happened? Is he in trouble?

Everything was happening too fast for Cory. What was going on?

Tyler looked at him, ignoring his mother's

demands. "Are you my dad?"

The world suddenly trembled, and the dark mouth of the beast opened up. Cory felt paralyzed.

He glanced down at the paper and realized the truth. Somehow the word had gotten out.

But I didn't say anything to anybody. Did I?

Tyler unzipped his backpack. Emma came to his side, still out of her mind with rage.

"I can't believe you'd use us like this," she said, moving Tyler toward the truck. "Get in the truck, Tyler."

"No!" Tyler jerked out of her grip and was fishing for something in his pack.

Then he turned and presented Cory with a box.

Tyler was holding the wooden box Cory had made so many years ago for himself and Clay. The one he'd gone out of his mind looking for in the barn.

"Here's your cards," Tyler said. "Your dad gave them to me. He used to cut our lawn. Before he — before he died."

As Cory took the cards, not knowing what else to do, the image of Dad cutting Emma's lawn was almost as crazy as his giving the cards to Tyler.

The monster who used to berate him daily

about baseball and chores and school and life . . .

He gave Tyler these because he knew who Tyler was. His grandson.

"Tyler —" Cory started, his voice weak and lost.

"I didn't know they were yours," Tyler said in a scared voice. "I'm sorry."

Emma cut off this moving moment by grabbing Tyler's arm and telling him again to get in the truck. The boy moved away from her grip and then walked to the truck, turning to face her before he got in.

"You lied to me," he said to his mother.

Emma didn't even bother looking at Cory as she got in, shut the door, and drove off.

Cory could see the tears in her eyes.

The truck drove off, leaving Cory standing there on the side of the street.

Alone with hundreds of mementos from his youth that now meant absolutely nothing.

He gets in the truck knowing he shouldn't be behind the wheel. But knowing he shouldn't do something has never stopped him before.

He shouldn't have left Emma behind when she told him the news.

He shouldn't have abandoned Tyler before he was even born.

He shouldn't have left in fear to follow his dreams while wrecking the dreams of so many others.

Cory drives to the one place he can hide. The only place in this world that has ever really, truly suited him.

CHAPTER FORTY: FOUL LINE

On the drive home Emma didn't say a word. She was angry at the situation, not at her son. She understood his need for answers — she would've been the same way. She also knew this wasn't the place to explain things to him — in the shadows of the truck on the drive back home.

Yet when she pulled into the driveway, Tyler was already half out the door before she had even finished parking. He bolted inside the front door and disappeared.

For a moment Emma just sat there in the silence. For so long she had carried this around with her, like the wooden box of baseball cards Tyler had been carrying in his backpack. She didn't know what it would be like, now that the secret was out and her backpack was empty.

She prayed for guidance, for God to give her the right words to say, for patience and clarity.

"God be with us," she said as she walked into the house.

She stepped through the open doorway and shut the door behind her.

James was gone, and Cory had never been and would never be part of the picture. It was just the two of them, and now Tyler was furious with her.

I was a kid once too, and I didn't have anywhere to go.

It had taken everything inside of her to leave Okmulgee and move to Claremore.

It had taken even more for her to finally open up to the army private who won over her heart.

Years later, she had to summon up the same courage to do it all over again after James was killed in Afghanistan. She made the decision for Tyler and her to move back to Okmulgee and start again just over a year ago.

All these decisions she had made on her own.

She heard something crashing in Tyler's room. Rage spilling out and not knowing where to go.

It's time I started making Tyler a part of those decisions. He's old enough to know some things. He's old enough to help make decisions with me.

Emma started up the stairs, knowing it wasn't going to be an easy conversation. But he deserved to know the truth about his fathers. The one who was wounded and died in a foreign land. And the one who was wounded and went out to live life in another foreign land.

Both were gone forever.

That was the only truth Emma knew and believed. The only truth she could share with Tyler.

Cory sat in the shadows of the barn, one lone, cold light shining a bleak glare his way. He was drunk and couldn't stop his mind from doing cartwheels in his head.

Everything that had happened in his life, these awful and broken pieces following him into the woods like bread crumbs tossed by a child, paled in comparison to this moment. All the nightmares with his father. The guilt from leaving Emma and Tyler behind. The booze and the women and the constant grind. The emptiness creeping up on him in full stadiums. The death of his mother. The failure to make amends with his father. His banishment from the game. His booting from the Grizzlies.

None of those things compared to this. To now. To the kid who had met him and idolized him and befriended him and then discovered the truth.

Tyler's real father wasn't some hero kids looked up to.

Tyler's real father was a coward who had left the one kid he needed to be there for.

The walls and the haunting draft inside the barn reminded Cory of all those times he'd felt confused and angry and in need. All he had ever wanted was a father who was there, who didn't scare him. A father who acted like a father should and loved him.

I'm no better than he was. In fact, I'm worse. Dad stayed around. I bailed.

Everything in him was broken. Everything in him couldn't ever be fixed.

This whole world sucked you dry and then some and then tossed you out without a care.

All people wanted was to take and take and take more. And they had done exactly that, and now there was nothing left to take.

Nothing at all left to take.

This feeling — the guilt and sadness and anger — felt like a blanket. Not one you'd put over a child to keep them warm at night, but the kind you'd put over someone's head to smother them to death. The kind you'd put over a dead body on the side of the road to keep it from being viewed.

Cory had done everything possible his own way — the good ole Cory Brand way — for thirty-three years.

Thirty-three lonely, empty years.

He couldn't go on like this.

Every time he closed his eyes he saw Tyler's eyes staring back at him. Confused. Hurt. Totally disappointed.

The sound of boots crunching the ground made Cory look up. He could see J. T. standing near the open door.

"Got your message."

Cory just sat there, looking up at J. T. without knowing what to say.

This man had been there the last two months, helping and guiding Cory, unasked. Cory had never been willing to let his pride go down and ask J. T. for his help.

J. T. walked over and sat down next to Cory. He didn't say a word, just looked ahead, patient as ever.

"What's going to happen to me?" The words leaked out of Cory. "I can't stop. I can't make myself stop."

Instead of a solution, or a quick fix, or a Bible verse, or a told-you-so, J. T. simply said, "I know."

Cory felt the tears hovering like grenades in his eyes. He fought crying like a baby but didn't know what else to do. All this time, and all he'd seen and done . . .

J. T. just sat next to him. Not giving him a brotherly pat on the back. Not sharing an anecdote.

The guy was there at his side and let Cory take everything in.

I need your help, God. 'Cause nobody's gonna be able to do it if You can't.

He thought of his mother, could see her walking on this property and smiling at Clay and Cory playing or doing something stupid.

Does she still see me? Is she still watching over me?

Maybe she could put in a good word for him up there or wherever it was she was at.

Cory needed help.

Cory wanted help.

The man next to him was silent, but in his head Cory could hear J. T. talking. He was remembering something J. T. had quoted when he gave his testimony to the crowd.

"If you confess with your mouth, 'Jesus is Lord,' and believe in your heart that God raised him from the dead, you will be saved."

Cory closed his eyes and let out a sigh.

Help me to believe this. Help me to confess this.

Help me, Lord.

Baby steps. That's the cliché of taking it easy or taking it slow or taking it one day at a time.

Cory takes that first step and finally starts. He finally really, truly starts, even though he's gone through all of this before.

Lesson 1. Principle 1. Step 1.

The words heard so many times now wrap themselves around him like a blanket. But this time it's a baby's blanket.

He reads the verse from Romans in the worn-out booklet that has his messy handwriting all over its pages.

"I know that nothing good lives in me, that is, in my sinful nature. For I have the desire to do what is good, but I cannot carry it out."

He keeps reading and finally gets to the questions.

He's done faking it, just going through the motions.

It's time. It's finally time.

Cory answers the questions without being

funny and without shading the truth.

This is where it starts.

CHAPTER FORTY-ONE: GRAND SLAM

The sanctuary of the old church surely held a wealth of history and stories. The afternoon sun streamed through the tinted windows as the CR meeting began. J. T. stood in the front, holding a basket of blue chips. Cory sat in a pew close to the front. Next to him sat Clay and Karen.

"The first chip is the most important, reminding us to surrender to Christ only," J. T. said. "If you've identified a new area you'd like to surrender to Christ, or if you've relapsed and are coming back, we hope you'll come forward and take a blue chip to remember this surrender date."

For Cory, it wasn't about a new area.

For Cory Brand, it was about the whole ship and every single area inside it. Every corner and crack and shadowy space.

He felt more nervous standing now than he ever had standing at the plate, awaiting the pitch. This was more important and held far more implications.

In light of the rest of time and eternity — yeah, this was pretty important.

Cory stepped out and began walking toward his friend and sponsor. As he pulled out a blue chip from the basket, J. T. gave him a big hug.

The kind a father might give his son.

"I'm proud of you," J. T. whispered.

Cory clutched the chip and sat back down next to Clay and Karen.

He wasn't alone anymore. And it wasn't because of these people surrounding him, either.

God, grant me the serenity to accept the things I cannot change . . .

Cory stood with the rest of the people at the CR meeting, reading the serenity prayer from his pamphlet. There were a hundred things he needed to do — no, make that a thousand — yet he knew he needed to take it easy.

There were a lot of things in his life he couldn't change.

Emma and Tyler. The Grizzlies and Helene. Tomorrow and next month and next year.

All I have is now.

He knew he had to take it slow. And keep this prayer in the back of his mind.

With his bags packed and ready to go, Cory had one more thing to do in this motel room. He couldn't say he was going to miss this deathtrap inn or his holding cell in it, but he was going to miss the simple nature of living here without much. Wealth and belongings and busyness could keep your mind off the important things. This room had been the perfect place for Cory to remember and to find himself again.

For God to find me and meet me halfway.

He glanced at the Bulldogs roster he had taped to the wall, then pulled it down carefully and placed it in a bag.

He was never going to forget the names on that roster.

Never.

. . . and the wisdom to know the difference.

Cory had given Chad his loaner truck back along with enough money to trade it in for a nicer one. Now he drove a car he'd purchased from J. T. The guy had practically given it away, but Cory had still insisted on giving him some money. He owed J. T. that much.

As he drove out of Okmulgee with the sun

just up, he passed the small bar where he'd tried to escape, the one where Tyler had found him. It was a reminder of all the unspoken words and undone things he was leaving behind.

This time, however, he wasn't running away.

This time, Cory was doing the best thing possible.

He was making his life healthy again. He was moving on and moving toward the future.

Maybe this was a door God was going to shut permanently. And Cory had to be okay with it.

Maybe someday in the future, he'd see them again.

What does that prayer say about looking back or looking ahead?

As he drove out of town and got back on US 75, Cory remembered the words of the prayer. He remembered them and whispered them to himself.

Living one day at a time, enjoying one moment at a time . . .

Cory felt like Kevin Costner's character in *Bull Durham* as he opened the door and smelled the aroma of fries and sweat in the manager's office. He'd skipped the minor leagues on his way to fame and glory. Now he stood across from the manager of the Tulsa Mustangs, an AA baseball team that was a long way away from the Grizzlies.

"Good to see you, Cory," Ron Knoller said, shaking his hand.

The old Cory might have said something witty like *It's not so hot seeing you, Jim* or *I didn't even know they had mustangs here in Tulsa.* But he just smiled and said, "Thanks for seeing me."

"Not many days we get an all-star walking through that door."

"I don't see any in this office."

Ron gave him a serious look. "Once you make that team, you're *always* an all-star in my book. And as far as I can tell, there are two of them in here."

Cory laughed, suddenly curious to know Knoller's background. "Glad I'm in the right place then."

"Have a seat."

. . . accepting hardship as a pathway to peace; taking, as Jesus did, this sinful world as it is, not as I would have it . . .

A few minutes into the conversation with the manager of the Mustangs, the no-

nonsense Knoller asked him a question.

"So just tell me — am I gonna regret making this decision? Is this gonna be a pain in the rear for me?"

Cory smiled. It was an honest question. "I certainly hope not."

"The guy who knocked over that poor batboy — is he gonna show up on the field anytime soon?"

"I don't think so. I don't plan on it. And that boy — his name is Carlos. He's my nephew."

For a second Ron tried to make sense of this admission, then he cursed and let out a deep laugh from his gut. "Now *that* is the funniest thing I've heard in a long time."

. . . trusting that You will make all things right if I surrender to Your will . . .

Cory held the uniform that read *Mustangs* across the front in his hand as he looked out onto the field from behind home plate. The view was a lot smaller than Samson Field in Denver.

He swallowed and looked up at the sky. Because this stadium was smaller, the view of the horizon was wider. The canvas of the sky looked like it had been splashed in blue and white and orange and red. The fading sun made everything look grand and end-less.

He let out a sigh. A nervous, tired, uncertain sigh.

For a dozen years he'd been doing it his way.

No, make that for thirty-three years.

That life was over. He'd tried it his way, and he had failed.

Staring at the sky, Cory felt inspired. He wanted to go back on this field and wanted to get behind home plate and do his job.

He wanted to appreciate the ability — the opportunity — of stepping up to the plate.

A man could run halfway around the world to try to find himself, only to find he hadn't gone very far after all.

He looked at the field and the sky and the fading sun with the newfound hope of a free man. A man knowing he didn't have to do it all and carry the weight of that around his shoulders every day and night.

All he wanted — all he needed — was to pray and trust God to make things right.

. . . so that I may be reasonably happy in this life and supremely happy with You forever in the next. Amen.

Happiness in this life isn't such an easy thing to come by.

Cory can feel the huge hole inside he used to fill so easily. And nights like this when he's alone and bored and restless, this hole seems to be shouting at him, demanding he do something, begging for one more refill.

He finds his iPhone and dials the number.

"Yeah?"

"It's Cory."

"Are you okay?"

Normally he would say yes, but normally he wouldn't be making this call. The old Cory didn't know how to say no. The old Cory didn't know how to ask for help.

"I've been better," he tells J. T.

"Where are you?"

"I'm fine. I'm at the apartment. Just bored out of my mind and itchy. I'd go work out, but my knee's killing me."

"I can leave in a few minutes."

"No, man. It's fine. I just — I just wanted to talk."

"It's fine."

"You're an hour away."

"Forty-five minutes. Tops."

"No, come on. Let me at least meet you somewhere."

"Are you sober?"

"Yeah."

At this point in their relationship, there's no need to lie to J. T. Cory's been sober for a while, but it feels like those weeks and months could vaporize in a single second.

"I'll be there soon. Just hang tight."

With that, J. T. hangs up, and Cory knows he's on his way.

And while it no longer surprises him, it's still amazing.

Cory sighs and swallows and waits. He can wait for J. T. to get there.

But it doesn't mean it won't be hard.

CHAPTER FORTY-TWO:
SCORING POSITION

Emma hit another grounder out to the team of zombies on the field. The ball soared past Tyler, who didn't seem too bothered and walked to pick it up. Carlos watched him at shortstop, his glove down and his head tilted in boredom. Wick was talking to Kendricks, and neither of them was paying attention.

The team was a disaster now that Coach Cory was gone.

"Come on, guys," Emma shouted out. "This is pathetic. You gotta at least try."

But Emma knew it was hard to encourage them to be motivated when stepping back out on this field felt like work now. Every time she saw a Bulldogs logo for the rest of her life, she was going to think of Cory.

Coach Cory, their hero.

Coach Cory who broke my heart. Twice.

"Hey," Carlos said with a laugh, "this is like the movie when that lady leaves the children and it's not fun for them anymore."

Tyler didn't know which movie he was talking about. Emma knew but didn't want to dignify the comparison. She still could hit the ball out to them. She wasn't *that* uncoordinated.

"What's that movie called with the nun and the singing children?" Carlos shouted across the field to Emma.

"*The Sound of Music*?" Tyler realized.

"Yeah, this is just like that," Carlos joked. "It's not fun anymore without Coach Cory."

She popped another ball out toward Carlos. "You're killing me, buddy."

Things were bad when the kids were comparing Coach Cory to Sister Maria.

The ball dropped to Carlos's side just as he looked out toward the parking lot, oblivious. Emma was going to say something when she turned back and saw Clay walking onto the field, followed by Karen.

"Dad's here," Carlos cried out, running toward him.

Clay's arm was no longer in a sling.

"Coach Clay is back," Stanton said as the Bulldogs circled Clay.

Everybody cheered his arrival.

Thank God one of the Brand boys came to save the day.

"How's everybody doing?" Clay said in a cheerful voice.

Emma let out a sigh and raised her eyebrows. "Wonderful now."

It only took a few moments for the team to get back into lifelike mode. Clay still had to take it easy, but he could throw with his right arm and he could get the team practicing again. Emma took a break and went to the sideline to sit with Karen.

"Look at how enthusiastic they are," Karen said.

Emma nodded. "Yeah. Wish I could get over it that quick."

Cory sat in the large sanctuary of the Tulsa megachurch, surrounded on all sides by strangers. He missed the small-town feel of the meetings back home.

Well, back in Okmulgee.

Right now, Tulsa was home. And he was okay with that.

The testimony for the large group was going to be given by a woman named Robin. She looked a little older than Cory and was dressed in business attire, like she worked in some sort of corporate environment, one of those places Cory knew nothing about but liked watching on shows like *The Office*.

Once again, here was a stranger telling everyone her story. It didn't feel strange or awkward anymore. It felt right.

"I grew up in a Christian yet dysfunctional home. We went to church whenever the doors were open. My father's work took him away from us most of the time. My stay-at-home mother was verbally and psychologically abusive. She was legalistic, and her expectations were unrealistic. She was a Christian, but she hurt me in ways no one else could."

Robin composed herself, looked out at the audience, then continued to read from her notes.

"Mom's rapid mood swings were really difficult. She would often send my sister and me to our room, where we were mandated to sit quietly, and then she would forget about us for hours. On more than one occasion, when I could no longer stand the suspense, I would leave the bedroom, knowing the yardstick would be broken on my backside and I would be picking out splinters for a week. But it was dark outside, and I was hungry. I also wanted to take the brunt of the punishment instead of my sister."

Cory knew that part of Robin's story very well.

"As a child, I lived in a constant state of fear. I believed in God, but I had a warped sense of who He was, and I couldn't trust

Him. Life, for me, was performance based. But after going through my step study, I'm encouraged. I'm changing. I now believe God is a *loving father.* He's not waiting to strike me dead and send me to hell for every mistake I make — no matter what my childhood experiences have taught me. I am valuable not because I am doing something well, but because I am God's child . . . and He doesn't make junk. Thank you for letting me share."

Cory joined everybody in saying thanks to Robin.

As they began to sing, he thought about God the Father. God as a loving father.

But how do I know — what's to show that He really, truly is such a loving father?

That same loving father gave up His one and only Son for him.

For you, Cory Brand.

The thought crushed him.

If — and that was a massive if — he ever could be Tyler's father — if he could start to be that young man's father — there was no way Cory would ever give that up.

No way.

And that's how much He loves you.

It was a pretty awesome thought.

Later on, in the open share group, Cory realized that he wasn't some anonymous guy in the room. Everybody knew who he was, and it showed in the looks and the hesitation. Yet nobody said the obvious. Nobody asked for an autograph or asked where he'd been or asked about baseball.

This story wasn't about baseball.

This story was about recovery.

After the rest of the men had introduced themselves, it was Cory's turn to talk. Nobody could see the blue chip in the palm of his hand.

"I'm Cory Brand," he said.

They all looked at him, waiting, watching.

"I'm a brand-new believer in Jesus, and I struggle with alcoholism and anger."

Without any awkward hesitation, the men all greeted him with warm, welcoming voices.

"Glad you're here, Cory."

"Glad you made it."

"Welcome."

"Good you could come."

He suddenly felt a hundred pounds lighter. Cory smiled. If he could see what it looked like, he'd probably not recognize this grin.

It wasn't the Cory Brand trademark smile.

This was a humble smile. A smile of thankfulness.

It's easy to start thinking about tomorrow and next week and next month and the rest of the nexts in his life. Yet Cory tries to remember this whole one-day-at-a-time thing. He thinks of the verse saying to not be anxious about tomorrow, that God will take care of it.

He wants to believe this, but it's hard.

It's hard because it means he has to give up control.

He has to give up and simply let God take care of it.

Chapter Forty-Three: Choke-Up

Emma thought she could outrun the sadness but discovered it had simply been tucked away and along for the ride. She assumed she could block out the pain but realized it tinted every single thing she had the opportunity to see. She believed she had moved on but found herself in the same spot she'd been at only twenty-two years old.

She knew she wouldn't change a thing, because changing it would mean Tyler wouldn't be here. Yet still she sometimes felt like she walked with the wreckage of Cory Brand following her every step. She could drive in the truck and hear the rumbling behind her, like tin cans attached to the back of some newlyweds' car. But she drove this car alone, hearing the clicking cans that had been there over ten years. Try as she might, Emma could not get rid of

407

those dangling, annoying, mocking reminders.

Cory had been gone eight months, but it felt like yesterday. He had been gone ten years before that, and then suddenly in two months last summer he'd made all these connections only to leave them again.

That was your choice.

Maybe so, but he still chose to leave them again. Without trying. The man who had worked so hard on his precious baseball life could have tried a little harder. But leaving was the easy thing to do, and Cory Brand was a master of easy.

She drove through the town to pick up Tyler, who was hanging out with a friend, when she saw the sign. Emma didn't realize she was passing by the motel, because the motel wasn't something you paid attention to. Unless, of course, some bigwig major-league baseball player was staying there. Or, of course, unless the first love of your life had to stay there as a form of punishment for being too much like himself.

She slowed down to make sure she was seeing the sign correctly.

Cory Brand Stays Here

For a moment Emma couldn't believe what she was reading. Then she saw the second sign nearby:

Ask About Custom-Stocked Mini-Fridges

The tears that suddenly popped out of her eyes went right along with the loud laugh she couldn't help giving.

For a moment she almost swerved off the road.

God, what are You trying to tell me?

Some things were simply impossible to avoid. Like Tyler's love of Arby's curly fries. Like Cory Brand and everything about him. Like the love she had tried and tried and tried to give up but could not let go of.

Emma wiped her eyes and wondered if Celebrate Recovery would allow her to come and give her testimony. "Hello, I'm Emma Hargrove, and I still somehow, in some way, love Cory Brand."

They would all understand. They'd welcome her with open arms more than anybody else in the history of CR.

Emma sighed and turned on the radio. She had to stop thinking about him.

The classic rock station blared "Open Arms" by Journey. Once again, it reminded her of Cory.

She shut off the radio.

She was beginning to think she was cursed. It was a disease. A bad case of Cory Brand.

She just needed more time. That was the key. Time to recover from the madness of last summer. Then she and Tyler could move on with their lives.

When she answered the doorbell that early April afternoon, Emma was surprised to find Karen standing there. "Hi?" she said, more question mark than greeting. Karen always told her when she was coming by. Something was wrong; she could read it on her friend's serious face.

"Hey, there. I know I'm kind of popping in unannounced."

"That's okay," Emma said. "Want to come in?"

"Um . . ."

This wasn't a good sign. Karen's voice never trailed off.

"Is Tyler here?"

"Upstairs," Emma said.

Karen gave her a nod and signaled her to step outside. Emma knew something was wrong now and went outside quickly, shutting the door behind her.

"Tyler called Clay," Karen said in a subdued tone. "He asked if we would talk you into letting him go to the game tomorrow."

Emma knew which game she was talking about. Even though Cory had been gone since last August, Tyler had been keeping tabs on him through news and other sources. Emma had learned from her son that Cory was now playing with the Tulsa Mustangs, a minor-league team. That news alone had surprised Emma, but she was done being surprised by Cory. She was done with him period.

"He called you? I am so sorry." Emma still couldn't believe Tyler was trying to work it after she had specifically told him there wasn't a chance in this world that they were going to go to the home game.

Somehow he must've gotten to Karen, because she gave Emma a look.

"Absolutely not," Emma said.

But Karen was strong and could be stubborn, and that look wasn't going away.

"Look, I really appreciate that Clay and Cory have worked through some stuff this last year, and your family is doing better. But I'm just not there."

"Emma . . ." Karen started.

"Karen. People don't change."

The woman who was the closest thing Emma had to a sister gave her a sad smile and an unwavering stare. "Emma, I love you. But the only person not changing here is you."

He's finally given up trying to be the captain of this boat.

He's finally let someone else take control of the wheel.

The future isn't the focus. He's not worried about how far he'll get or how fast he'll get there. He's fixed on these deep waters around him and the furious storms that will surely be coming.

The sun beats down on Cory, and he finds himself thankful. In this moment. In this now. To know that God has shined down on him and that there is still a reason to look up, to get up, to be UP.

Each breath and each beat, no longer stretched out and left broken.

He is here on these waters, and he's not about to jump overboard. He's staring straight ahead, ready for whatever's going to come at him.

Ready for wherever the captain is going to take him.

CHAPTER FORTY-FOUR:
COMPLETE GAME

This day was all about starting over. It was the opening day of the baseball season. Even though it was only AA ball, it was still something. Cory had a job. He had a game he could still play. He was sober and in a good place and this day was another landmark in his recovery.

Maybe they'll show up. Maybe.

He was on the field, giving an interview, being asked the same questions he had been asked for the last eight months.

"One day at a time is all I can tell you," Cory said. "I'm in Tulsa now, so I'm focusing on doing a good job here."

These weren't trivial clichés thrown out there just so he'd be heard saying the right thing on ESPN. He meant these words. He wasn't thinking about how well he might do and whether or not a team like the Grizzlies or any other major team would invite him back to the show. This was where he was for

414

now, and he had to make it count. Thinking about the future only made the present even more difficult.

As he was sharing his thoughts on the opening game, he saw Clay and the kids walking onto the field toward him.

"Excuse me, I've got some very special guests here."

He rushed toward them and greeted each kid with a hug.

"Hey, guys," Cory said. "It's so good to see all of you."

Carlos and Wick and Stanton and Kendricks — all of the Bulldogs were there. All except one very important Bulldog.

Cory hugged Clay and Karen.

"Good to see you," his brother said.

"How are you?" Karen asked.

"They couldn't make it, huh?"

"You know how it is," Clay said.

"Yeah."

Cory had to live with the reality of how it was every day. He had tried a few times to reach out to Emma, but she hadn't returned his calls or emails. He understood. It had taken him ten years just to go back home, and that had been because of a forced publicity stunt.

The kids talked Cory's ears off, and he welcomed it. The only thing that would have been better would be to have Emma and Tyler joining in the conversation.

"Did you say anything about the Bulldogs to that reporter?" Carlos asked.

"Don't be stupid," Stanton said.

"We get that station in Okmulgee," Wick announced to nobody in particular.

"Do you get a player's discount in the gift shop?" Kendricks asked.

The constant barrage of questions and comments made Cory laugh. He looked at Clay with an amused glance.

I miss these guys. I miss all of you.

It was his second at bat, and Cory stepped up to the plate, feeling the pressure.

For a moment, as he got into his stance, he could feel his father looking down at him. Waiting impatiently. Waiting to throw the ball and make Cory pay. Watching to make sure he did everything right. Waiting and watching and willing to hurt Cory if he had to.

The buzzing intensified, and soon Cory had to step back out of the box and collect himself. He held the bat as he looked at the pitcher.

It's not Dad. It's just some kid fresh out of college.

He stood back at the plate and focused.

Cory knew he no longer needed to bat off all the hurtful objects coming his way.

He wasn't batting to protect himself and his little brother. He wasn't batting for his life.

I'm here to do the thing God gifted me to do.

The pitcher released the fastball, and Cory knew he had all of it. The bat blasted the ball high and long to the heavens themselves.

It cleared the fence easily.

God gives some people certain abilities, Cory, and He sure gave you one. To hit home runs.

This, indeed, was a beautiful and glorious home run.

Cory could hear the cheers and knew they sounded different. He was no longer running *for* them. He smiled and felt satisfaction, but *this* — this job and this game and these people and this stadium — did not define him. He wasn't doing it for them. And he was no longer running away from the memory of a man who was no longer alive.

Cory Brand, the starting left fielder for the Tulsa Mustangs, rounded the bases and heard the cheers from the Bulldogs.

His old team.

Coach Cory was making some strides and doing okay. Slowly but surely.

A day at a time.

Cory's car was the last one left in the empty lot. As he walked toward it after leaving the locker room, he couldn't help thinking of that moron who had knocked over his adopted nephew and then found his brother waiting for him.

A lot had changed in that span of time. A lot.

Tonight he was the last one left simply because he had been talking with Clay and Karen on the field, along with signing balls for all the Bulldogs. The Mustangs had won by five runs. His two home runs were the talk of the game, and Cory had to admit it felt great. It was good to remember what winning felt like. What *caring* felt like. What contributing really meant.

"Excuse me, Cory Brand? This boy belong to you?"

Cory turned and saw one of the security guys for the stadium standing with Tyler.

"He sure does."

Tyler rushed toward him as Cory tried to understand how he got there. For a second he was worried until he saw Emma standing behind the guard.

"Sorry we missed your game," Tyler said when he reached him.

Cory had been waiting for this moment for a long time. He hadn't known how badly until he thought it might never happen. He got down on one knee and pulled Tyler close to him.

"Come here, bud," Cory said.

Time stopped as Cory held his long-lost son.

Thank You, Lord.

There were tears in his eyes, and he didn't care whether anyone saw them. Cory looked Tyler in the eyes but couldn't speak. There was too much to say. He didn't even know where to start.

Emma slowly walked up to them. Cory smiled as he stood, wondering whether to hug her or not, then deciding a nice genuine smile would be enough.

"Hey, Emma," he said. "Good to see you. Thanks for bringing him."

She glowed, reminding him why he had fallen so hard for her. He had missed that beautiful smile. He had missed both of them a lot.

"You look good, Cory. Healthy."

The words and the declarations and every big and little thing Cory wanted to say were all stored away, waiting for him to unload them. But Cory knew this wasn't the time.

They were there, and that was enough.

It beat hitting two home runs on opening day, and that in itself was pretty special.

"Hey, how about a tour?" Cory said.

Emma didn't hesitate this time. She gave him a polite nod.

Of all the things she imagined might happen on this evening once she'd decided to bring Tyler to the game, this was not one of them.

The stadium lights were still on as they walked onto the soft grass of the field. Cory had grabbed sodas for all of them. Tyler gushed over every little thing. Cory looked like a proud father, talking about the stadium and pointing things out to him. It was a side of Cory Emma had never seen.

As they stood in the outfield, Cory asked Tyler if he wanted to play some ball. Tyler looked at her, and she gave him a nod.

She wasn't going to deny Tyler this moment. Tyler and Cory.

She watched them throwing the ball back and forth. A simple image of a father and son playing catch.

Yet as Emma watched, the emotions seized up inside of her.

Years ago, the moment she had first known

she loved Cory, she had secretly dreamed of this moment. When she discovered she was pregnant, and even after Cory left and Emma moved away from Okmulgee, she still had dreamed that one day this moment might arrive.

The father throwing the ball wasn't just any ordinary baseball player. And the son catching it wasn't just any ordinary kid.

She wiped her eyes as Tyler threw a long ball over Cory's head, causing him to turn and spring and then snag it and fire it back to Tyler.

Tyler had to go back to grab it, but he did.

"Nice catch," Cory shouted.

Tyler launched another long ball, making Cory sprint and dive and barely catch the ball.

"Whoa," Tyler said.

Emma knew Cory was showing off for Tyler, and for her. It felt good. It had been years since she could remember Cory showing off for anybody except himself.

Careful, Em.

This scene was cute and special, but it didn't change a decade of not-so-cute and not-so-special memories. She knew she had to tread very lightly on this ground.

"Time to go, Tyler."

Tyler scooped up the ball but threw it again, obviously hoping not to have to leave yet.

Cory caught it and began to run toward them. "Time to go, slugger."

As they headed off the field, Cory told them to wait a minute.

"What is it?" Tyler asked, still breathing heavily.

Cory grabbed the duffel he'd brought out onto the field from his car and came back a moment later carrying the wooden box with the metal latch.

"You can't leave without your cards."

Tyler beamed as Emma looked at the box in Cory's hands.

Some things in this life didn't need any explanation. And some apologies didn't need any words.

"Whoa — these are really mine to keep?" Tyler asked.

"They're all yours," Cory said.

Before Tyler could take the box, he wrapped his arms around Cory.

The two of them stood holding each other while Emma watched and tried to fight off the tears.

Sometimes God made you wait for moments like this. And sometimes, when they came, you weren't so sure what to do with them.

Sometimes, all you could do was thank God above.

That was exactly what Emma did.

They were ready to leave. When they would see Cory next, Emma didn't know. She hadn't woken up this morning expecting to bring Tyler to this game. She hadn't expected the evening to be so . . . so magical and moving. But she still didn't know what to make of everything or what might happen tomorrow or the day after that.

Like Cory, Emma knew she needed to take things a day at a time.

Cory and Emma stood next to her truck while Tyler waited inside. The stadium parking lot was empty.

"Thanks for coming, Emma."

She gave an unsure shrug, not knowing what else to say.

"I know there's nothing I can do to make up for what I've done, and what I haven't done. For what I put you through. And Tyler. I have to say, I'm sorry. I'm so sorry, Emma. I hope you can forgive me."

Emma could see Tyler's face watching them from inside the truck. She tried with everything she had inside to control her emotions.

She'd waited a long time to hear those words.

"Yeah," she said weakly. "Okay."

"I'm not asking for anything," Cory said. "But I love this family. I believe in this family. And I'll be a part of it — as much or as little as you want me to be."

This was a Cory Brand she had never seen. There had been the cocky Cory and the angry Cory and the distraught Cory, but never this one.

This was the man she always hoped and believed Cory Brand would become.

Emma nodded and then turned to get into her truck. She still didn't know what to say to him about expectations and tomorrow. She would figure that out when tomorrow came.

As she climbed inside and shut the door, Tyler watched her carefully. She couldn't help tearing up as she started up the truck.

All she could do was look down at her lap and try to control the emotions inside.

I don't know what to do because God knows I still love that broken and bruised man walking away from us.

She gripped the wheel as she waited for a moment. Tyler shifted in the seat next to her.

"Nothing good happens when you hang back, Mom."

She looked at the face of this beautiful and sweet soul. The two of them had been through a lot. He didn't know it, but they had.

Emma sighed and smiled and then hugged her son.

Cory walked toward the players' parking lot, feeling full and empty at the same time. The restless feeling was beginning to swirl around again in his head and his gut. He knew he might have to call J. T. and talk with him or even meet with him. This night had been full of peaks and valleys.

The old me never wanted those peaks to go away.

He prayed for guidance and peace as he walked, closing his eyes for just a second.

Then he heard footsteps coming toward him and his name being shouted out.

By Emma.

That sweet and pretty girl he'd fallen in love with in high school hadn't changed much. She'd just grown into a beautiful woman and mother, and he hadn't been there to watch the change. He'd missed every good and glorious part about it.

But Emma was there now.

She walked toward him and then embraced Cory for the first time in ten years. Their last embrace had been cold and had signified good-bye. This one signified hope.

Cory stepped back for a second to make sure it was really her, to look at her face.

Those eyes looked at him once again without any walls or barriers between them.

Cory might have been a fool and might still be a fool, but he knew this woman still loved him. Anybody could see that.

He wanted to say that everything was going to be okay and that he was going to take things slowly and that he would never *ever* leave their family's life again if they would allow him back into it.

He tried to show this all with a smile and a nod.

Emma knew. She knew him a lot better than he knew himself.

Cory looked toward the truck and saw Tyler's gawking face of disbelief in the window. It made him laugh while Emma stood back and seemed to regain her composure.

She cleared her voice. "You hungry?"

He needed to wrap his mind and heart and soul around what was happening here.

Please, God, don't let me wake up in the roach motel, watching ESPN and staring at the Devil's fridge.

Cory smiled at Emma and regained his composure as well. "Always."

Tyler was out of the truck and had reached the two of them.

Only two fans were left in the stadium parking lot of the Tulsa Mustangs after their home game, but Cory Brand definitely did not feel alone anymore.

When the night is over and Emma and Tyler are gone, Cory doesn't collapse back into his own little world he's made for himself. He doesn't panic or have a pity party at being left again.

This time, Cory simply says a prayer of thanks to God who forgives. To God who answers prayers. To God who has mercy, just like the woman who's allowing him back into her life.

It used to be that emotions like this terrified him because ultimately they would let him down. Cory no longer believes that. He no longer fears the silence and the shadows. He's no longer afraid of the void inside of him, one that will never truly be filled until the day he steps before his heavenly Father.

Cory thanks God for one of the best nights of his life. He believes there can be more of them, God willing.

But right now he remains in the moment and remains thankful for this day.

CHAPTER FORTY-FIVE: HOME RUN

These pieces of you, imperfectly sewn and patched all over, blur by like a blinding pitch.

That image woke Cory up at three in the morning. He'd been able to go back to sleep for a while, but the picture had stayed with him as he drove back home to Okmulgee for an important occasion.

It was there as he passed his sweet home-away-from-home and spotted the sign outside the motel that said Cory Brand Stays Here. The old Cory Brand would have stopped and told them to stop using his name; now he found it oddly amusing.

The image had been there as he spotted Hank's Tavern, where his father used to drink and where Cory had found himself at a crossroads of his life.

It was especially there as he drove past the Little League field.

Now that his moment had arrived, it felt like he'd been building up to it for the past thirty-four years. Cory stood in the large church sanctuary before a crowd of familiar and loving faces.

Suddenly he could see all the broken strands of the story intersecting.

The man in the front pew still resembled that pesky and annoying little kid who always seemed at his side wherever he was. He would forever be the little brother who loved him unconditionally. No matter what.

Next to that man sat a pretty girl who had grown into a lovely woman, still lit up with all the potential she somehow saw in Cory even when nobody else could have ever imagined it.

He pictured the boy belonging to this woman, a boy who looked a lot like the one threatened and abused on a farm around here years ago. If that boy could be here at this moment, he would be a portrait of happiness and hope and pride.

Karen sat in the pew with Emma and Clay. While children weren't allowed in CR meetings, Cory knew that Tyler and Carlos were close by. He would see them soon. J. T. sat a couple of rows back.

He had pictured their faces all day, but now he saw them in light of this story, of *his* story that he was going to be reading. He had failed all of them at one point or many points along the journey. Yet ultimately there was only one person he had failed time and time again.

But God graciously continued to love Cory Brand despite all he did.

"I'm a believer who's in recovery and struggles with alcoholism and anger," Cory started out, a statement now as familiar in his mind as the act of stepping up to the plate.

The room gave him a rousing greeting that brought chills over his skin.

"Some of you know that I occasionally play baseball," he said, a line that brought the sound of laughter.

He needed to hear that because he was so nervous about these words he was saying. As usual, he made the joke to feel a little better. Yet in this case, he wasn't hiding from anything.

Not a thing.

Cory shared pieces of that broken puzzle. His relationship with an abusive father, his desire to take care of his brother. He shared his love of baseball and how it opened doors and how it also shut doors.

"I was given a gift many years ago, but I was too stupid to realize it," Cory said, looking at Emma and thinking of Tyler. "I thought that gift was the ability to hit a ball into the stands. I didn't realize that gift came in the form of a new life, a precious baby boy that I didn't want to think about, that I ran away from. Even then, all I could think of was myself and my career."

Cory paused and composed himself, smiling a sad smile at Emma.

He continued to detail the journey into having his dreams come true and how that took everything good and whole from him. Alcoholism and women only dulled the pain of the past he'd run away from.

"I have spent my life replacing the love and attention I never had from my father and covering up the pain from that neglect with alcohol. But every drop of alcohol, every drunken tirade, every one-night stand — none of it would ever erase the ache inside of me. An ache only God could fill."

Cory looked down and remembered the expression on Tyler's face as he'd yelled at the boy in the bar. The moment when it had all come full circle and he knew he couldn't do anything about all the broken pieces surrounding him.

"I tried to change," Cory said. "But I failed every time."

A sense of strength and hope soared through him, and it wasn't from a crowd chanting his name. It had nothing to do with him. Cory believed that with every fiber in him.

"I know now that I am powerless without God, but with His help I have found a freedom from my pain and my habits I never believed possible."

The faces staring at him smiled and nodded and gave him affirmation. For a second he pictured the face of Michael Brand, the man he had spent so many years trying to escape from. But Cory knew he didn't have to run away from that beat-up man anymore.

"My family has suffered for generations. I suffered because of my father's pain. He suffered because of his father's pain. But this is where it stops. This is how it changes."

The pieces of his life and his story blurred by like a blinding pitch.

A blinding pitch that he finally connected with.

"Today, I begin a new story," Cory said with joy and pride. "I am a child of God, and I have a Father who loves me — on and off the baseball field."

In his mind, Cory pictured Emma and Tyler. His joy and his pride.

"Thank you for letting me share."

The crowd erupted with an applause he'd never quite felt as strongly as he felt it now.

As they stood and cheered, J. T. walked up to the podium and gave him a hug.

It was a year to the day that Cory got sober. He wasn't at this church because of some publicity event or some public outing he got paid for.

This truly was a celebration of one year of his life. A very good year, in fact.

Cory Brand hoped and prayed there would be many more years like this to celebrate and thank God for.

He approaches the bronze plaques in the ground. The ground around the plaques has been groomed a bit. Now the plaques are easier to see.

Nobody else knows he's here. Nobody but God above and maybe his parents if they can see him. Cory kneels and places a gift by each name.

The dozen fresh red roses go by Alicia Brand's name. They're nothing in comparison to the gift she gave him so many years, but they're something.

"I'm sorry I didn't grant your request," he says out loud, hoping she can somehow hear him. "But I finally did come home. And it was the best thing that ever happened to me."

He slips a ball out of his pocket and puts it down by Michael Brand's name.

Seeing that ball next to that name brings tears to his eyes. He didn't think it would, not after all this time, but then again, every new day something surprises him.

Cory Brand knows something now.

There are two ways a heart can grow. It can either harden or grow softer.

"I forgive you, Dad."

He looks long and hard at the name and the ball next to it — the ball from the first home run he ever hit in the major leagues.

There's only one person who ever deserved to have that ball.

Maybe deserve isn't the right word, Cory thinks.

But then again, none of us deserves the grace we're given.

That's the beauty of it.

Chapter Forty-Six: Perfect Game

Cory sat in the crowded wooden bleachers next to Karen and J. T. The Bulldogs were up by five and playing great. Tyler had connected with a couple of monster hits that reminded Cory of someone else he once knew. The second hit had gotten a basking mother's brilliant beam coming his way. Cory knew Emma was thinking all the things he was thinking.

Well, most of them.

The early evening still had a little sun left in it for the July day. He'd been able to stay a couple of days after his testimony at the CR meeting before heading back to Tulsa to hit the road with the Mustangs. He wasn't thinking beyond this moment, sitting here and watching Tyler and Carlos and the rest of the ragamuffins playing out there while coaches Emma and Clay worked their magic.

For a second he looked into the endless

Oklahoma sky and felt at home.

If Cory could write the script that would become the film of his life, he knew how he would end it.

He wouldn't write a scene that echoed *The Natural,* as Robert Redford's character stepped up to the plate and blasted the home run that sent down a steady glowing stream of sparkles and explosions while the music played in the background. That was a spectacular ending for Roy Hobbs.

Nor would Cory choose the touching conclusion of *Field of Dreams,* a guy throwing a baseball with his father. That was a beautiful moment in a wonderful film too, but that wasn't in the plans when it came to Michael Brand and his son.

No.

Cory would end things just like this. Sitting here watching his son play ball. Watching the only true love of his life be willing to invite him back into hers after he'd been gone so long. Holding a one-year CR chip in his hand. Knowing not to get ahead of himself, not to worry about tomorrow or the next day.

He knew God made his life complete when He placed all the pieces before him. Cory also knew he was promised that once he got his act together, God would give him a fresh start.

All the pieces were in place.

The fresh start would come every morning. For the rest of his life.

■ ■ ■ ■

AFTER
WORDS

. . . A LITTLE MORE . . .

■ ■ ■ ■

When a delightful concert comes to an
end, the orchestra might offer an encore.

When a fine meal comes to an end,
it's always nice to savor a bit of dessert.

When a great story comes to an end,
we think you may want to linger.

And so, we offer . . .

AfterWords — just a little something
more after you have finished a
David C Cook novel.

We invite you to stay awhile in the story.

Thanks for reading!

Turn the page for . . .

THE BEGINNING OF *HOME RUN*

Inception. It was January 2010, and film producer Tom Newman had not worked on a feature film in several years. After pitching a three-picture deal to prospective partners for most of 2009, Newman still found himself waiting. Fed up and determined, Tom challenged his longtime colleague and video/TV producer Carol Spann Mathews: "Let's do a movie — *this* year — for just a million dollars." Mathews agreed instantly.

Miracle. Normally Mathews would barrel down a road and then ask God to please bless it and guide the endeavor. But this time was different and would set the pace for a thousand prayers on the filmmaking journey. So Mathews, alone in her office after others had gone home, simply asked God, "What do You want to say in our movie?" There was no fasting. There was no repeated ritual of praying and waiting. The answer came swiftly and clearly: *I want* *people to know that I can heal them of their addictions — that I can free them; that change is possible.*

The Original Home Run. There was an unscripted story idea entitled "Home Run," conceived by Tom Newman's son, Eric: a major leaguer, horribly heart-wounded by his father, finds himself coaching a Little League team in the rural hometown he had avoided for years. Mathews called Eric Newman and asked him if he felt he could give the ballplayer an alcohol problem, eliminate the mentorpreacher character, and incorporate a faith-based twelve-step program as the device to share God's truths in the script. Eric Newman and colleague Candace Lee began working tirelessly to bring a new set of characters and a new angle to Eric's original story.

Celebrate Recovery. Every time Mathews saw a Celebrate Recovery testimony at her church, she saw the undeniable hand of God at work. In each story, a brave soul revealed his or her darkest struggle to shine the brightest light of hope on those who listened. Mathews believed the Celebrate Recovery program could be the very backdrop for a troubled protagonist-addict on a journey toward wholeness. The film would have no preachy mentor-type characters. But the true stories of broken people whose lives were completely changed by Jesus would shine a hope-filled light for our character (and the film's audience). Mathews believed these stories would preach without being "preachy."

John Baker. The producers had to garner permission to use the Celebrate Recovery name in the film. The only problem was that CR's founder, John Baker, was based out of Saddleback, one of the largest churches in America. He was also one of its elders alongside "America's Pastor" Rick Warren. This wasn't going to be as easy as a simple phone call. Fortunately, the producers received the wise counsel of a local CR state rep, Norma Murphy, who suggested a few steps to take prior to reaching out to Mr. Baker. One, the producers and screenwriters should attend a Celebrate Recovery meeting. Two, the producers should attend a CR "One-Day" where the ministry is unpacked and explained to those interested in implementing CR at their church. These were the prerequisites before she would introduce the producers to her *dear friends,* John and Cheryl Baker.

Testimony Night. The producers' second CR meeting was "testimony night." The man telling his story was a recovering drug addict. It was the most courageous and honest thing Mathews had ever witnessed. In the buckle of the Bible Belt, at a large Southern Baptist church, there was a man telling his story of drugs, sex, alcohol — and stealing from *their* offering plates. He told of the transformation in his heart, the love he found from those in the room, and the hope he had that God would now work on his alcohol addiction. He was on his journey. He hadn't arrived, but he was experiencing true healing. The raw honesty of this man, and the honesty of the others in the room, was a part of the Christian church they wanted to portray in their film. One that perhaps others wouldn't believe even exists. And the more they attended CR (which included going on their own journey through the twelve steps), the more the CR experience would shape the storytelling of their movie.

Another Miracle. With prerequisites fulfilled, Mathews and Newman were now ready to meet with CR founders John and Cheryl Baker. Forever grateful to Norma Murphy's sound advice, the producers were clearer than ever about the message of the film, the importance of this message, and the beauty of incorporating Celebrate Recovery into it. They were told to keep their expectations at bay, however, as Baker would not give permission quickly, and, an avid protector of his brand, he would not be afraid to say no. But after meeting for an entire afternoon and attending CR at Saddleback that night — they prayed together, and he gave his unreserved blessing to a first-time film producer from Tulsa, Oklahoma, who had no money and no script. This blessing would prove to be the rocket fuel in the project's engine that propelled this movie forward in many, many ways. What felt like a good idea for a script would prove to be a *God* idea on many levels.

The Script. Eric Newman and Candace Lee, also now regularly attending CR, began working on the script. Mathews then brought in Dreamworks story analyst and screenwriter Brian Brightly, who worked with them for three months. Under Brightly's leadership, the team stood the script up and tall with strong structure, good pacing, and solid characters. Still, Mathews thought something was missing. A certain pathos. This is where screenwriter Melanie Wistar came in. According to Mathews, Wistar put the "soul" in the characters with her honest dialogue, great sense of humor, and clear understanding of the film's message. After seventeen months, the script was complete.

WHY *HOME RUN* MATTERS

The audience for the film — and this book — are Christians who are tired of faking it. The shame from the choices they made or the habits they can't break or the abuse they endured creates a condemning weight on the shoulders of good-willed believers who sit in a church pew and simply feel trapped. For *them,* the praying and the worship and the Bible study just doesn't work for this *one dark area* of their lives. They love Jesus. But they have found that the promised peace and real-life change elude them. The worst of it is, *they feel alone.* They are certain that those seated next to them in their small group have it all under control and wouldn't possibly understand, much less accept, this struggle. *This movie is for those people.* Those who feel alone. Those who feel condemned. It's for those who think things will never change.

The unflinching honesty of *Home Run* resonates with a growing part of the church that rejects the assumption that once you're saved, everything is okay. And to the world *outside* the church that never bought that claim in the first place, *Home Run* is an honest and hopeful message for them.

In the film the characters are *not* neatly divided into the "have Jesus" group and the "messed up" folks. Everyone is portrayed as having a struggle of some kind . . . because that's true in real life. *We all struggle, but healing is possible!* But not by being better or just acting right or signing the oath or making the resolution or privately trying to fix the problem all by ourselves. Change and freedom are ours by *surrendering* to Jesus.

This is what makes Celebrate Recovery an amazing backdrop for this story. This ministry, currently in over nineteen thousand churches across the country, is creating a culture of telling the truth about the Christian walk. It teaches the biblical truths underlying the twelve steps of recovery. The people participating in Celebrate Recovery are telling their stories from pulpits and lecterns around the country: God loves us, and *He* can heal us.

It's time to start this conversation in our churches. What's holding Christians back from living the life they were created to live? *What happens after the altar call?* What do we do with the broken pieces, the shameful places of our hearts and lives? Why do we try to fix our struggles on our own? Why do we resist the pain and process of healing? Why are we afraid to give it to God and trust Him?

Home Run would like to help ignite this important conversation.

The employees of Thorndike Press hope you have enjoyed this Large Print book. All our Thorndike, Wheeler, and Kennebec Large Print titles are designed for easy reading, and all our books are made to last. Other Thorndike Press Large Print books are available at your library, through selected bookstores, or directly from us.

For information about titles, please call:
  (800) 223-1244

or visit our Web site at:
  http://gale.cengage.com/thorndike

To share your comments, please write:
  Publisher
  Thorndike Press
  10 Water St., Suite 310
  Waterville, ME 04901